Totally Bound Publishing books by Deana Birch

Single Book
Love Repaired

with Amelia Foster

Single Book
Luca's Lessons

I0607504

LOVE REPAIRED

DEANA BIRCH

Love Repaired
ISBN # 978-1-83943-879-0
©Copyright Deana Birch 2019
Cover Art by Erin Dameron-Hill ©Copyright July 2019
Interior text design by Claire Siemaszkiewicz
Totally Bound Publishing

LOVE REPAIRED

Dedication

To the three loves of my life — A, M and Z

Chapter One

The Cupcake

Amee

I parked the loaner SUV in line next to the other shiny overpriced automobiles, did a final check for personal belongings in the seat next to me — no need to learn the same lesson twice, my cell phone had spent the day in my car — and headed into the office. With the sun set, the cool evening air hit my cheeks and I perked up as I walked. My Cayenne sat in front of the large metal garage doors, a sparkle reflecting its recent wash. At least luxury came with attention to detail.

When I reached the glass door, I tugged it toward me only to find it locked. *Jesus.* I'd even failed at picking up my car. I stood on my tiptoes and rapped my knuckles against the glass. On the other side, the room was dark and the half-circular reception desk was abandoned, a black office chair pushed into its place. But from the hall behind it, a light peeked out — my ray of hope.

I knocked again and pressed my lips together while readjusting my shoulder bag. I shifted my body weight from side to side and banged louder.

Florescent beams flooded the showroom and I blinked. My skin flushed, and my mouth went dry. A legal aide at the firm had once said something about man candy, but I thought that was like a unicorn — not real, a legend in a forest I would never visit. But Man Candy had a warm smile, combed-back dirty blond hair and a build that screamed heaven through a tight, black, untucked work shirt. The last few buttons were open and matching pants hung low on his waist. He was also headed right toward me, tapping a wrench in his hand.

With dimples in his smile, he slipped the tool into his back pocket and unlocked the door. His sea-blue eyes must have been designed for skinny dipping.

"Mrs. Benton, I presume." The low, scratchy voice matched the light stubble on his cheeks. His dimples deepened, and the warm showroom air hit my already-heated body.

"Ms." I couldn't resist the urge to brush against him, and as I did, the perfect blend of motor oil and earthy spice came with me.

Testosterone, how I've missed thee.

I walked over to reception and placed the key fob on the desk.

He followed and squinted down at the neat paper piles next to the flat computer screen and keyboard. He picked up my keys from the tail of the stuffed squirrel that held them and dangled it like a time piece.

"Nice keychain." After a quick arch of his eyebrow, the damn dimples reappeared with his tight-lipped smile.

"Thanks" — I glanced at his chest — "Ben." I took the stuffed animal from his grease-stained hands and slid the other key toward him.

"Did you fill it up?" he asked.

"Uh...no." Add one more failure to my day.

Ben shook his head and grabbed the fob before popping it into a drawer. "No one ever fills it up. You know it costs double, right?" He peered up with one eye closed.

"Well, it was either fill it up or make you wait longer."

"Either way, it's my time. I'll have to do it Monday." He rubbed his face with both hands and a tattoo poked out from the tight sleeve around his bicep. His very full bicep.

I cringed and lifted a shoulder. "Sorry. Anyway, I only drove it to my office and back."

Ben walked out from behind the desk and over to the door. Holding it open for me again, he motioned for me to leave.

I'm too young to suffer hot flashes, right? And I was not dreaming of ways to sabotage my brakes or engine. That would be silly — and a further inconvenience that my schedule would not allow.

"You had a failed fuel pump. It's a pretty common problem. That was what was causing the stalling."

Note to self — Get another failed fuel pump.

When we stood in front of my car, he pulled up on the handle, swung the door open, and I froze. A big white pastry box sat on the passenger seat.

"Fuck me."

"Pardon?" he asked with an airy chuckle.

I brought my hands to my face and pulled them down slowly, probably ruining the effects of the anti-aging cream I'd put on that morning. "Fuck. Fuck. Fuck."

"Are you okay?" Ben leaned in closer.

"I forgot the fucking cupcakes. Fuck me. *Fuck.*" I let my bag fall off my shoulder and dragged my feet over to the steel garage. My back met the cool wall and I slid down to the rough concrete. I stomped my sensible beige heel before slumping into a ball and whimpering into my hands. My entire day, week, month... They had all been colossal fails.

The motor oil and musk were back, now touching my wrist and seated on the ground next to me.

"Shitty day?" He draped his defined forearms over his knees with his fingers interlaced.

"I wish I could say it was the shittiest, but it just seems to be par for the course. *Fuck.*" I stomped again.

"You have quite the potty mouth for a lady."

"Did you just call me a lady? Oh my God, now I'm really going to cry." Forgetting Shae's cupcakes was the cherry on top of my botched-Mom sundae. But being one step away from a 'ma'am' was the rainbow sprinkles. Asshole-expensive face cream... It obviously wasn't working. And I wasn't even forty.

"You wanna talk about it? I'm a pretty good listener."

If that were true, then Man Candy truly was a unicorn and I *was* in an enchanted forest. But the words flew out before I could stop them.

"My client lied to me and made me look like a fool in a deposition. I forgot my phone in the car this morning, which means my older daughter has probably called it three hundred times. And because I was behind closed doors with said lying client, I couldn't call her.

"It was my little one's last day at dance camp and I was supposed to bring the cupcakes. Which, as you can see, I did not do. Oh, and their father is in prison for vehicular manslaughter. Sorry you asked?"

He frowned and shook his head. "Where are they now? Your girls?"

"My sister takes care of them so I can keep working." I wrapped the hem of my skirt around my legs.

"Who takes care of you?" The smile and dimples were gone, but the warmth stayed in his eyes.

"Me, I guess." I shrugged and tried to recall any moment my ex, Pete, had ever really taken care of me, and I drew a blank.

He narrowed his blue eyes. "Is that enough?"

The beautiful stranger next to me had gotten as far as my walls would let him. Although, I had to admit, someone being concerned about me might have made a tiny crack.

"That and the half-bottle of Chardonnay waiting in the door of my fridge."

"That's depressing," he said, getting up. He offered me his strong, rough hand and I clasped it. With a gentle yank, I was on my feet. "You ready for me to add insult to injury then?" He wet his lips and tilted his head.

"Oh, God. I don't even care about the bill. Just tell them to send it to me." I smoothed the front of my skirt and dusted off my rear.

"It's not that." Ben cleared his throat.

I scanned my car for a scratch or dent.

He continued, "I'm really sorry, but I ate one of the cupcakes."

I darted my eyes back to him and he hunched as if waiting to be smacked.

"You eat cupcakes?" I leaned back a little. Whatever moment sugar had spent on his lips, it was not spending a lifetime on his hips. *Bastard.*

"It's my cheat day. And those damn things were next to me in the car all day. Staring at me. Taunting me. Like, *'Ben, you know you want me.'*" He wiggled his fingers. "Then you were late, and, well…I made some kind of weird justification that I could have one. I'm really sorry."

"You ate one of my daughter's pink frosted cupcakes?" I planted my hands on my hips.

Ben nodded with a clenched jaw.

"You're a fucking unicorn." I picked up my bag, tossed it in the back and climbed into the car.

With the seat belt fastened, I reached for the door, but he held on to it stopping me from closing.

He blinked hard. "Did you and your potty mouth just call me a unicorn?"

"We did." I smiled at the mythical man candy creature, shut the door and drove out of the enchanted forest.

* * * *

"Want a cupcake?" I slid the box onto the center island of my spotless kitchen. My older sister, Jude, sat on a barstool at the other end with her ankles crossed and feet dangling over the white granite countertop. She swiped her phone a couple more times and looked up at me with gray-blue eyes that matched my own.

"Epic fail on the mom front today." The grin shifted from smug to sympathetic in a flash.

"Who's more pissed, Carly or Shae?" I opened the box and let my finger dip into the melted pink frosting. *Irresistible.*

Jude set the phone down on the counter and locked her fingers behind her neck. She leaned into the back of the stool and said, "Carly is reading that book again and the ballerina mob boss is tending to Lasagna."

Shae had random names for her many, many—most likely too many—dolls. Lasagna had been christened the night Pete had brought the brown-eyed baby home—the same night we'd told the girls we were getting divorced. 'Lasagna' had initially seemed like a joke, a way for Shae to rebel against her parents splitting up, but the name had stuck. I had to admit, she was my personal favorite doll.

I licked the frosting from my finger and closed the lid. "She wasn't too disappointed?"

Jude yawned and stood, planting her hands on the gleaming counter. "It's fucking weird." She scratched her short hair that was adorable no matter what she did to it. "She practically made a grown man cry for putting the wrong topping on her frozen yogurt yesterday. But when it comes to you, it's almost like she knows how hard you're trying. She told her friends your car broke down and you were waiting for a tow. Did you eat?"

I shook my head as Jude reached for the handle of the fridge. Everything she had said about my baby girl was true. Shae defended me above all else. But that didn't change the fact that I would need to tread lightly with her older sister.

With my hand on the banister, I climbed the stairs. Colorful paper flowers and butterflies plastered Shae's door, a summer project she and Jude had adopted. I pushed it open and my baby girl was busy, as always.

Her blonde hair was still in place from ballet, a perfect bun with only the thinnest locks having escaped at the base of her neck. But instead of her tutu, she wore a purple T-shirt, a yellow-and-black bumblebee skirt and red ladybug rain boots.

"Is Lasagna sick again?" I walked over to the bed, sat down on the floor next to her and kicked off my heels.

"She's afraid she's a cannibal. I fed her spaghetti." She cradled the doll and stroked her plastic head.

"Did Jude teach you that word?"

She ignored the question, but the mature vocabulary pulled at something deeper inside me. My six-year old had grown up too fast already and there was no going back.

Initially, Pete and I had been on the same page about exposing the girls to life. There were no nicknames for body parts, and we were honest about current events — no matter how brutal. Pete and I shared our matter-of-fact views on science and religion. But when their daddy had become the news on television by driving drunk and killing another father, I'd wished for drapes and shutters on our glass house of reality.

I'd had no idea how to protect them from the truth and therefore didn't do it. After I'd told them Pete would go to prison, Carly had stared at me like it was my fault — and maybe it was. I had asked for the separation. I had been unhappy. I'd broken up our family. At least our divorce had been final before his accident. But even that seemingly made me selfish somehow.

But it was Pete who'd spiraled into drinking more. His art had never taken off, so he'd busied himself with distractions, the biggest being golf. *Fucking golf.* My free-spirited painter had hung out at the clubhouse and drank with the retired businessmen, pretending he belonged. Wanting to belong. But he couldn't — and he didn't — which made it all the worse. To be fair, he'd never fit in as an artist either. With his Oxford shirts and clean-cut style, he was more in line with what his fellow painters were moving against.

Shae, with her hazel eyes the same shape and color as her daddy's, tucked Lasagna into a toy crib. She gave her a butterfly kiss on her cheek — just as Pete would have done for her and Carly when he'd said good night to them. The months of anger were over and my heart broke for my girls every time they held on to their father's memories and the good times.

A single tear fell down my cheek. I held my arms open for my sweet girl and said, "I'm sorry about your cupcakes."

She climbed into my lap, legs straddled around my waist, and laid her head on my shoulder. Shae rested there for a moment before pulling back and saying, "It's okay. You have more jobs than anyone I know. You're a lawyer, a mommy and a daddy. You're a grandma to all my babies and you're planning the Fall Festival for our school." She wiped a tear away from my face and added, "Don't cry, Mommy. We all make mistakes or forget."

I brought her head to my shoulder again and inhaled that sweet, busy-little-girl scent. "You want me to read to you?" I kissed her head next to the bun.

She popped up and went to her book case. "No, it's okay. Jude said if I can read this whole book, she'll buy me a new baby and I can name her Fortune Feimster." She kicked off her boots, slid into bed and Jude appeared in the doorway. Maybe she'd been there a while. There was no sign of snark in her eyes.

"Carly's waiting." Jude came into the room and sat on the edge of Shae's frilly bed.

With a kiss on Shae's forehead and a battle of who loved who more, I said goodnight to Shae. I snatched my shoes on the way out and went to my own room to change.

In my pajamas, and with the stupid night cream that promised to hide my wrinkles rubbed into my tired face, I headed down the hall. Behind my soon-to-be nine-year-old's door, a single light shone from her bedside table. She continued reading her book as I walked over and lifted the covers. My cold feet found her warm little legs and I nuzzled into one of my favorite spots on earth.

"I'm mad at you," she finally said before tapping my head with her paperback. She frowned, but it lacked conviction.

"I'm trying, Carly. I really am." I plead my case with sincere eyes, but the guilt of never being enough soured inside me.

She shifted onto her side, set the book on the table and turned off the light. Facing the wall, she said, "I want to go and see daddy for my birthday. That's all I want, not even a cake." Her quiet confession tore at what I was sure was my last layer of strength.

I snuggled her tight and moved my fingers to her hair. I twirled and gently tugged, as was our ritual since she had stopped being a bald baby and turned into a toddler with thin, silky locks.

"Whatever you need, bunny."

"I need you to never forget your phone again." She interlaced her sweet fingers into mine and moved our hands under her chin.

"I'm sorry." I was. I truly was.

She nuzzled her cheek into my forearm. "Those words don't help."

Not much did. Jude was right. I was an epic fail.

Chapter Two

The Unicorn

Ben

A drop of sweat plopped on the ground as I curled upward for another abdominal crunch. *Cupcake.* That was what I was calling her. I tightened my crossed arms on my bare chest. If she was going to give me a totally ridiculous nickname, she'd get one too. Although, I admit there was nothing ridiculous about Cupcake.

Reps complete, I swung down and my feet stomped on the concrete of my garage floor. Well, Uncle Teddy's garage. Attached to his house, not mine. I grabbed the jump rope and skipped into my routine. *A fucking unicorn. What in eternally burning hell does that mean?*

The whoosh of the rope and its snap lulled me into a welcome trance, but it wasn't long before my thoughts went back to Amee Benton. She was probably a few years older than me and definitely smarter — and beautiful, even in a boring-ass business suit with shoes that should be snapped in half and thrown away. Gorgeous women didn't need too many accessories.

And even though her face read tired, with her fit little body and dark blonde hair, she remained exceptional.

Shit. I'd almost said, *'you got it'* after she'd said, *'fuck me.'* I chuckled through the rest of the rope workout at her profanity. I was a sucker for a dirty mouth—without fail.

I tidied up my makeshift gym and headed into the house. Little Man sat at the kitchen table spooning cereal into his mouth, the milk dripping into the bowl below and his dark hair fully snarled in bedhead. In front of him was the physical newspaper he insisted on reading and having delivered every morning.

"Your mom up yet?" I opened the fridge and pulled out the milk for my protein shake.

"Uh-uh." He wiped the back of his hand along his chin and swiveled in his chair to face me. "She got in late again."

Our gazes held, transmitting the true meaning of his words. He spun around to the four-person wooden table and dug the spoon into his bowl. The crunch and slosh of cereal in his audibly open mouth made me shudder.

"Chew with your mouth closed, Nate. And please try to remember that Monday at lunch when you start your new school."

He rolled his brown eyes and took another loud bite.

"Dude. Seriously."

I prepared my shake and he brought his empty bowl over to the sink, rinsed it and stuck it in the dishwasher. I leaned against the counter and sipped.

Little Man faced me, and I caught the quick twitch of his mouth.

"What?" I asked.

He sighed. "She didn't get the shirts. I reminded her all week, but she never got them. The store isn't open on Sundays and I can't go to the new school without the uniform. It already sucks being the new kid." His dark eyes softened. He hated asking me more than he hated the disappointment in his mom.

I ruffled his shaggy hair and smiled. "I'll take you. Just let me shower."

The twitch was back, followed by a side bite of the bottom lip.

"What else?"

"It's at the mall." Nate cringed.

I faked puking up my shake until he laughed. "That's how much I love you, Little Man. Saturday-morning-at-the-mall love."

* * * *

Teenager girls moved in packs, staring down at phones and somehow not running into people. Middle-aged men wore tucked-in Polo shirts with random labels on the breast. Their khaki pants were topped off with dark belts. They held bags and pretended not to ogle the underwear on display in the window of Victoria's Secret. The smells of overly sweet soap mixed with fast food made a stew that churned the bile in my stomach.

It was hell, my own personal mall hell. Half of me expected one of my ex-girlfriends to pop out from behind one of the kiosks and scream, "Boo!" It was enough for me to ask Satan for a hug.

"Where is this store, anyway?" I searched the pastel-cased map but could only find overly branded shops with shit that no one actually needed, except maybe

Victoria's Secret. Every woman needed lace, as far as I was concerned.

"There's an information desk over there." Nate pointed to a circular stand not far from the food court.

We walked over and were met by a willowy, pimple-faced teenager whose voice cracked when he asked if he could help us.

"Dude," I said, shaking my head as we headed toward the exit, "you could have told me the store had an outside entrance and we would have been able to avoid all this." I waved my hand around and snarled.

"I didn't know. And I wanted to make sure there was a Mr. Pretzel."

The metal frame of the door scraped against the floor as I pulled it open. I dropped my jaw and bugged out my eyes. "You drag me to the mall then you're gonna eat carbs in front of me? Does ice run through your eight-year-old veins?"

He was still taunting me with all the food he would enjoy after we picked up his shirts when I saw her. Well, the back of her anyway. But there was no mistaking my Cupcake.

Black skinny jeans hugged her legs and outlined a firm little ass — an ass that her work attire had somehow failed to accentuate. She had on a simple white T-shirt and black flats. Without the heels from the day before, our height difference put me at a bigger advantage. I dug my top teeth into my bottom lip and tugged it back.

She stroked the long, light brown hair of what must have been her older daughter. Her fingers stopped at the neckline, twirled a strand then pulled it down to the ends.

Over and over, she repeated the transfixing movements.

A shove in the arm brought me back to reality, and Nate yanked at my sleeve so my ear was at the level of his mouth.

"Staring is rude," he whispered out of the corner of his mouth. I journeyed the length of her once more, lingering on that fine little rear.

Nate hid his eyes behind his hands. "You are *so* obvious," he said into his palms.

"Sorry." I straightened my posture and debated saying hello.

The customers in front of her finished and everyone in the line stepped forward.

"Hi. I'm here to pick-up St. Regis shirts. Amee Benton," Cupcake said to the round, bald man behind the counter.

St. Regis. Nate was headed to the same school as her daughters. She and her perfect little body were officially part of my future. But celebrating would have to wait. I was stuck in that awkward moment of social purgatory. Say hello and seem too eager or say nothing and come off as an unobservant dick, especially with the emotional scene she'd showed me the night before.

"Can I get a frozen yogurt while we wait for Shae and Jude?" her daughter asked as they both spun around.

I smiled a tight, what I hoped was friendly, smile. A simple silver chain flickered in the light and caught my eye. It lay in the opening of her white V-neck and separated two perky mounds of Cupcake heaven.

Amee blinked once, like she'd just seen…well, a unicorn.

Little Man bellied up to the counter and said, "St. Regis shirts for Nathanial Fulton, please."

"Hi." I tilted my head a bit, hoping to unlock a smile from her stunned face.

"Mom?" Her daughter waved spread fingers in front of Amee's head. I liked that kid already. Amee remained frozen. Maybe she needed an out.

"Have a nice weekend," I said and put my arm around Nate.

I handed the Weeble Wobble behind the counter my credit card and Little Man's mouth twisted. It was one thing that his mom had failed him and quite another that he worried about my spending. "It's fine. I can afford your shirts." I messed up his hair.

Behind me the door jangled and closed.

Bye-bye, Cupcake.

"Thanks. I forgot to ask her for money. But I do have enough for my pretzel."

I signed the thin white miniature paper, grabbed the plastic bag with his uniform and said, "Please tell me you're not going to put that yellow goo claiming to be cheese on it."

We walked back into the mall. Thankfully the food court was close to the entrance. Chatter and grease filled the air and we found a small table in the center of the chaos. Nate left to get his carbohydrate and gluten-filled treat and I pulled out my phone, only to find no missed calls from his mom.

"I feel like I should explain for last night." Amee Benton slid into the chair across from me. She tucked a loose strand of her straight hair behind an ear.

Hello, Cupcake.

I set my phone facedown on the table and interlaced my fingers. "For calling me a fucking unicorn?"

"No," she said with a quick shake of her head. Amee rolled her shoulders back, and she placed one hand on top of the other at the edge of the table. "I regret you had to see me like that. And I apologize for putting you in an uncomfortable position."

I cleared my throat. "You're fine. Don't worry about it." I shortened the space between us then whispered, "Your dirty mouth is safe with me, Cupcake." I licked my lips and a pink flush traveled from her chest to cheeks.

"Potty mouth. You said I had a potty mouth. And did you just call me 'Cupcake'?" She shifted in her chair and crossed her arms.

"I did." *Shit. I did. Out loud. Mercy.*

"So, what you're saying is that"—she checked her thin silver watch—"in the course of less than eighteen hours, you've upgraded me from potty to dirty and given me a nickname?" An eyebrow rose, and her gray-blue eyes bored into me. Her attempt to be mad was weak. There was a smile underneath her act.

"Now that I know you think dirty is an upgrade, there's no telling what I can come up with in the next eighteen."

"Holy shit. Are you flirting with him?"

We both whipped our heads around and a blonde with the same button nose and light eyes as Amee peered down at us.

"Jesus Christ, Jude. Stalk much?" A wide-eyed glare followed Amee's words. "Ben, this is my annoying sister, Jude. Jude, this is Ben." After the introduction, Amee dropped her head into her hands and shook it back and forth.

Jude and I exchanged pleasantries, then there was a moment of silence. Maybe Amee would take it as a parachute to escape our conversation.

"So, you gonna ask her out on a date? She could use one," Jude said.

I fought a smile. "I was thinking about asking her to coffee." I squinted to Jude and Amee's head stayed in her hands.

"Fantastic. She's free tomorrow morning. You can meet at Duggan's on Third. Say nine-thirty?"

"Works for me."

Amee lifted her head and her gaze ping-ponged back and forth between her sister and me.

"Great. Then my work here is done. See you at the car, Amers." Jude walked off, joined who I supposed were Amee's daughters and ushered them to the exit.

Nate made his way back toward the table, carrying not one, but two pretzels and a bottle of water.

"So... Do you want to have coffee with me?"

She bit her lips inward and stared me down. Nate arrived at the table with big, disapproving eyes. Amee's tight lips turned into a little smile. "Yeah, I do." She rose out of the chair and said, "See you then, Unicorn."

She swung her hips all the way to the door and the massive grin on my face dropped when I finally looked over at Little Man.

"Seriously?" he asked with high-pitched voice.

I shrugged.

"I'm going to make this painful for you." He ripped off a piece of the soft pretzel and took a bite. "Mmm." Slow chews and more satisfied sounds surfaced. "So salty."

I unscrewed the cap of the water bottle and leaned into the hard chair.

"So carby." Nate did his best impression of an actor in a food commercial.

With a tight grin, I held in my laugh. "'Carby' is not a word."

He stopped mid-pull on the pretzel. "I know that's not a word. I told you that when you said it to Grandpa Teddy last week. You said, '*I can't eat that casserole, it's all carby and cheesy and shit.*'"

"Don't say 'shit'. You're eight."

"Don't hit on moms from my new school."

I drank from the bottle and set it back on the table. "Might be too late for that, Little Man."

"That's what I was afraid of." He crumpled up the wrapper and made a tight ball.

"Sorry. I promise I won't hit on any more moms. Don't be mad at me, okay?" I frowned.

"It's hard to be mad at you when you're the only one who pays attention to me." His words hung in the air, their truth too painful to grasp.

"Okay, mister." The chair scraped against the floor as I stood. "You need anything else while we're in this godforsaken zoo?"

"I have a list." A hopeful but hesitant smile joined his shrugged shoulders.

"I thought you might." I rolled my eyes. Man, I *did* love my cousin's kid if I was ready to endure Mall Hell for him.

Chapter Three

Coffee

Amee

"You called him a *what*?" Jude sat cross-legged on my king-sized bed and sipped her green tea.

In my mismatched bra and underwear, I went to the doorway of my walk-in closet and parked my hands on my hips. "A unicorn. No. Actually, a *fucking* unicorn."

Jude pursed her lips and closed one eye. "You can't wear that."

"No shit, Judy. I'm looking for those navy pants. I think I wore them last time we saw Pete." I spun around and went to the side of the closet that wasn't bare.

"I'm talking about your underwear, grandma."

Grandma? Those were fighting words. I stormed over just in time to catch a smug smile on her face.

"He's not going to see my underwear."

"*No one* should see that underwear." She set her mug on the nightstand and stood up. Crossing to my dresser, she asked, "When was the last time you had a date?" Wood brushing against wood created a low hum as she opened my top drawer. "You need to wear something sexy underneath—*not* those hideous pants you wore to visit your ex-husband in prison—to help your confidence game. It's not about showing. It's about knowing."

I belly flopped onto my bed and whimpered. "Why is this so nerve-racking?"

"Probably because he is massively hot…with tats. I mean, sheesh. He's enough to make me consider going straight." She tossed matching black lace next to me on the bed and headed to the closet. "Why'd you call him a unicorn, anyway?"

"A *fucking* unicorn," I corrected, but wasn't going to give my older sister any more fuel for her teasing fire. "I can't date him, right?"

"Why the hell not?" She examined a black cotton dress on a hanger then hooked it onto the top of the door.

"He's younger than me. And, well, I don't even have time to date. There would be no future. What's the point?"

"Why does there have to be a point?" She plopped down next to me and I sat up. "You're meeting a hottie for coffee. Just start there."

"What if I see someone I know?" I whined.

"Amee. It's fucking coffee. Besides, all those bitchy moms from school don't go to coffee on Sunday mornings. It's their only day to sleep in."

"Christ. Dating advice from a Tinder ho. I'm fucked." I fell back onto the bed again and fake cried. "I don't even have his phone number to cancel."

* * * *

Duggan's was a not-too-hip, not-too-chic coffee shop downtown. It had its own parking lot and outdoor seating with canvas umbrellas for overly sunny days.

Ben — I didn't know his last name — was sitting at a table for two toward the edge of the terrace. His long-sleeved army green Henley was pushed up to the elbows and his casual sprawled posture opposed the nerves brewing in my belly. He stood when he saw me, those damn dimples pressing into his cheeks with his smile.

Time to face the unicorn.

He side-stepped around the table and pulled out the wicker chair for me. The earthy scent from Friday night returned, this time without the motor oil.

"Hey."

The grittiness of his voice made me swallow hard, and I sat in the chair. He reached up to adjust the angle of the umbrella to protect us from the sun. What promised to be the perfectly formed V of his lower abdomen peeked out from between a black elastic waistband under his jeans and the green shirt.

Unicorn cupcake eating man candy. Shit. I was in over my head. He was *way* out of my league. My workouts consisted of me taking the stairs and vacuuming with headphones on. I hadn't even been on a date since Pete and I had divorced. I shouldn't have been allowed to play ball.

New plan – Excuse my behavior from Friday night, tell him I was not ready for any kind of relationship, go home and take a long, long shower thinking about his stomach.

"Sorry I'm late," I said as he took his seat.

"I assumed you would be." He scooted in, and before he could say anything else, the waiter came over.

I ordered a fluffy complicated sugary mess of caffeine and Ben asked for just a water.

"You don't drink coffee?"

"Nope." He crossed his arms. "So, let's hear it, Amee Benton."

"Hear what?" There was no way in hell I would tell him why I'd called him a unicorn. *A fucking unicorn.*

"Your list." His blue gaze challenged me from the opposite side of the table, then he blinked.

"What list? I don't have a list."

"Yes, you do. You have a list of why you're not going to give me your phone number and agree to see me again."

I sank a little into my chair before puffing out my chest, mulling over my next move.

"Maybe you should tell me *your* list." Every muscle on my cheeks wanted to smile but years of questioning witnesses had polished my game face. I shaped parallel lines with my forearms on the black wire tabletop.

"Which one do you want me to tell you about?" he asked with a casual grin.

Stupid dimples. His dimples were dumb. Dumb like puppies.

"How many are there?" I raised my eyebrows.

"Many. Many. So many lists…" Leaning in, he licked his lips. He lightly traced a semi-circle on the top of my hand. "Grocery lists, home repairs, back to school…"

The breath from the base of my lungs rose up my chest and escaped slowly through the 'O' I'd formed with my mouth. I hadn't been touched like that in ages and mundane tasks had never sounded better. *Christ.* I was practically panting.

His recoil startled me and he cleared his throat. The waiter set down our drinks, breaking the beautiful tension.

Creamy froth parted as I blew into the mug before taking a cautious sip. Without the haze of his touch, I regrouped. I placed my coffee on the table and he drank from his water bottle.

"Why?" I asked.

"Why what?" He screwed the cap on and set the bottle on the table.

I'd studied body language. I knew liars and I knew nervousness. His open legs and arms were neither. He was confident, honest. Real.

"Why me?"

A small airy chuckle accompanied a shake of his head and his blond hair brushed against his shoulders.

"Why *not* you, Amee Benton?"

Questioning soon-to-be-ex-spouses was much more satisfying. They weren't allowed to answer questions with questions.

"What's your last name?" I squinted.

"Mathis. And because I like you."

I sipped my coffee.

He propped his elbows on his knees and searched my eyes. "And you're kinda beautiful. Beauty and a dirty mouth are a weakness of mine."

"Like cupcakes?" I fought the smile, but when his dimples appeared, I lost the battle.

"Just like cupcakes." He shifted in his seat and pulled his phone from his back pocket. Quick tapping from his thumbs hit the screen before he slid it to me.

"May I please have your phone number?"

Yes. He could. *Shit.*

I picked up the phone. Under the heading New Contact, there was one word. Cupcake. I giggled, like a school girl in a candy shop. *Pitiful.* I typed in my number, hit new message and sent myself a text.

Satisfied, I grinned and handed the phone back to him. Instead of reviewing my handiwork, he set it face-down on the table.

"You're not going to check? Make sure it's the real number?"

"Nope." He popped the 'p'.

My toes twitched in my flats. The remainder of my coffee and foam clung to the edges of my cup and trailed down to the empty bottom.

"Are you free Friday night?" Ben asked with a rasp.

Coffee had been one thing. *Safe.* The sun was shining. Friday night would be a date. *Risky. Dark.*

"What did you have in mind?" I asked. The man had other lists. Lists hidden in his dimples and heavenly touch.

"A movie. Popcorn." He lifted a shoulder.

One small step for Ben Mathis and a giant leap for Amee Benton. *Crap.* A firetruck and its sirens raced by on Third Avenue and the intrusive sound gave me a minute to think. *This is what I'd wanted when I'd divorced Pete, right?* A chance for something deeper before I shriveled up and had as many cats as Shae had dolls.

But then Pete had gotten drunk and killed another human being. He'd pleaded guilty to a lesser charge and had been taken away to a correctional facility within months, locking away my bright future behind bars with him. Instead of free weekends to build a new life, I had one hundred percent parenting duties twenty-four-seven, not to mention my career.

But Ben's touch had answered a faded call — a call to be selfish, a call to be human.

"Can I meet you there? I'm not sure the girls are ready for their mom to be on a date."

"I'll text you." He flipped over the check and dug into his front pocket.

With the money and check secured under my used coffee cup, Ben walked me to my car. When we arrived at the driver's side door, I turned around to face him. He pushed his arm into the window and crowded my space.

"I gotta admit that I'm a little disappointed." He was close. *So* close. And the hair on the back of my neck stiffened with the scratch in his voice.

I could have kissed him. I could have absolutely kissed him. Right there. Broad daylight. Sunday morning. Did. Not. Care.

I summoned any courage I had and asked, "Why's that?"

Soft stubble caressed my cheek as he leaned into my ear. His warm breath brushed my neck as he whispered with his ridiculous rasp, "I was looking forward to your dirty mouth."

My expression must have been his desired response, because when he stepped back and freed the heat between us, his grin stretched from ear to ear.

"See ya Friday, Cupcake."

He swaggered away and climbed into a beat-up truck.

Revised plan – Shower and a lonely orgasm.

* * * *

I finished my coffee and placed the paper cup in the drink holder of my car. Barbed wire curled above a chain-link fence opposite my black shiny hood. I'd rescheduled a meeting and put Jude on morning drop-off duty to visit Pete alone before the girls and I came out together for Carly's birthday on Saturday.

I passed the initial guard — who verified my ID — and took a gray plastic crate for my bag. Another guard waved me through the metal detector then hooked his blue-gloved thumbs back into his belt loop.

"This way," he said. *As if I don't know.*

Distant doors buzzed, and my heels echoed down the stark hallway. A chubby guard opened the door to the visitation room, where another uniformed man met me. The younger and more physically fit guard nodded his hello and I searched for a table, preferably as far away as possible from the strung-out blonde in the corner, scratching her already-irritated skin. I'd seen her before, and her stench of cigarettes and body odor had been embedded into my olfactory system's permanent memory. *No need to re-live it.*

I sat and crossed my legs. Experience told me I had fifteen minutes before Pete would show up. The stale air in the windowless room reflected the motionless moments of prisoners' lives. Outside the walls, life carried on. Behind them, nothing changed.

My phone had stayed in the car so there was no way to re-read the text Ben had sent late Sunday night. When I'd been across from him, I'd written, *This number belongs to a fucking unicorn.*

He'd replied, *Your dirty mouth* was *there. No longer disappointed. BTW, interesting choice of words...*

Then nothing. The dot dot dot must have meant that he would get back to me. I'd checked at lunch on Monday, after work and again that morning, each time reopening the chat to make sure I hadn't missed a notification. *Am I obsessing? Probably.* I'd even searched for him on the first day of school. The little boy he'd been with on Saturday had also said St. Regis. *Is that his son?* There wasn't a lot of resemblance.

Why didn't I ask him about the boy when we went for coffee? Maybe he was having second thoughts for Friday. *And what will Friday be like? Will we kiss?* I bet he was a fantastic kisser. Forceful, hungry.

"Haven't seen that smile for a while." Pete's hollowed-out cheeks and pale face looked down at me. His beige inmate uniform hung off him, and each time I saw him, his frame shocked me. "This is a nice surprise."

Pete tapped the table twice and sat down with a straight back and a slight grin.

"How are you?" I always tried to be civil. We had a history. We had children. I'd witnessed firsthand too many bitter ex-spouses.

His hazel eyes rolled. "Shitty. I'm in fucking jail, Amee."

Oh, there he went. *Pete's Pity Party*, take one.

What had the family therapist told me during my solo sessions? Zen garden. I was in a Zen garden. A Zen garden of bullshit, but still…

"No need to get hostile. I was just being polite. Christ."

The door opened and another inmate in a matching beige jumpsuit joined what was most likely his lawyer at a center table.

I continued, "You'll be out in three months, Pete. Less than a hundred days."

"You counting down?" he asked with too much hope.

Not that. Not that head tilt and pleading in his eyes.

"The girls miss you. Carly said she didn't even want a cake for her birthday. She's read that fucking book you gave her countless times and I think she sleeps with it." My best attempt at chipper would have to do.

"But *you* don't miss me." He crossed his arms then lifted a hand to cradle his chin. "Not even a little."

"This is exactly why I came by myself before Saturday. I don't want you to bring this up in front of the girls. They've got their own shit to deal with. It would be cruel to give them false hope of us patching things up." *Asshole.* I would pat myself on the back later for leaving out the 'asshole' part.

In a quiet voice he said, "What am I supposed to do in three months? Huh? Get a job bagging groceries? I will forever be an ex-con."

I pushed my elbows into the plastic table and two fingers into each temple. I closed my eyes.

Pete continued, "I won't even have a place to live. It will be easier for everyone if I move back in. I can stay in the guest room. I can help with the girls."

"No. It will be easier for you, but it won't be easier for everyone."

"When did you get so fucking selfish?" he spat.

Bait. I recognized it. Name calling. Trying to guilt me into believing I was the bad person. That if I hadn't filed for divorce, he wouldn't have had to drink. Then drive. Then go to jail. My Zen garden was a mirage. I was actually in a landfill — and it reeked.

I trailed my fingers down my cheeks then rubbed my jaw. "I don't want to fight with you, but you need to be clear on one thing. You will *not* move into my house."

"*Your* house?"

"My house. I paid for it. I got it in the divorce. *My* house."

"God, you really are a bitch. I'm here, away from *our* family — you know, the one we made together — alone. Do you know how much I miss those girls? How sorry I am for driving that night? The irony isn't lost that two families are fatherless because of me." He bit his tongue and squinted as he shook his head.

"Our family was already broken before your stupidity." My words were flat and I hope they'd ring a bell in his damn head. I'd sure as shit said them enough in the past.

"Are you so heartless that you won't let me make up for lost time? With them? With us?"

"There is no more 'us'." Another repeat.

As we stared at each other, the wrinkles around his eyes tightened. He glanced down then up.

"Are you dating someone?" His face gnarled, and mouth gaped.

"That's none of your business." I folded my hands on the table then twisted my watch.

"Jesus Christ. Are we done here?" He shoved against the table and the chair screeched under him. His nostrils flared. *Ugh.*

"No." I pushed my palms into my eyebrows. "I need to know what you want to get Carly for her birthday."

He stood with a snarl. "Another book. This time, check the self-help section. I think there's one called, *What to Do When Your Mom's a Heartless Bitch.* Get that one. She's gonna need it."

Chapter Four

Popcorn

Ben

The TV blared the slow southern drawl of a baseball announcer and I found Uncle Teddy in his recliner. The drapes were drawn, just an orange sliver of the sunset peeping through and highlighting the dust particles in the living room.

Nate was sitting on the floor with the light blue laundry basket. He was folding Uncle Teddy's worn-out boxer shorts. *Poor kid, always paying penance for his mother.*

"Hey," I said and plugged my phone to charge on the table in the entryway. Nate looked up, but Teddy stayed focused on the red-and-white team on the box in front of him. "Come into the kitchen and tell me about your week."

The familiar twist appeared on his lips and he glanced down to the full basket of clean clothes.

"It can wait," I said.

"But then everything gets wrinkled." The little plea in his voice, the part of him who loved perfection, was too much to resist. After all, if he didn't have that tiny glimmer, his life would be totally different.

"All right," I answered and shook my head with a smile. "Bring it to the table, and we'll do it together."

His large, satisfied grin pierced my heart. *What eight-year-old finds joy in folding white boxers with holes around the elastic waistline?*

I washed my hands — the grease of my job had a way of following me everywhere — and met him at the table. Nate grabbed one of my white T-shirts and snapped it straight. He laid it flat, smoothed out the remaining bumps and folded it into a neat and even rectangle.

"Do you have a part-time gig at The Gap I don't know about?" I asked.

"I'm too young to work, although I saw they're hiring at the mall."

I shuddered at the memory of mom jeans and toddlers trying to escape their loaded-down strollers.

"So... Give me the good, the bad and the ugly." I rolled my gym socks together and tossed them onto the table. "I want to know all about your week. Between me putting in extra hours, night school and getting up to work out, I missed the details."

He focused on another pair of Teddy's underwear fit for zombies and his little chest rose and fell intently.

"And I missed you too, Little Man."

He blinked his warm brown eyes and scratched his head. "Well. My teachers are pretty cool. Except the music one, she has weird teeth and abnormally curly hair." He grabbed another T-shirt of mine. "The food at lunch is really good. Lots of healthy stuff, you'd be happy."

I smiled. He had started in my precise order — that had been the good. "Okay, so the bad?"

"I'm the new kid and I'm kinda a geek." He scrunched his button nose and laid my shirt on top of the other in a pile. They'd never been so wrinkle free.

"You're not a geek."

A loud snore resonated from the living room. Baseball was more powerful than any sleep aid on the market.

"It's okay." Nate's little shoulders wiggled. "I'm smart and suck at sports. The sooner I learn to deal and accept my geekiness, the sooner I can figure out who the other nerds are."

With everything folded, I loaded the basket. "All right, so what's the 'ugly', then?"

Nate slid into a chair and chewed his lip. I flipped the seat next to me, straddled it and crossed my arms over its high back. "Spit it out, Little Man."

"I don't want to say it out loud. I'm afraid it makes me a bad person." Nate frowned. He blinked several times, tears threatening to drop.

"Hey." I pushed the plastic basket to the other end of the table. "You can say anything to me. I won't tell a soul. And you are *not* a bad person. Don't ever, ever, think that."

After a swallow and a nod, he said, "There's this fall welcome thing next Saturday. It's supposed to be super fun, like a carnival. I want to go."

"Then you should go."

"It's for parents, too." Nate dropped his gaze from mine and he focused on the linoleum floor below.

Just above a whisper, I said, "You don't want *her* to go."

He blinked hard, releasing a long tear down his cheek before turning to me and confirming with a slow shake of his head. The earlier puncture wound in my heart transformed into a gaping hole. An embarrassing mother would indeed be the worst thing for him. While Kim had always teetered on the edge of depression, her current rut was particularly deep. We all silently moved around her, hoping something would trigger some healing.

Entrance into that school had required my uncle to actually get up off his ass and help his only grandchild. Teddy had called an old buddy from his lodge who was on the board of the private school and he'd pulled some strings. When Nate and Kim had moved in at the beginning of the summer, we'd had to act fast. But once it was a sealed deal, Teddy'd washed his hands of it. Maybe he'd felt like I had it all under control and he could revert to his life of naps, sports and frozen dinners. Maybe seeing his daughter shrivel away in front of his eyes prevented him from actively loving Nate.

But not me. Nate's dad had been my friend and his mom my family. I was even paying part of the kid's tuition, although I would never tell him that. I was ready to take care of him, whatever it took.

At first, there had been fights and screaming matches between Kim and me. I hated how she neglected him. But they'd only upset Little Man, so I'd surrendered. I'd waved my white flag of acceptance, for his sake. And even though he wasn't my son or my true nephew, he was my Little Man. Helping Nate be happy, healthy and as normal as we could get was my number one priority.

"Can I take you?" I asked.

"But…you're not my parent." He squinted his puppy dog eyes, and I snickered inside — Nate loved his rules.

"We can say she's sick. No one will know, I promise. And you know what? In a way, she is. And just like being sick, she's gonna get better. You'll see."

Nate scratched his head and I decided not to push it. He had his own checks and balances of morality to weigh. I swiveled in my chair and opened my legs. "Come here." I waved him over to me and he got up and obeyed. I hugged him tight and, in his ear said, "I got you, Little Man. We may not have known each other long, but I love you and I got you." I gave a quick peck on his temple and he squeezed me tighter.

"Aw. You two are downright adorable." Kim's voice mocked us from the archway into the kitchen. Her thin, highlighted hair streamed below her shoulders and her out-of-date tight clothes signaled she wasn't going to snuggle up on the couch and watch a movie later.

Nate stepped back from the embrace and said, "Hey, Mom. I finished folding the laundry and I did all my homework on the bus already."

Kim zeroed in on me like her child's good behavior was me trying to get revenge her for being absent. But life had dealt her shit — and if it helped to blame me, so be it.

"That's great, baby," she said, her words hollow. She snarled at me then chimed, "I'll make you and Grandpa some mac and cheese. Then Mommy's meeting some friends."

"I need to shower." I pressed into my knees and stood. I shot Nate a quick wink and mentally flipped off his mother as I left. I was tolerant, but far from perfect.

* * * *

Sitting on a wooden bench in the park across from the movie theater, I checked my phone yet again. I was sure she was the kind of woman who would cancel if she wasn't coming. She also had a habit of being late and I teetered between both possibilities.

Maybe I had no business trying to date an older woman, totally out of my league and miles out of my tax bracket. But there was something. A spark, friction, lust. Yeah, there was lust, especially after those jeans. *Mercy.* And there was more. An attraction to her need. A desire to give her...

What could I give her, anyway? *Something better.* I could be better than what she'd had. She didn't need money. She needed someone who saw her. The real question remained if I could prove that I was that person—if I even was that person.

Quick movements in the crosswalk caught my eye. There she was. I rested my elbows on the top of the bench. Her light hair bounced with her steps. She wore a hippie sheer blouse and those damn jeans. She clutched a small purse in her hand and when our eyes met, she smiled.

As she got closer, I stood and slipped my phone into my back pocket. First dates sucked. No kissing hello and hugging was, well, kinda pussy awkward when one barely knew the person. I settled on a smile I hoped read 'no pressure'.

"Sorry I'm late." She shrugged and bit her bottom lip.

"Is that something you're going to be saying to me often?" I winked. I didn't care that she wasn't on time. She was there. We were officially on a date.

"Maybe we should see how tonight goes before we commit to future tardiness."

Right. *Slow down, Benji.*

We walked to the corner and I pushed the button to cross the street.

"What do you want to see? There's that comedy" — I pointed to the huge poster of a disgruntled couple and four dogs — "or that action re-telling." We both looked over to the famous actor's face with multiple explosions behind him.

"Action."

Was she flirting with me? Either way, I'd won. I did not want to sit through a rom-com. I would have, because well…her. But no way in fourteen mall hells did I want to.

"You sure?" I asked as we stepped into line for the box office.

"I am so sure. Thank you. As a divorce lawyer, I can't watch those romantic movies anymore. I just end up dividing all the assets and wondering who gets the dog. That one seems to have four."

I smiled, paid for our tickets, and we went to the concession stand. With a popcorn for me and water for both of us, we headed to the theater.

Once we settled down, the salty sin crunched in my mouth and I must have let out a moan or sigh.

"Cheat day again?" She raised one of her thin eyebrows.

"Mmm-hmm." I tossed another handful in my mouth.

"Is it always Friday?"

I finished chewing, ran my tongue quickly over my teeth and turned to her. "Always."

She rubbed her shoulders and shivered. "Why is the air conditioning always full blast?"

I fought my smile by adding more popcorn to my pie hole. *My arm. Around her. Soon.* The popcorn needed to be destroyed. It was the only thing standing in the way of physical contact.

"You want any of this?" I tilted the bucket to her.

"No, thanks. I ate with the girls."

The previews rolled in front of us. I battled between not coming across like a dog in heat for popped kernels with fake butter and too much salt, and getting my arm around that woman. *Thank God, I opted for the small.*

When I got near the bottom, I offered her one last chance to share in the cheat. Her warm smile and small shake of her head made me think she didn't want to take away any of my food happiness.

Boom!

Massive bass opened the movie and she sat a little straighter. The light from the screen bounced off her face as her eyes raced to follow the images. Her silhouette hit me in the chest. There was something different about her energy. I wondered how long it had been since she'd done something as simple as go to an adult movie on a Friday night.

I set the bucket on the floor and took a drink of my water. I briefly debated faking a stretch but pretending would have been out of character. I reached my arm over her shoulders and nudged her in my direction.

Still staring at the silver screen, she rubbed her lips together. Then, it happened. Her posture melted and her elbow touched my stomach. By the time the end credits rolled, her knees were in her chest and my thumb brushed against her leg. She'd curled perfectly into me.

We picked up our litter and side-stepped to the exit. At the trash and recycling station, she paused.

"You didn't finish your popcorn?"

"I'm good." I threw the bucket away.

"Does that mean we can get ice cream?" Her slate-colored eyes lit up.

"Hell yes, we're getting ice cream."

"Come on. There's a gelato place not far." Amee reached for my hand, threaded her fingers in mine and pulled me out of the door.

On the street, we probably talked about the movie and its plot, maybe even the actor and the latest gossip about him. It didn't matter what she said. It was how she said things, so easy, relaxed. Amee Benton chilled out was ten times more beautiful than before, and I didn't think that was possible.

"I'm getting two scoops. I don't even know how to have one anymore," she said in the brightly lit shop. "It's like I'm incapable of having chocolate without coconut."

We ordered, and she insisted on paying. I couldn't decide if I was relieved or heartbroken when she hadn't got a cone. The skill set of her dirty mouth had been on my mind for a week.

Sugary goodness in hand, we walked back to the bench where I'd waited for her at the beginning of the night. The crowd from the movie had dispersed, but country music from the sports bar next to the theatre seeped out of its open door and onto the street.

"So." She hooked a foot under her butt and turned to face me. "I realized I was a shitty coffee date."

"Oh yeah?"

"Yeah." Her spoon dug into her ice cream. First, a bit of chocolate, followed by the white coconut next to it. It was the same pattern she'd executed since she'd started eating it. "I never asked you about yourself. Tell me something."

Tilting the paper bowl, I scraped the last melted bits down in a puddle then scooped them up with my tiny plastic spoon. I swallowed my last cheat of the week and peered at the traces of creamy, melted-sugary heaven. "It would be wrong to lick this, right?"

"Don't do that." She rolled her eyes.

"I won't. I mean, it's tempting, but I won't." I set the spoon and empty bowl next to me on the bench. When I smiled back to her, her face had fallen.

"No. I mean don't answer a question with a question. It drives me nuts."

"Is that why you became a lawyer? So people have to answer your questions?" I stretched out like a board, arms over head and toes pointed.

Her gaze lingered down at my waistline then met mine. "Tired?"

"Nope." I scooted back into the bench and blinked a few times.

"Liar. But I'm not going to let you go home until you tell me something about yourself." She stood, swept up my bowl and walked over to the trash. Her incredible and needed-to-be-squeezed—and a whole list of other things I was still working on, 'cuz I had a list—ass wiggled the entire way. When she was done, she perched her hands on her hips in front of me. "Come on. One thing."

"Well, you already know where I work. That's one thing." I rubbed my hand over my beard. *What can I tell her? That my cousin is a faltering mother, her son is my only real connection in the world and my uncle is an uninvolved conflict-avoider? That I go to night school to try to better myself but that I barely understand anything the teacher says?*

She crossed her arms and scowled. Not a real one, but she was trying.

"Fine." I held up my hands. "I get up at the crack of dawn and work out every morning in my garage."

"Not what I had in mind, but I didn't know that, so I guess it counts." She held out her hand and I had an urge to pull her into my lap. Instead, I clasped it and stood.

"Walk me to my car?" she asked.

"With pleasure." Anything to spend more time with her.

Hands locked, we walked over to the parking garage in silence. When we stood in front of her Cayenne, I asked, "Do I get a third date?"

She spun to face me and pressed her lips together. A quick nod allowed me to step closer. Her perfume was faint but like crisp sunflowers in a distant field. I searched her face for more approval, any tell that it was okay to kiss her. Her eyelids fluttered — not unlike the beating of my heart — and I closed my eyes.

As much as I wanted to push her against the car and find out how she really kissed, she deserved better. I brushed my lips across hers as she released an exhale. I hovered, not wanting to budge from the perfect fit I'd been longing for. Eventually, I let go and stepped back. I licked my lips and the residual coconut and chocolate mixed together on my palate.

"Fuck." Her airy tone made me smile.

"Your dirty mouth tastes nice, Cupcake." I winked and walked backward with a grin.

She opened her little clutch and found her keys with the hilarious stuffed squirrel. She was halfway into the driver's seat before she said, "You're a fucking unicorn with ridiculously soft lips."

The car door slammed as if she were mad. But before she drove away, she smiled and rolled her eyes.

I rode the high all the way to my pickup, then my heart hit the concrete. *What the hell am I going to do for date three?*

Chapter Five

Cake

Amee

The unmistakable buzz and click of the heavy door unlocking resonated in the vestibule. I ushered the girls over to security and we placed our belongings in plastic crates on the conveyor belt. My heart sank. No matter how many times we'd shuffled through the routine, the gravity weighed me down. My children had to pass through a metal detector before they could see their father.

I rolled my shoulders and reminded myself why I was there. *Carly.* My daughter wanted to be with her daddy. She was starved for his contact, wilting in the absence of their daily bond. When I reached down for Shae's sweet hand, I squeezed it twice, our secret signal of love. Carly walked with determination in front of us and waited at the visitation room door. When we caught up, the guard opened it and we sat in silence at a Formica table in the corner. The stale air hung over us.

Each visit was a glimpse of happiness for some and a reminder of hardships for others. Well, hardship was the nice way to put it. The desire to vomit was perhaps more in line with my sentiments.

Carly smoothed the rainbow-striped fabric cover of her sketchbook. Pete's idea, it was filled with drawings she'd done for him. Each visit she brought it to share, and after every goodbye, it returned home. I'd often wondered if Carly used it as proof she had been thinking about him.

Shae fiddled with her new doll's shoes then hugged it into her little body. Our inmate finally appeared with open arms for his girls. I stood while Carly gripped him tight.

"Happy birthday, baby!" Pete lifted Carly off her feet and kissed her cheek. Their embrace was longer than usual, no doubt Pete sensing her need.

"Hi, Daddy." Shae's tone was as if she'd seen him ten minutes prior. "How's jail?"

His tired eyes pierced me like daggers, as if I could control what came out of our younger child's mouth.

"It sucks, because I miss you all so much." Pete sat in the chair where Carly had been and she slid into his lap like a hand into a glove.

"This is Fortune Feimster. Aunt Jude bought her for me since I'm really good at reading." Shae lifted the doll's little arm and Pete shook its plastic hand. "She says she's delighted to make your acquaintance but won't be coming back. She doesn't like the way it smells here."

"Oh my God, Shae. You're so rude." A big sister's judgment was never far away and that one came complete with Carly's stink lip. She would have made a great Elvis.

Shae shrugged, the comment rolling off her red-and-white polka dotted back.

Addressing the doll, Pete said, "Well, thank you for making the effort today, Miss Feimster. It's greatly appreciated." He turned his attention to Carly's book and kissed her cheek again. "Show me what you did this week."

Our elder daughter explained to him her page of eyes and how she had been trying to understand the different shapes they could make. Shae and I assumed our seats as witnesses to the undeniable bond on the other side of the table by solidifying our own. She slid onto my knees, I kissed the top of her blonde head and ran my fingers up and down her arms the way she liked.

I would have to talk to her about the comment and try to weigh how much of it was her being blunt or her trying to tell us something more. She had only been four when I'd filed for divorce and her connection with Pete had suffered from it. He'd clung on to Carly because she'd reached out to him while the little one, confused and overwhelmed, had retreated to me.

After the sentencing, when we'd learned he would have a year of confinement, Shae had changed. As if understanding that her sister needed more attention, she'd balanced by becoming stronger. Shae was more vocal, more independent, and had fourteen times the attitude of her bigger sister. Out of necessity, she'd become my rock while we both tried to be strong for Carly. Shae's new role was unfair — she was still a baby in my eyes — and I hoped someday to free her of it.

Our time was up, and Carly and Pete scowled with my reminder. Shae said a simple goodbye with a kiss on her father's cheek and a wave from Fortune

Feimster. Carly clung to her daddy while she bawled into his shoulder. Tears puddled in his own bloodshot hazel eyes and he whispered all the comfort he could muster in her ear.

When they finally pulled away, Pete cleared his throat and stood straight. "I'll see you next week." He let out a long breath through his mouth then forced a smile.

No, he wouldn't see us the following week, and once again I had the familiar duty of bad cop. "Next week is the Fall Fest. We'll see you in two weeks."

His face dropped, and he shot me a quick, cutting glance. "Well, Fortune Feimster will be happy." He winked over to Shae, who smiled back.

"I'm sorry," I said under my breath and went to console Carly, whose face was red and puffy. I reached down for her hand and she glanced over her shoulder as the guard held the door open for us.

Outside, and free of the bleach and industrial cleaner, I released Carly's hand when we got to the car. She stayed on the passenger side as Shae and I looped around. Before I opened the little one's door, I whispered, "Be nice."

The forty-minute drive was in silence, as were the many that had preceded it. When we got home, I could smell Jude's sweet brilliance from the entryway. Like dogs who'd picked up a scent, the three of us walked down the open hall to the kitchen.

My not-so-big sister stood over the middle island. She wore the white apron I'd given her the previous Christmas. It said, '*You Are What You Eat*' and had a graphic rainbow above the black font.

Jude finished piping out a flower and looked over at Carly. She set the icing bag down on the counter and shrugged. "I know you said no cake, but it's kinda what I do."

Jude outstretched her arms and she frowned to Carly, who walked over and let her aunt hug her tight.

"What flavor did you make?" Shae hopped onto a barstool and was practically nose-to-pastry.

"Strawberry and buttercream layered."

Shae made several little smacking sounds and rubbed her hands together.

"Mom?" Carly asked as she walked closer to the counter.

I raised an eyebrow and smiled.

"Can we have my cake for lunch?"

Shae widened her eyes to the size of golf balls and looked back and forth from cake to mother. The silverware clanked in the drawer as I opened it and I pulled out four forks. The end of the silent treatment and my daughter's birthday both deserved a sugar reward. "We can absolutely have cake for lunch."

"You're the smartest big sister on the planet. I take back everything bad I said about you yesterday," Shae gushed to her sister.

Once the forks were distributed, the four of us hovered over our meal.

"We're not even gonna get plates?" Jude leaned in on her elbows.

"Nope."

Later, after an equally unhealthy meal of delivery pizza and a movie with adult language that Shae was probably too young for, the girls were asleep. Jude had gone out with friends and I curled up on the couch.

I didn't want to be *that* girl and call Ben. But, damn it all, I wanted to call Ben. He would offer a real escape from my epically shitty day. At the movies, when I'd snuggled into his arm, it had been a connection to something other than my role as mother or lawyer. And the biceps. Those muscles had given me a lot to think about.

What would he be doing on a Saturday night anyway? A huge part of me doubted that he would in any way be at a bar. Maybe he was working out. I pictured the glimpse I'd gotten of his abs on our coffee date and the night before when he'd stretched. There was a definite six-pack waiting for my fingers under his shirt. And Christ, as worn as his hands were, his lips had been the softest thing to ever touch me. Maybe it would be a rebound or a fling or some kind of secret affair. It didn't matter. Jude was right. I needed it.

I stretched behind me and grabbed my phone. Typing the words made it realer than real and heat flushed my neck and chest.

I want to kiss you again.

I hit Send and tossed my phone onto the couch like a hot potato. I covered my eyes with my hands, but I peeked out at the screen through the slits in my fingers.

Thankfully, the torture of the wait was brief.

Where?

Where? I stared at my phone. Like on his body? *Um…your abs, Ben. Duh. Wait no, the mouth. Definitely the mouth. And the neck.* Yes, kiss his scruffy neck while my fingers counted the ripples in his belly. That needed to happen. And soon. Very soon.

I dropped a pin on the phone to show him my location and replied.

Here.

Before I could think of the implications, the phone vibrated next to me and his nickname appeared on the screen. *Shit.*

I clenched my jaw and swiped the bar to answer.

"Hi."

"Hey..." *Triple-layered shit.* His deep voice was about to reject me. "What are you doing?"

I swallowed. "I'm trying to do something to make myself happy."

"Is this your home address?"

"Yeah, the girls are asleep." Lord, I sounded desperate. "Do you want to come over?" I ground my teeth and squeezed my eyes shut.

He chuckled slightly. "I'll come over on two conditions."

"Okay..." I opened one eye but kept the other closed, unconvinced that our conversation would go well.

"First, you can't change out of what you're wearing now into something to impress me."

I looked down at my plaid pajama pants and tank top. *Uh-oh.*

"And second, I'm not going to come in." The other eye flew open.

"What? Why?"

"Amee, I don't want your daughters walking in on me grinding on top of you."

Grinding on top me? Holy shit. That sounded fucking fantastic.

"I'll be there in twenty." He hung up and I wondered if twenty minutes was long enough to build a case about the grinding behind a locked door somewhere in my house.

* * * *

With my hands in the pocket of the cardigan that I'd grabbed, I sat on the steps of my front porch and examined my toes. I was going to need to revisit regular lady grooming if the thing with Ben went any further.

The purr of a motor came from down the street. The closer the headlights approached, the faster my heart raced. *Is this feeling the same thing rule-breaking babysitters go through when they have their boyfriends illegally visit them while on duty?*

Ben's big black truck pulled into my driveway and the sound and shine died. I stood and walked over to the driver's side where the window was halfway down.

"Hey, Cupcake." He rubbed his beard and leaned back.

"You sure you won't come in?"

"Positive."

He gestured to the other side of the truck and said, "Hop in."

I closed the car door as silently as I could and tried to find any residual confidence the second-guessing of the prior twenty minutes hadn't washed away. "I hope you weren't in the middle of something."

"Nah. Nate and I watched Laurel and Hardy all night and I had just put him to bed."

"He doesn't look like you." I thought back to the little boy from the mall.

"No reason why he would." When I tilted my head, he continued. "He's not mine. Unfortunately. But I love him like he is."

A man who steps up to the plate? Yes, please. I repositioned myself to get an eyeful of Ben Mathis. Between my front porch and the streetlight, there was enough of a glimmer to bounce in his blue eyes.

"He's my cousin's kid. His dad died in Iraq."

"Oh. I'm sorry."

Nate was another fatherless child. Between work and my personal life, I'd seen too many.

"What about you? What led you to want to do something nice for yourself? Which, as it turns out, sounds nice for me too." His dimples deepened, turning me into putty in PJs.

I dropped my head behind me and exhaled.

"Every Saturday morning for the last six months, I've driven the girls to see their dad. The little one doesn't want to go anymore and the big one would prefer if we lived across the street from the prison."

"That must be tough." He stared ahead at my closed garage door. "For him. For everybody."

"It's definitely not easy. And we can't go next week, so he and Carly are pissed. And I'm their favorite punching bag."

Ben turned to me and narrowed his eyes.

"Figuratively."

"So, you called your favorite unicorn? You think I can make you feel better?" He lifted one of his thick blond eyebrows as if he were daring me to be bold.

"I have a lot of baggage. Two kids, I work all the time…"

"Ah, the list. I knew you had one." He chuckled to himself and stretched. His clothes were just as casual as mine, black sweatpants and a plain white T-shirt. He crossed his arms and smirked over to me.

List or no list, I needed to be honest. I continued, "I don't have a lot to give. I mean, I don't even know if I believe in love at this point. Not that I'm..." *God, the horror. What am I assuming we would be?*

"It's okay. Get it out. Tell me all the shit inside your beautiful head. Then I'll know what I'm up against." His gentle words coaxed their way to the other side of my wall.

I pressed my palms into my forehead. "I just don't—"

"Say it. Ask it. I promise. I'll answer."

"I don't get it." I dropped my hands as the curiosity bubbled. "Why me? I mean, you're hot and sweet and single. Why would someone like you want all the fucked-up shit suitcase that is my life?"

"Fucked-up shit suitcase?"

"Yes. So why?" I slipped off my flip-flops and tucked my foot under my rear.

He looked forward and blinked a few times.

Crap, maybe my sales pitch of how messed up I am worked.

"I honestly don't know. That first night, I thought you were pretty, then funny. And I was sure you were going to be pissed at me for the cupcake. But instead, you called me a unicorn."

"A *fucking* unicorn," I corrected.

His eyes met mine and he smiled. "Exactly. Then, when I saw you in the mall, I just wanted to know you. Who the hell knows why there's a spark? But there is. I'm just trying to figure out what it means and respect you and your family on the way."

I let the words settle between us and used my thumbnail to push back a cuticle on my other hand. "What if this doesn't go anywhere?"

"Then it doesn't. I mean, I'll probably still check out your ass when I see you again, but we'll both live."

The grin on my face was hard to hide. "You check out my ass?"

"Every chance I get." He wet his lips. "Which leads me to your original message."

"I have plenty of rooms with locks on the doors in that house." I tried my sexiest voice, as rusty as it was.

"I told you...I'm not going in there." His deep, breathy words dripped with ultimatum. "Whatever it is you want, you're gonna have to come and get it."

Unicorns were beautiful. Unicorns were magic. But they had no idea what two years of middle-aged sexual frustration and solitude could do to a woman. I climbed over the center console and wedged myself between him and the steering wheel.

Straddling him, I gazed down into his eyes as his hands skimmed my hips then traveled to my ass. As he squeezed, he tilted his head onto the headrest behind him. I played with the thick hair at the bottom of his neck. My breasts perked, and my old but ever-so-welcome friend arousal joined the party. I needed to taste him, to devour him, to breathe him. Aware of my thin cotton pajamas and the soft fabric of his sweats, I swayed my hips once.

He exhaled, leaving his mouth barely open. As gently as I could, I touched my lips to his. I peppered delicate pecks down his jawline to his ear. I flicked the lobe and pulled on it with my teeth. When I reached my hand under his T-shirt and caressed his hard stomach, it was way better than I'd imagined. Rock solid and ripped. *Thank you, unicorn gods.*

"I want to do dirty things to you, Ben," I whispered in his ear. With another grind of my hips, I found the stiffness in his pants and rolled over it again. "Dirty things, with my dirty fucking mouth." I kissed a trail to his lips and he strained to meet me. Instead, I pulled back and smiled. "You sure you don't want to come in?"

Ben grumbled and he moved his hands from my ass to hips. With a sexy smirk, he asked, "Are you teasing me?"

I brought my other hand under his T-shirt and I shrugged.

He grinned. "One, I fucking love it. Two, sorry, Cupcake, I'm not coming in. Not tonight."

I moved closer and kissed him once. I looked over his face for any signs to stop. He dug his fingers into my flesh and drew me nearer.

That time, the kiss was his. It was deeper, harder, rougher. His whiskers scratched my face and the friction and intensity of his movements were well worth the cost of the burn. I intensified the grind, eager for what might someday await. My skin tingled. Had kissing always been that fantastic? I honestly couldn't remember.

He slowed, pulling back between the brushing of our lips, then withdrew completely. "You should go in."

I slumped down and rested my forehead on his thick shoulder. "When can I see you again?"

"Friday night?"

When I sat up, he reached for the door handle.

"That's a long time," I protested.

The click of the release brought the cool night air and I climbed down.

"You're worth the wait, Cupcake." He winked.

"How do you know?" My arms crossed.

"You just showed me."

We said good night and I walked to the door, hoping my pajama pants-clad butt was worth watching.

Chapter Six

Meatloaf Sandwich

Ben

"Flexting." My buddy and regular sparring partner Trev said as the Velcro from his boxing gloves screeched off.

That isn't a word. Is it?

I squirted some cool water on my face, shook off the drops and reached for the towel hanging over the ropes.

"You're flexting her. Flirting via text." Trev's bald black head glimmered with perspiration and he ducked under the top rope and pushed on the bottom to make room for me to climb out of the ring.

I tossed my gloves in my open bag on the floor, wiped around my neck and collapsed onto the bench. Maybe I had worked out too hard. I still had a date to go on. Or maybe I'd done the right thing. Too much energy and seeing Amee after almost a week of her teasing me from a distance would be incredibly frustrating. I didn't think she was ready for the things she hinted at, even if she thought so herself. And after too many rushed relationships in my past, I wanted to try the slow lane.

Trev joined me on the bench, took a drink of a cloudy concoction he'd created to restore 'only his' muscles and hunched over.

"I don't flext." I shot Trev a dirty look. "I'm not an eighteen-year old cheerleader. But I flex." I hunched and pressed my pectoral muscles together while engaging my biceps for a full-on body builder pose.

"Bro." Trev's face turned sour. "Don't use that."

I scratched my wet hair with both hands then clasped them on the top of my head. "What are you doing tonight, anyway?"

"As much as I would like to be in the presence of a beautiful woman like you will be, I have to study. Lame, I know. Med school is poison for a social life." He pushed on his knees and stood. "How's that night class going?"

I dropped my head back and looked up to the ceiling with an exhale through my mouth.

"That well, huh? Jesus, it's only been two weeks." He grabbed his bag and swung it over his bare shoulder.

"I honestly don't know what I was thinking." I side-eyed Trev.

"You were thinking that one day you want your own business and you need to understand accounting to do that." As he walked into the locker room, he said over his shoulder, "Let me know if you need help. And I'll throw the basket in the bed of your truck when I leave."

Four classes of basic accounting and I was already more lost than a debutante in a crack house. I'd opened and closed my textbooks so many times that their previously pristine bindings were already worn. But I couldn't quit. It would disappoint Nate. And I wouldn't do that to him.

But the words and numbers were muddled. Every time I thought I understood a concept, my instincts were wrong. Numbers were nothing like taking apart an engine. Under the hood of a car, everything had a function and place. It was a puzzle waiting to be solved. But a balance sheet, credits, debits, red, black... I couldn't make sense of it. It didn't help that the numbers I plugged in were usually wrong as well.

I checked the large, round clock that hung over the entrance of the club. *Time to shower.* Amee might be fine showing up late, but it would be out of character for me.

* * * *

Two small heads peeked out from behind curtains as I sat in my truck idling in her driveway. I had offered to meet her in a parking lot and go from there, but she had insisted I pick her up at home. The thought of those two cute girls already disapproving bothered me, but it was Amee's call, not mine.

From the window, the shorter one waved in my direction. I checked over both shoulders then pointed inward to myself in a 'Who me?' gesture. Her reply was a smiley nod and the older one disappeared. *Maybe only one of them isn't on board with her mom dating me. Still...*

Commotion at the front double doors caught my eye. Jude shoved Amee out onto the front steps, waved once to me then closed behind her.

As Amee walked down the pathway in her long skirt and denim jacket, I wiped my palms on my pants. I hopped out of my side, leaving the door open, and escorted her around the front of the truck to the passenger side. She slid in, and I jogged back to my door.

In the cab, I nodded to the little girl still observing us. "You sure they're okay with this?"

She smiled tightly as she checked the window then looked back to me. "They have to be. Jude and I talked about it. A lot. They *have* to be."

I shifted the truck into reverse and winked over to the tiny blonde, who now had a doll waving to us. "She seems to be okay."

"Yeah." She let out a half laugh, half scoff. "You should have seen the tiara she wanted me to wear. Let's go. I'm ready to be off mom duty. Where are you taking me, anyway?"

I backed out of the driveway. When we got to the stop sign at the end of her road, I grinned. "What if I'd rather show you than tell you?"

Amee's lips were pursed, and she stared back at me. "You're not going to abduct me, are you?"

With a wink, I said, "I'd like to after all those damn texts this week. But no, just a date."

She rolled her eyes and said, "I actually fucking love surprises."

I did so adore it when the dirty mouth showed up. She moved her elbow to the base of the window and cradled her chin with the palm of her hand.

"And it's been a long time since I had one. A good one anyway."

"No pressure." I turned off on to the gravel road.

We rode in silent but comfortable anticipation until I reached the spot I'd found the Sunday prior when I'd taken Nate for a hike. I reversed into the clearing and killed the engine.

"I need five minutes," I said as I scratched the back of my head.

With the headlights still on for a little guidance, I hurried to the bed of my truck. I arranged the blankets and opened the basket Trev's mom had prepared. Once the setting was as good as I thought it could get, I jogged around to open her door.

Amee was fiddling with her fingers in her lap. It was hard to tell if she was nervous or bored. Neither one a good sign on a date.

"One second." I reached over and pulled out the keys, extinguishing the headlights.

With a small smile, I offered her my hand. She took it with her own timid grin and I guided her to our starlight picnic. When we were just in front of the bed, her neck was exposed and with her so vulnerable, I couldn't resist brushing my beard along the crook of her shoulder and giving her a gentle kiss.

Her shiver was the perfect reaction, and for a brief moment, I thought about tossing her onto the blankets and worshiping the shit out of her.

In time, Benji. In time.

Her eyes fluttered. In front of us were all the city lights and what I hoped would be an acceptable date. She brought a hand to her mouth and stared.

"You like?" I reached around her hips and drew her back to me.

Her head fell onto my shoulder and I gave her a quick peck on the cheek.

"I like," she said and turned to me.

"Good. I'm starving, and my friend Trev's mom makes the best meatloaf sandwiches and peach cobbler in the world." I climbed up and sat on the outstretched blanket. "Come on." I patted the spot next to me.

"What do you eat on non-cheat days?" She joined me on the covers, her feet kicked to the side, and she leaned back.

I twisted off a beer cap and handled her a bottle. "Lots of chicken and veg. And protein shakes. Maybe a banana." I shrugged and tapped my bottle neck against hers. "Cheers."

"Cheers." She tipped her bottle to me. "To my first night picnic. I love it. Thank you."

The smell of Trev's mom's cold hamburger mixed with her special spices sent my taste buds into overdrive. I tore off a bite and savored it. "Oh my God." My stomach purred its approval.

As we ate and drank, she filled me in on her week at work and with the girls. I skirted around the subject of my own. A drunken cousin on a Monday night, me struggling with homework and Nate getting mildly bullied didn't seem like much to brag about.

I repacked our trash into the basket and watched the lights glimmer below us. When Nate had suggested a picnic for a date, I'd thought it was silly. But when I'd realized it would have to be at night and I couldn't really afford a fancy restaurant, it had clicked into place. Luckily, I'd fixed Regina's car and offered for her to pay me in meatloaf and dessert.

"You cold?" I opened my legs and she nudged her way over.

"I'm always cold." She rubbed her hands together as she snuggled her back to my stomach.

I reached for the other blanket and draped it over her knees and feet. Bringing her hands into mine over her shoulder, I blew a warm breath into them. "Better?"

Her gentle sigh was a perfect response.

The city flickered in front of us and a lonely cricket chirped from the woods. Amee stared ahead, probably going through one more of her lists of why I was wrong for her—which, in all fairness, I was. Poorly educated, cheaply bred and no real future that I could assure. At least my Uncle Teddy's house was paid for and my rent was affordable, but with the addition of Kim and Nate, the four of us lived from paycheck to paycheck. And there was only one of those to speak of—mine.

Both of our situations were complicated. I wasn't exactly proud of my living conditions. A beat-up double bed in a finished basement was far from a bachelor pad. And she had two young girls at home. At least the ex-husband was out of the picture. I couldn't imagine letting go of a woman of Amee's caliber was easy, although she did have to see him every week.

"This has been truly perfect. Thank you."

I hooked my chin on her shoulder and squeezed her a little closer. "You ready to go?"

She turned to face me, and gave her head a slow, sultry shake. The back of her hand brushed against my beard. Amee stroked my ear with her fingertips then curled them into my hair.

When she let go, she touched my shoulders then journeyed down my arms and up again. I longed to reciprocate but sensed there was more meaning than feeling my muscles.

At my waist, skin met skin with her fingers on my stomach. I fell back onto my elbows and she climbed on top of me, her flowing dress forming a circle on the blanket. *Holy shit.* The only thing standing between more flesh was her underwear and my pants.

"You been thinking about our texts?" Her voice was almost a whisper.

"Best part of my week."

She pushed down, and my very obvious erection wrote thank-you notes at the contact.

"I can tell," she said with a small grin.

I hit the blankets below and searched the stars for restraint. Lucky for me it was a cloudy night. I shot up, flipped her over, and we were nose-to-nose within seconds. I ran my hand over her smooth leg, exposing it to the night.

"You still cold, Cupcake?"

With a brush of my lips, she shuddered. I kissed her again, then again, deeper but just as slow. Her warm, sweet mouth was too much, and I needed to rub for some relief. I took a hold of her little ass, and when my fingers found lace, I dug in. A whimper accompanied her leg as she hooked it around my lower back, guiding me to continue my grind.

Our kiss amplified, the below-the-belt friction only making me more ravenous. I moved my hand from her ass to her breast and moaned. Even through fabric I could tell her breasts were sensational — a perfect size and no doubt under-appreciated. When my thumb skimmed the pebbled center, she arched her back even more.

I kissed down her neck, and at the base, I had to nibble. It was too much. She was too sweet, too selfless. I needed to make sure she was real. I kissed the spot I'd just claimed as my own and trailed a line with my tongue to her ear.

"So...beautiful." My throaty whisper made her seek out my lips. Amee scraped her fingernails along my neck and tugged hard at my hair. She released one hand and scratched down my back. How she'd known it fucking turned me on more, I had no idea.

Jesus Christ. I wanted to get inside that lace. She would be dripping. I touched her thigh and could already sense her warmth. After another gentle kiss on her sure-to-be-swollen lips, she dropped her head to the blanket below.

"Condom. Please tell me you have a condom," she groaned.

Wait. What?

Did she think I was going to have sex with her? No doubt I wanted to. *Shit*, I needed to. But she barely knew me. Counting coffee, it was only our third date.

Double shit. I'd taken it too far. I rolled off her and fell on my back, my dick shouting profanities at me for the lack of contact.

"Please. Please. Please tell me you have a condom in your pocket." She propped up on an elbow. "Ben." Her hand found the flesh of my stomach and she climbed on top of me. I closed my eyes and let her rock in her rhythmic bliss. She leaned down to my ear and said, "I want you to fuck me."

Am I in purgatory? Because it was equal parts heaven and hell. Meanwhile, my dick had a new best friend and her name was Amee Benton.

"Ben?"

"I don't want to have sex." I hated every word in that sentence. Every syllable. Every letter.

Fuck you, sentence.

"Oh." She stopped her tease. Protests, including signs and chants, called out from behind the zipper of my pants.

"I mean I do. Obviously, I do."

She unhooked her legs from my hips and plopped down next to me, facing the opposite way.

"Hey." I shuffled over to see her face.

Amee frowned and hugged her knees.

"No. No. No. You don't get to do that."

"What?" She pouted. Actually pouted. *Mercy.*

"First of all, let me just say that your fat lip is adorable. But" — I unfolded her arms and pushed her down on her back — "you don't get to take this as a rejection."

With her bottom lip in a full pout, she said, "Feels like rejection."

"Really?" I rubbed against her one more time to offer the proof. "I'm just not ready to take that step with you."

"Exhibit A says you are." She smiled.

I kissed her again. "Guilty as charged. But we're not there yet." I breathed her in one last time then pushed to my knees. "Come on. It's past your curfew."

Crawling around the blanket, I collected the remains of our meal. Amee hadn't moved and was studying the sky.

"You're not helping?" I asked, not really caring, just curious as to what she was thinking about.

"I'm on strike and staying here until you change your mind." She turned her head to me and batted her eyes with exaggeration. "Any chance of that happening?"

I hopped off the truck and held out my hand. "Not tonight, Cupcake."

On the drive home, she played with my free hand while she stared ahead, lost in her thoughts. It was after midnight when I pulled up along the curb to her house.

"Thank you for a beautiful night."

We kissed again, and when she pulled away, she touched her cheek.

"You better hope this whisker burn is gone by tomorrow. I can't have all the school moms clucking around me at the Fall Fest I organized." She winked and reached for the door handle.

"Oh, right. See you then," I said and cleared my throat.

Her hand stayed on the handle, but she didn't open the door. Instead she turned to me and asked, "What do you mean 'see you then'?"

"I'm taking Nate. His mom..." *Is a drunken embarrassment.* "Can't make it."

"Oh." Her smile was off. "See you there. Night." She hopped out of the truck and walked up the pathway to her front door. When she turned around and waved goodbye, the corners of her mouth were curved the wrong way.

Chapter Seven

Cotton Candy

Amee

The athletic field at St. Regis overflowed with bouncy castles and carnival games. The student body ran wild while parents formed familiar huddles and exchanged pleasantries. A light breeze brought the confirmation that the petting zoo had successfully installed itself on the opposite end, and the sun hid behind white puffy clouds.

The first year I had organized the Fall Fest, it had taken a lot of work. The budget approval, finding and booking of vendors and the selection of booths had sucked up every last minute of my free time. But, three years into it, I'd showed up to a meeting, set the date with the principal and had written a few emails. Fall Fest at St. Regis School was a well-oiled machine.

Except for the Cake Walk. *Who knew walking around on colored footprints to win food can be so damn complicated?*

The Cake Walk station was a political debate and debacle among parents. Nuts, no nuts. Too much sugar. Let them eat cake! Store-bought shame. There was a social status for desserts and the cheating was ridiculous. The previous year the dad in charge had rigged it so his kids took home all the best frosted prizes. I had an entire folder in my email inbox dedicated to the complaints. *So much for 'you get what you get and you don't get upset'.*

And thus, while Jude let Shae and Carly scarf down cotton candy and manhandle baby goats, children walked in circles like zombies in front of me to the happy tunes of Taylor Swift.

"You look like shit." Michelle Simmons sat down in the metal folding chair next to me and slid a coffee in my direction.

"You look perfect, you fucking bitch." We clanked our paper cups and turned to the miserable massive wheel of kids rotating in front of us. I took a sip and the shot of caffeine tickled my hypnotized brain.

Ah, sanity.

Michelle was *the* mom. Her house was spotless. There was no trash in her car. She ironed sheets, fucking *sheets*. And she had four boys. Four. Her treats were the best, birthday parties amazing and her kids' clothing never had holes. Everyone despised her — except me.

I loved her. We had been forever bonded in our mutual hate for Carly's and her youngest son Logan's evil first-grade teacher and our love for swearing. Sometimes she sent me texts that read, *Ffffuuuuccccckkk!* I think I was the only mom she let see her weaker side. We were also each other's go-to person for forgotten homework and the lost dates of important events.

"What gives? Why do you look like you haven't slept?" Michelle brought a finger to the corner of her mouth and wiped away an invisible drop of coffee while not taking any of her dark lipstick with it.

The music stopped and beckoned me to tend to my Cake Walk Manager duties. I distributed Jude's Chocolate Caramel Delight to a little girl with braids and glasses, wondering if she was in Shae's grade. With Carly, I knew every kid from every class in every year. Shae, not so much.

When I returned to the table, Logan stood next to his mom, asking to sleep over at one of his friend's houses. I grinned at their banter. Negotiations in the Simmons family always involved her boys cleaning something.

The empty-handed children cleared as I swiveled in my chair to try to find my girls in the crowded field. I landed on the ring-throwing booth and my chest tightened. Ben was tossing plastic hoops around bottles with no problem as Nate cheered next to him. He had on the same tight green Henley he'd worn at our coffee date, dark jeans and dark work boots. And he had that damn dimple-bending smile. I touched my cheek, remembering the scratch of his beard.

He had every right to be there, just like the rest of us, but I wasn't ready to be the subject of mom gossip yet again. And Michelle was right, I lacked sleep. I'd tossed and turned all night stressing about my two worlds colliding. I stared at my fucking unicorn and wondered how to make him momentarily invisible.

"Who the fuck is that?" Michelle's voice was just above a whisper and she leaned so our shoulders were touching.

"Uh... No idea. Must be new." I turned back around just in time for the music to start again and kids of all shapes and sizes walked in merry-go-round fashion in the large circle with cut-out color footprints.

Maybe if I stayed facing forward, he wouldn't see me. After all, it wasn't his 'cheat day', so he probably wouldn't come near all the sugary temptation.

"Logan!" Michelle, who was still staring in Ben's direction, snapped her fingers several times at a sharp pitch. Her child spun around, slumped and drug his feet until he was in front of us again.

"What?" he groaned. "I'm not picking up the dog poop. You promised that Cal had to do it."

"Who is that boy over there at the bottle ring booth? I've never seen him before." Michelle picked nonexistent lint off her son's Polo shirt then smoothed the spot.

Logan peered over his shoulder. "You mean L.P.?"

Michelle's brow furrowed as she waited for further explanation.

"It's the new kid Nate. Can I go?"

"Why do you call him L.P.?" I asked. I could have been in a neck brace, my posture was so stiff.

"Last Pick. L.P."

"Please go." Michelle cradled her cheeks with both hands and her head shook with disapproval. "I swear, as soon as it's legal, I'm selling that one on eBay." She took another drink of her coffee and instructed me on who should get what cake. I laughed and ignored her. I didn't need more emails.

After more pop music punishment and the caffeine from my cup pumping through my veins, only three cakes remained. So far, Ben hadn't spotted me, and my confidence grew that my two worlds could coexist without gossip. I could call him later and laugh at 'how weird' it had been that we'd missed each other. My crisis was three treats away from being averted.

But as soon as I'd lulled myself into believing I could avoid Ben and the sure-to-be watchful eyes of the other parents, he and Nate stood in front of me. *Shit.*

Nate grinned from ear to ear and my heart warmed. Happy kids were the entire point of the Fall Fest.

Ben cleared his throat and Michelle stood. She reached out her hand. "Hi, I don't believe we've met. Nate is in class with my Neanderthal son Logan. I'm Michelle."

They shook hands, and both sets of eyes fell on me.

"This is Amee Benton, Carly's mom." Michelle beamed down at me.

Repeated blinking was the only motion I could muster. I could talk for hours to a judge or question a witness, but social awkwardness was my kryptonite and I froze. I loved Michelle and I didn't think she would talk about me behind my back for dating a younger man, but I remained mute nonetheless.

"Yeah, I know." Ben rubbed his neck, the same neck I'd worshiped with kisses the night before. The same neck that had that blond scruff and a warm, inviting smell.

A sideways smile crossed Michelle's face and she arched one of her pristine brows.

Ben leveled his blue eyes, and I moved my mouth in various directions but no sound came out. I hated that I was dead in the water, but I didn't know which move was worse. Telling Michelle I knew him would be one thing. Admitting to going on a date was another.

In the end, it didn't matter. My non-action had already spoken for me.

An airy, quiet scoff escaped from Ben's throat and he turned back to Michelle as he put his arm around Nate. "Nice to meet you. Maybe Logan can lighten up on the new kid nickname." He guided Nate away from the table and Michelle sat down with a blank expression, having literally been put in her place.

"Okay, liar. You know him. Spill it."

I shook my head to rattle my brain. "He works at the Porsche dealership."

"Like a car salesman?" she asked with a squishy frown.

"No. He's a mechanic." I rose to deliver the sugar-free vegan carrot cake that no one wanted and rubbed my temples.

"He could look under my hood," Michelle said with a head swagger.

I rolled my eyes then apologized to the child in front of me for the crap dessert. Michelle didn't question me further, perhaps assuming I had committed a minor social faux pas instead of a colossal intimate insult. We wiped off the tables and folded the chairs in silence. She did a little check in with me before leaving and I sold her my best lie about being great. I added a line about not having to drive out to see Pete for more believability. Michelle hated Pete. She prayed that he dropped the soap in the community showers.

That night, after tucking in the girls, I poured myself a glass of wine and curled up with my favorite soft throw blanket in the living room. The sweet liquid hit my palate and I set the glass next to my phone on the table behind me.

Calling him and apologizing would have been the right move. I had been rude—really fucking rude. It had come off that I was embarrassed by him—and maybe I was. He was too young for me. And even if I was pretty, Ben Mathis belonged on calendar without a shirt. And with a puppy.

If my secret affair, that wasn't even an affair, hit the PTA moms, there would be chatter behind not just my back, but the girls' as well. They didn't need another scandal. Pete had no idea of the backlash our daughters had suffered at school from his accident. I would not put them through more shit. I cursed my ex and the mess he'd left me.

Jude tapped on the wall, keys jingling in her hand, then pressed her upper arm into the corner. Her short hair was spiked and her open denim jacket revealed a simple white tank top. "You're drinking by yourself? Was Cake Walk duty that stressful?"

A witty comeback was too much work for my brain. "I fucked up with the unicorn."

"The fucking unicorn?"

With a sigh, I reached for my glass and took a sip. "I acted like I didn't know him in front of another mom."

"Ooooo. That's low, Amers. Why you gotta sabotage your sex life like that?"

I dropped my head into the corner of the couch and moaned.

Jude flipped her keys in her palm. "Don't pull a Pete and finish the bottle. I'm headed out. Call your unicorn and grovel. He's a nice guy." She waved from over her shoulder.

"Wait. How do you know he's a nice guy?" I sat up straighter.

Jude stopped in her tracks and spun around dramatically. "Because I talked to him for, like, half an hour today."

"What did he say? Was it before or after I was a douche queen?" *Please let it be after and shed some light on his Amee hate meter.*

"You are such a douche queen. That is a great name for you. DQ from here on out. Did I invent that or you?" She narrowed her eyes.

I shivered at her lack of attention span. "What did he say about me?" I tucked my feet under my butt and pressed my lips together, waiting for her answer.

She slumped and shook her head. "See? This is why you're a douche queen. We didn't talk about you. He asked about *me*—like about my interests and what I go to school for and why."

"You mean my name never came up? You didn't try to insult me in front of him or tell him how often I change the batteries in my vibrator?"

"Too often." She held back the smirk I knew was dying to appear. "But no. We talked about me, the school and the kids. Sorry. Maybe it was after your suicidal sex life flub and he was just being polite. God, did you smell him? Insane. You're so stupid." She turned on her heel and left. The garage door hummed its opening and closure, leaving only the small buzz of emptiness.

The screen of my phone reflected the light from the kitchen, mocking me and reminding me it was there. I couldn't decide what was more difficult, picking up the phone, apologizing and moving forward—*with what, some kind of relationship?*—or putting an end to whatever we'd started, thus surrendering on my first chance of repairing my love life.

Ben wants something with me, right? I'd practically begged him for sex the night before and he'd been the one to put on the brakes. If I was just a cheap date to him, he would have taken his shot. But, him at the school had been a reminder of not only our gaping age and social difference, it had also unearthed some wounds I'd previously thought healed.

Then there was the fact that dating a younger guy would bring out the chatter-moms. And from that point it took one kid. Only one clueless kid would need to overhear something to start the teasing of Carly or Shae. I pulled my hair at the roots. *Is it really that difficult to be selfish?* I'd thought that by getting a divorce I had chosen myself, but the girls had to come first.

"Mom?" Carly's half-open eyes glimmered with sleep from the archway and she stood barefoot in her mid-length striped nightgown. "When are you coming to bed?"

"Now, baby. Sorry. I was just unwinding from the day." The blanket fell to the ground in a puddle as I stood. I gave Carly a tight smile and said, "Go on up. I'll brush my teeth and come snuggle you."

The cool tile of the kitchen assailed my feet as I walked to the sink. I dumped the wine down the drain and added the glass to the dishwasher. With the lights dimmed to facilitate Jude's return, I climbed the stairs.

Alone.

Chapter Eight

Chocolate

Ben

After a final scan of the underbody of the white Porsche Panamera overhead, I wiped the grease from my hands with a red rag and tossed it onto the steel workbench behind me. *Who the hell comes to see me at work? Kim? Please, not her.* I would rather have a tax collector show up than have her come in and ask for money in her state.

I trudged out to reception, ready for the eye assault of Kim Fulton and her acid-washed denim, and thankfully found no such thing. Instead, the spikey hair and single rainbow wave of Jude greeted me. I ushered her out of the door—there was no need to let the receptionists hear my business. They already gossiped enough about the head of sales and her 'deal sealing' abilities.

"Apparently, it's your cheat day and you like cupcakes." Jude shoved a Tupperware offering in my direction.

I scratched my neck and peered down at the plastic container with a promise of a sugar-loaded bomb. "She sent you?" I lifted an eyebrow.

It had been six days since I'd spoken to Amee Benton. Six days since she had made it perfectly clear that her intentions were to use me and leave me. She hadn't called. She hadn't even bothered to apologize for her rudeness. And I didn't even care about her blowing me off. All right, that was bullshit. I was fucking pissed about that. But what really fucking boiled my blood was she had done it in front of Nate.

Nate, who had been snubbed all week as the dorky new kid, had witnessed his hero getting shot down by a parent of the same classmates who were dicks to him. That was the blow. That was why I was going to tell the ever-waiting cupcake to go fuck itself.

"Sorry, Jude. I bet it's amazing, but I'm not interested." I turned to walk away.

"She is."

I looked over my shoulder. "I was talking about the cupcake."

Jude's blue gaze pleaded, something I had a feeling didn't happen very often. "I wasn't." She stepped toward me. "She messed up. She knows it. But what you don't know is that last year when all the drama with her ex was going down, the girls got teased. Bad."

"Kids can be cruel," I said in the most dismissive tone I could muster and ignored the tiny promise of sugary goodness coming from her hands.

"Yes. They can. But trophy moms are cutthroat brutal. I know you like her. You would be so good for her, Ben. You know why she calls you a fucking unicorn?"

That I had to hear. But I would stay strong. "No clue. Don't care."

"That's the biggest bullshit sandwich I've ever been served." Jude rolled her eyes but continued, "Because she thinks you're a magical beast."

Jude's words were just as tempting as her cupcake, but I wouldn't let them work. "I'm a mechanic. No Prince Charming here."

"Apparently, men like you are hard to find. And a chance for something better is why she divorced Peter in the first place. She doesn't give a shit what you do. She sees your heart. Why don't you show her more?"

My mouth watered as I imagined licking the cupcake wrapper clean. *Shit*. I was going to be a one-two punched by her plastic box and kind words.

No.

Restraint.

I knew how to resist.

"Listen, Jude. It was nice to see you and I appreciate the effort and the vote of confidence. I really do. And maybe if it was her standing here, things would be different."

Jude crossed her arms and her mouth-watering present got farther way. *Good. I can get my own damn cupcake, thank you very much.*

"But it's not her. It's you," I said with a firm voice. I hoped she understood we had no deal.

Jude flared her little nostrils and squeezed her lips together. She took a few deep breaths before uncrossing her arms, and her tight expression transformed into a wry grin. She peeled off the lid of the Tupperware and revealed my biggest weakness.

"Chocolate with peanut butter frosting." Jude took out the cupcake and flaunted it before me.

Its transparent blue wrapper promised rich, light chocolate cake. And above was a perfectly formed mountainous swirl of peanut butter frosting. At the peak were crumbles of Reese's peanut butter cups. Pools of saliva formed in my cheeks and forced me to swallow twice as I beheld its perfection.

"Two questions. What do you want for that cupcake? And how did you know it was my favorite?"

Her smile grew and met her eyes. "I bribed Carly to ask Nate. Sorry. I knew I would have to bring my big guns. And I want you to go over and talk to her tonight."

Ambushed, I'd been ambushed. That pesky little pixie was going to make me see Amee again. *Nope. Not going to happen. Not enough cupcakes in the world.*

"There's an entire batch of these on her counter…"

She was no cupcake fairy. She was a scheming mini witch.

"Ben, please. Just talk to her. I promise she's worth another try."

With that, I couldn't argue. Amee was probably worth endless tries. I slumped my shoulders and stretched my neck.

"If she wanted me, she would have said something."

"Oh, she wants you." The innuendo dripped from her voice.

I rolled my eyes. "I'm not interested in a one-night stand. Sorry."

"Neither is she. Although my sister needs to get laid…like seriously soon."

I played the air trumpet with my lips and my stomach screamed to snatch the dessert still taunting me.

"Come on. Just one talk. The girls both have sleepovers and I'm going out. She'll be home alone starting at nine." There was a small, mildly adorable whine in her voice.

"Did you orchestrate this entire thing by yourself?"

"I did. And if you don't take this damn cupcake and go see my sister tonight, I will get an entire lesbian pitchfork army after you."

I closed an eye. "That's not a thing."

"It could be." The confidence in her voice and stance was mildly disturbing.

I looked down at the cupcake and back to Jude.

Mercy, mercy, mercy.

"Don't grumble. Just..." She pushed the cupcake into my chest. "Please."

It was too much, my favorite dessert coupled with the ounce of truth bubbling that I did indeed want to see Amee again.

"Fine." My mouth and stomach shouted victory as I grabbed the cupcake and signaled for the box. The little piece of heaven I held would be devoured as soon I could properly wash my hands. *When did I become so easy to bribe with food?*

Jude clapped twice and said, "Oh...and don't even think about eating that and not showing up. I will hunt your man-candy ass down and cut you." She spun around, climbed into her blue hybrid and drove off.

After work, I went straight to the gym to meet Trev. He kicked the crap out of me, taunting me the whole time. After a particularly weak defense, he dropped his gloves, pulled out his mouth guard and cocked his head. "All right. This is pointless."

"No. Sorry, man. I'll focus." Droplets of sweat dispersed around me as I shook my head to concentrate.

"Nah. You're good. I'm going to Ma's for dinner anyway." Trev threaded through the ropes and hopped down from the ring. "You want to come? You obviously have something on your mind."

Defeated, I joined him on the lower level and bitched to him about the previous Saturday's events as we showered and dressed. He listened and nodded with occasional grunts to prove he'd heard me.

Finally, while we sat on the bench in the locker room and he tied his tennis shoes, he spoke. "How many chances have you given Lazy Crazy Kim?"

"That's different." The sharp hum of the zipper to my bag punctuated my words. "She's family. And you know she's been through hell."

Trev shifted toward me on the wooden plank. "My point is, you don't even like Lazy Crazy Kim and you've given her countless chances. Crap, man, you pay for her groceries and take care of her kid."

"By the way, don't use your nickname in front of Nate. He loves his mom, as he should." I stood up and swung my bag over my shoulder, and Trev did the same.

"I'm just saying… You like that chick. Give her a break."

* * * *

I killed the engine in her driveway and pulled the keys out from the ignition. Amee's massive brick house sat in front of me. Another sign of our differences.

No. Fuck that. I would not let her list of bullshit seep into my head. Trev was right. I liked her. I loved the way she put her girls first. *Damn it.* The fact that the reason she had treated me like dogshit was to save them had lessened the blow. But she had still done it in front of my priority, and for that, she owed me an apology.

When I got out of the truck, I adjusted my junk and tried to decide if I wanted her to be in those stupidly cute, yet hot, pajamas again.

Images flashed from a bay window as the only sign of life from the interior. I swore a few times up the walkway and let my finger hover over the doorbell for one last indecisive second. Worst case, she would be a bitch, and it would be over quickly. I pressed the bell and let my mind skip down the road of the best-case scenario. She was home alone...

The door opened, and her little body appeared in front of me. But she wasn't wearing the pants. It was worse...and definitely better. Amee bunched the neck of a long sweater at her chest, barely covering the above-the-knee baby blue cotton nightgown underneath.

Mercy.

After a brief stare down and another sprint to best-case scenario by my overly active imagination, I managed to say hi.

"I..." She searched my face.

Jude's full disclosure had obviously only applied to me.

"Thought you'd gotten rid of me for good?" I dipped a shoulder and she widened the threshold.

"The girls are..." She closed her eyes as she shook her head, stray strands of otherwise pulled-up hair brushing her neck. "Fucking Jude."

The door clicked behind her, and if I thought the outside of her house was a wedge of a reminder of our economic differences, the inside was the Grand Canyon. Even in the dimly lit entryway, I could see state-of-the-art everything. A huge open staircase led to the upper level and a marble counter top and stainless-steel appliances gleamed from down the hall. To my left was a massive living room and the source of the flashing images.

I dug my hands into the pockets of my hoodie, and when she padded past me, I realized how inappropriately dressed she must feel. "Do you want to go change? Sorry. I probably should have called..."

She halted and looked down at her perfect braless cleavage. "I'll be right back. Make yourself at home." Up the stairs she went, and I half hoped she would reappear in one of those full-body adult pajamas or her work clothes with those ugly shoes. Resisting her hotness had to be my first priority. We needed to clear the air before we moved forward.

I unzipped my hoodie and walked back to the kitchen. On the wall, I found a dimmer for the lights. I rolled it halfway and pulled out a barstool at the center island. The counter shone. There weren't any fingerprints on the fridge and even the sink was pristine. Someone liked her house clean. *Dang.*

"Can I get you something to drink? I don't think I have any beer. There might be some wine..." Amee walked around the island. She'd changed into a white tank top, a bra with its straps sticking out at the shoulder and those goddamn pajama pants. They were rolled down at the waist and there was no way she was wearing underwear. It was like she'd sidestepped her sexy to…well, sexy.

"A glass of water would be great." *Anything to cool me down.*

When she turned around and reached up to the cupboard for a glass, the small of her back peeked out. She had a perfect little curve in her lower spine that led to that beyond-fantastic ass. An ass my fingers itched to remember. I curled my tongue and let out a long, slow breath.

She served me the water and said, "I owe you an apology." Her chest deflated. "That was a dick move. I'm sorry. If it makes you feel any better, Jude's been calling me douche queen ever since. DQ in front of the girls."

I considered her words as I lifted the glass to my lips and drank. When I set it down on the counter, I asked, "That's it?" As I leaned into the barstool, I crossed my arms. "You beg me to have sex with you then twelve hours later ignore me. No wait, worse." I lifted a finger. "You pretend you don't know me in front of Nate, who knew you were lying, then don't even fucking *call* me." I moved in so that my stomach pushed against the sharp granite edge and closed the space between us. Quieter, I asked, "But it's okay because Jude called you a name?"

She pulled back and her eyes fell to the floor. "I'm sorry."

"You mentioned that."

Her hands framed her body on the countertop behind her. "Why did you come here?"

"Do you want me to leave?"

"Don't fucking do that!" *Hello, Amee's angry voice. Holy crap.* I'd struck some kind of nerve.

"What?"

Calmer, she said, "Answer a question with a question. Please don't do that. Cryptic kills me. Why are you here?" She cradled her arms and one hand went to her shoulder. Her gray-blue eyes sank lower, and she rubbed her opposite arm.

I bet she'd worked all day. Her house was spotless and there she was alone. I remembered something I'd asked her the first time we'd met. *Who takes care of her?* I had my answer. *No one.* Sure, Jude helped out and her daughters probably adored her. But no one nurtured Amee. She didn't need to be punished or judged. She needed to be held — and eventually worshiped.

The barstool screeched on the tile as I stood, and desperation pooled in the corners of her reddening eyes.

"I don't want you to go," she whispered.

I walked around the island and stopped in front of her. "I wasn't leaving." I tilted her chin with my thumb and the skin-to-skin contact shot a spark down my spine. I grazed my knuckles against her silky cheek.

"I want to do this, Ben. I want to date you." Her skin flushed, and she blinked a few times. "I just don't know how." A single tear marked her confession and stained down her face. I wiped it away with my thumb and pulled her into my arms. I rested my chin on her head, and while circumstances weren't ideal, our fit was perfect. She continued, "I don't want to fuck them up any more than they already are."

Moisture seeped through my T-shirt and warmed my chest.

"I know. Believe me, I know."

When I went to pull away, she reached under my shirt and up my lower back. She pulled me closer, and I wondered how long it'd been since that beautiful woman had just been held.

We stood there, locked in our embrace for what seemed like an hour. Her crying had stopped but she wouldn't let go. Finally, I said, "I should get going."

She shifted her head and looked up at me. The message in her eyes had changed from sadness to something else. *Flirtation?*

"I'm not going to stay. Don't bother asking." I fought the smile she seemed to be searching.

"You're giving me a complex with all your rejection." She slid her hands over my ribs and up to my pecs. There was no denying that her teasing touch was divine, but it was for another time.

I fished her hands out of my shirt. "Slow down."

"You're too tempting." Her eyes glimmered and she brushed her lips on my neck between my beard and ear. *Damn it.* She'd found my spot. It was better than the cupcake I'd inhaled after Jude had left. I fought off a shudder and ignored the twitch in my pants. As relieved as I was to see her feeling better and as undeniably amazing her tiny kiss felt, it had to end.

"Amee." I stepped back and hit the island edge. "I'm not like that. I don't do flings. I don't race into bed with a woman." Because that lesson had been learned. Cheap hook-ups built faulty foundations and I was ready for more.

The sexy little blonde glared at me. "Fucking unicorn. I knew it. Fine." She huffed. "You want me to court you? Win you over? I can do that." The confidence in her voice was downright adorable.

"I can't wait." My small laugh turned into a huge smile.

"Are you free tomorrow night?" She puffed out her chest, daring me to deny her.

"It just so happens that I am."

"Great. You're coming over for dinner. With my girls. No hiding."

Dang. Cupcake was going all in.

"Are you...?"

She lifted a hand. "They come with me. We're a package deal. I don't want to sneak around behind their backs." She stared me down. Maybe that was Amee's work voice. It was almost scary, but it was also one hundred percent hot.

I smiled. "Fine. But I bring Nate. He's part of my deal."

"Fantastic."

I shortened the distance between us as I decided how I would kiss her. Because I was absolutely going to kiss her. She stumbled and reached for the counter behind her. Bending down, I scratched her neck with my scruff.

"I fucking love those pajamas." I took her earlobe in my teeth then ran my tongue in a circle, catching the sharp point of her studded earing. I found her hipbones and pulled her to me. Her ass was too close, too tempting. I dug my fingers into it and moved my mouth to hers.

She panted her longing. I bet she wanted a repeat from the truck or picnic, but she wouldn't get it. I kissed her once and withdrew.

"See you tomorrow, Cupcake. I'll let myself out." I gave her one final wink and turned to leave.

"You have to be fucking kidding me," she said to my back.

My massive smile stayed facing forward as I headed for the door. I answered with an over-the-shoulder wave and left.

Chapter Nine

Spaghetti

Amee

Carly slid into the back seat and I pushed the car door shut, sealing out the crisp fall morning breeze. The concrete driveway at her friend's house was not the ideal setting for telling my girls I was bringing a man and his little sidekick home for dinner, but time was not on my side. It rarely was.

In the front seat, I gathered my courage and, instead of starting the car, I turned around to face them. Shae was a vision of rainbow glory. Her pink and purple striped tights covered her little swinging legs. A click sounded the security of Carly's buckle and snapped my attention to the task at hand.

"Okay, so we're having guests for dinner tonight."

Shae silently clapped and her eyes grew to the size of saucers. We hadn't had guests since Pete's accident and Mini Me loved to entertain. She was probably already planning the proper attire for each one of her dolls.

Carly, on the other hand, looked like she was sucking on a lemon wedge. *Crap.*

"Who?" My elder daughter was not one to beat around the bush. *No idea where that came from.*

"Ben, the man I'd like to start dating, and Nate from your class."

"Mommy?" Shae's palms continued their happy quiet rhythm. "Can I put glitter on the table?"

"Yes." I nodded and smiled at her excitement.

"Pink and blue glitter?" Shae bit her lip.

"Yes."

"Oh my goodness. Oh my goodness. You're the best mommy ever."

That brought a full-on, but entirely expected, scoff from her sister, who was now staring out of the window with her chin in her hand.

"Say it, Carly. Tell me. Do you not like Nate?"

She delivered an epic eye roll and a disgusted frown.

"There's nothing wrong with Nate. He's really smart actually." She turned to face me. "What about Daddy?"

There it was. I'd known it would come.

I dug up the speech I'd spent the morning preparing. "We talked about this when Daddy and I got divorced, baby. I love Daddy as your daddy and a friend. But he and I don't work as a couple. I'd like to try to have a relationship with someone else while I'm still young enough to do so. I don't want to spend my life alone. I have to start dating. I need this. Please."

"Why can't you just spend your life with Dad if you don't want to be lonely? Plus, we live with you. You're not alone." It was so simple for Carly.

"She doesn't love Daddy the way other mommies love daddies." Although Shae had every right to speak,

Carly took it as an attack. Two against one. I could practically see the wall of defense construct around her.

"No one's talking to you." Carly glared at her sister.

"Hey." I shot my own corrective eyes to Carly then softened. "Look… it's never going to be a good time to do this, but I have to. I love every single minute of being your mom, and at the same time, I need to make myself happy. If I'm not happy, I have less to give you guys. This isn't about you two not being enough. It's about me deserving something special." I smiled to Shae and tilted to find Carly's eyes. "I know that might sound selfish, and trust me, I'm still struggling on how to make it all work. But I have to try…for me."

Shae studied her sister from the other side of the car. When Carly gave me a small nod of approval, the little one exploded into an adorable shoulder shimmy dance. She sang, "Glitter? Check. Perfect dress? Check. Food? Don't know how to do that yet. Name tags? Oh! Carly, will you help me spell everybody's names?"

Shae's jubilant energy was too contagious, even for Ice Queen Carly.

"Sure."

* * * *

After five minutes of Shae's repetitive song about everything she needed for the perfect evening, I turned on the radio to a pop station the girls loved, and they belted out lyrics from the back seat all the way to the correctional facility.

Shae's mood stayed bubbly and excited, but the reality of passing through security and the pending betrayal of her dad dampened Carly's pep. The unfortunate odor of familiar cleaning product accompanied us down the hall and into the visitation room.

We waited for him at a table in the corner, while residual whispers and random dance moves from Shae reminded us of the evening ahead. Carly's eyes locked on mine. Shae would tell their dad about our plans within two minutes of seeing him. The rainbow squirt between us was bursting with too much joy to contain herself.

Big hugs greeted Pete, and I offered him a cordial kiss on the cheek. When it all boiled down — all that shit between the two of us — I did truly want us to have a working relationship. Even if it was me who did most of the work.

"Two weeks was too long. I missed you guys so much," he said and gave them both another squeeze.

We settled at the table, falling into our positions of Carly on his lap and the squirming Shae on mine. Pete and Carly went through her sketch book and Shae cupped her hands to tell me a secret.

"I'm very excited about our date." Her hot breath tickled my neck and made me smile.

"I know, baby. Thank you." I kissed her sweet cheek and refocused on Carly's latest drawing of a calico cat with long whiskers. She had definitely received her father's gene for art talent. He asked her about school and she told him about the sleepover from the night before.

With Carly's need for Pete's attention fulfilled, he turned to Shae. "What about you, peanut? What's up with you?"

"We have a date!" Shae bounced on my lap.

Carly's head dropped, and Pete's face fell.

"I'm sorry, princess. You have a what?"

"A date. Well, Mommy has a date, but we get to go along. Well, not really along since it's at our house. But we get to be there. I'm so excited, Daddy." Shae's hands cupped her chin. "I've never been on a date before."

A snarled smile covered Pete's sunken face then dropped. I recognized the new expression as the exact same one Carly had given me an hour prior in the car.

Carly readjusted in his lap and Pete worked his jaw. "You have a date?"

I pressed my lips together, sealing in all the things I really wanted to say. I slowly nodded the confirmation and prayed whatever anger he might be feeling would be caged like the irresponsible criminal that he was.

"With who?"

Nine years of a turbulent marriage and ridiculous accusations were enough for me to read him. He had been sure I'd cheated on him with a colleague and had loved to spit his theory at me whenever we were in a heated argument. His frequent cocktails had been a constant fuel to the fire.

"You don't know him." I tried to keep my voice flat.

"His name is Ben," the ever-helpful Shae said.

"Well, Ben is a lucky guy." Pete's gaze drifted to the table, and after the bitter silence, he looked up and away. "Sorry to cut this short today, but Daddy has some stuff to do." Pete's bloodshot eyes and tight smile were enough for Shae to reach out her purple manicured hand.

"Don't be sad, Daddy. Mommy needs this." She patted his forearm.

A blink set free a tear and he rubbed the top of her hand with his thumb.

"I'm not sad, princess. I'm jealous. I wanted to be your first date." He kissed Carly's cheek and pushed her off his lap. "See you guys next week." The hugs were quick and tight and he disappeared behind the steel door, returning to his self-inflicted hell.

* * * *

To say I was a good cook would have been untrue. Since Pete had stayed home with the girls and possessed massive culinary aptitude, he had been in charge of the meals. Jude cooked since he'd been locked up, and if she wasn't around, we usually had take-out. But I did have one dish—Spaghetti Carbonara. I'd mastered the right balance between over-done and undercooked bacon and the perfect temperature to add the egg yolk so it didn't go hard.

As the girls sprinkled glitter around Carly's perfectly folded napkins in the dining room, I sliced the pancetta and added it to the pan on medium heat.

Jude appeared at the end of the counter and flipped her keys back and forth in her hand. They clanked in a succinct rhythm as her eyes narrowed in on the huge steaming pot of water.

I couldn't stand her silent judgment any longer. "What?"

She caught the keys in her palm and asked, "That's what you're going with?"

"It's my go-to meal. I can't make anything else. You know that." I thought she liked my spaghetti. "Everyone loves this. You're freaking me out."

Her mouth moved around, and she bit her bottom lip. "If Ben eats that, he really is a unicorn. Tie him up and never let him go." She snapped the keys once more and turned to leave.

"What the fuck, Jude? I'm nervous enough for him to meet the girls. You can be so thoughtless sometimes." I chopped more bacon.

She snickered. "Whatever." When she reached the door leading to the garage, she called out a goodbye to the girls and smirked at me from over her shoulder. "Good luck, DQ."

I set the knife down and flipped her the bird.

"Love you, too." She air-kissed me and left.

Five minutes later, the doorbell rang and frills and ribbons raced by me in a blur to be the first response. Shae swung the door open as I wiped my hands on a towel and walked down the entryway to greet our guests.

Nate, in an oversized black hoodie that matched his hair, stood in front of Ben, who draped his arms over Nate's shoulders. The child's hands held a bouquet of wild flowers with tin foil at the stems.

"I'm Shae. Are those for me?"

Ben's dimples deepened, and he introduced himself and Nate. "The flowers are for all three of you," he said as he shook her ring-bedazzled hand. Nate handed Shae the flowers and she skipped off, saying she knew the perfect vase for them.

I flopped the tea towel over my shoulder and motioned for them to enter. Knowing that I'd messed up with Nate, I said, "I'm Amee. Sorry about the Cake Walk. I was just surprised to see Ben there."

His lip twitched to the side, then he looked beyond me and waved.

"Hey." Carly's unenthusiastic tone traveled from the base of the stairs.

"Carly, this is Ben. Ben, this is Carly."

They silently waved to each other and, to my surprise, Carly said to Nate, "Come on. I'll show you that volcano book I told you about." She led him up the stairs and I stared for a minute in disbelief. I mean, I knew Carly read books, but I didn't know she owned the one about how to act on your mom's first joint-kid date.

"That went better than expected." I risked a peck on his blissfully scratchy cheek by standing on my tiptoes.

"You look gorgeous." Ben winked quickly as I lowered to my heels.

If only he'd known about the forty-five-minute battle royal between Jude and Shae on what I should wear. I'd finally settled on my favorite pair of jeans and a low-cut green silk blouse.

I dug my fingers under his white T-shirt, found the tight muscles of his abdomen and rubbed my thumbs over the small hills. "Gonna be hard to keep my hands off you."

"I thought you were courting me. Do I smell bacon?" He stepped back, and my hands dropped to my side.

"Yes," I confirmed. "I hope that's okay."

"Who doesn't like bacon?"

I mentally sighed my relief and told Jude to suck it. *See? My meal will be fine.*

Shae skipped over to us and she studied Ben. "You wanna meet everybody else?"

His head tilted to the side. "Who else is there?"

"Shae, I don't think Ben wants to meet your dolls."

"Mommy. Don't be rude. Fortune Feimster got her nails done especially for our date."

It was hard to know what to tackle first—the fact that Shae had most likely acquired nail polish without permission, that she had a doll named Fortune Feimster or that she thought we were all on a date.

Thankfully, Ben answered for me. "I would love to meet your dolls. Where are they?"

"They're all waiting in my room. Carly said Nate wouldn't want to meet them but I knew you would. I could tell from the smile you gave me last time you were here." Shae's fingers wiggled like worms as she waited for my blessing.

"Is that okay with you?" Ben asked me.

The fact that he checked in somehow helped. He was still new. We were still very new. And I'd seen him with Nate. Ben Mathis may not have been a biological father, but he was a natural one.

"Yep. I'll come and get you when dinner's ready."

Back in the kitchen, I added the pasta to the boiling water. I thanked every lucky star in the universe that the introductions had gone well. The girls might be bickering pains between each other on a regular basis, but their manners were solid. I lined up the deep plates and cracked a yolk in each one.

With only minutes to go on the spaghetti, I headed upstairs to call down the troops. In Carly's room I found her and Nate on the floor silently reading books. They lay on their bellies, feet swinging.

"Carly, can you show Nate where to wash his hands? Dinner's almost ready."

Nate returned my smile and closed his book. Down the hall, I heard Shae's voice and stopped short of her doorway.

"This is Annabelle. Her favorite color is white. She likes your T-shirt."

"Pleased to meet you, Annabelle. What's your favorite animal?" Ben's deep voice was an adorable contrast to the pink frills surrounding him.

"Bunnies, you silly. They're white!"

I giggled at the thought of anyone calling Ben 'silly'. Ben sat on the floor with his legs crossed at the ankle and Shae kneeled next to him with her blonde doll Annabelle. They both looked up at me and smiled.

"Dinner's ready."

"Can Annabelle come to dinner? There's an extra place and she likes Ben. He's wearing her favorite color." Her eyes widened in disbelief, like white wasn't the most common color of clothing.

"Is she going to behave?" I teased.

"She will. She promises. She loves your pasta. It's white!"

Ben pushed to his feet and extended his hand to help Shae get up.

"Go wash your hands. We'll meet you at the table." I shooed Shae down the hall in the direction of the bathroom.

"That's a lot of dolls." Ben and I walked toward the stairway and at the top he gestured for me to go first.

"Bribery. Divorce, Daddy in jail, getting her to not scream in public..."

"Or maybe she's lonely." He shrugged and winked. "I mean, I'm no expert, but Nate does the same thing with books. They're all over his room. Thank God for the school library. I almost went broke buying them this summer."

Carly and Nate waited for us at the kitchen island and the cooktop beeped the pasta's readiness. I touched the electric timer to stop the noise and said, "Carly, would you help me serve? Shae, you can show Nate and Ben their places."

Ben chose the path between me and the counter. He brushed against me a little closer than called for, and beautiful heat shot up my spine and flushed my cheeks. I shivered it off and he shot me a quick smile before heading to the dining room.

The stress from my shoulders eased out. Well...our family date was going well.

I loaded up the plates, mixed in the yolks and sent Carly on her rounds of delivery. With everyone served except myself, she stayed at the table and I joined them with my portion. I slid into my high-back chair at the head and told everyone to dig in. Ben was on the opposite end, the large salad bowl separating us. Nate and Carly sat next to me and Ben was surrounded by Shae and Annabelle.

"Thank you for the flowers, guys. Did you pick them yourselves?" I asked while twirling my pasta into a spoon.

"We found them on the bike trail," Nate said.

"Oooo! I wanna learn how to ride a bike." Shae sprinkled cheese over her plate. "Ben, would you please serve Annabelle some cheese?"

"I'd be delighted. How much does she like?" He took the little dish from Shae and paused before shaking the cheese off the spoon.

"She likes the same as me." Shae leaned closer to Ben and out of the side of her mouth said, "I have to eat it."

"Mind if I start with the salad?" Ben asked.

"Help yourself. Anybody else?" I gazed around at the kids, who all had strands of spaghetti in varying lengths coming out of their mouths, and let out a breath. Dinner was working. We were working.

Ben checked for takers of green leaves and vegetables but found none. He served himself a huge portion and the five of us ate in silence until Shae blurted out, "Nate, is Ben your dad?"

Nate finished chewing and turned to the small, nosy blonde to his right. "No. He's my mom's cousin. My dad is dead." Ben and Nate exchanged quick glances.

"Our dad is in jail."

Thanks, Shae.

"He must miss you guys very much." Ben gave Shae a sympathetic smile and took a bite of salad.

Carly picked at her plate and I reached out and squeezed her hand. Shame and guilt were a terrible combination for children. We had spent many nights talking about what Pete had done, many hours in front of the therapist, the fact that his actions needed to be punished and the battle between relief and horror that he would come home one day but the other daddy never would. Pete's own demons remained a secret that I never invited him to share.

"Who taught you how to ride a bike?" Shae asked Nate.

"Ben did, this summer. I never had one before."

"Can you teach me?" Shae's eyes lit up, and her fingers did that wiggle move as further proof of her excitement.

Ben served himself more salad and said, "Sure. If your mom's okay with it. Do you have a bike?"

Shae looked over to me. She'd been asking Jude to show her without the training wheels, but Jude was a crappy teacher and lost patience and interest quickly.

"Sure. It's too dark today, but another time."

"Mom?" Carly asked. "We're all done. Can the kids be excused?"

I checked their empty plates and nodded.

"Thanks for dinner, Amee." Nate stood and picked up his plate. He followed the girls into the kitchen and the dishes clanked on the counter.

"You're far away," I said to Ben and scooted my chair back.

He rose at the same time and tossed his napkin on top of his plate. We met halfway around the table and he tucked a strand of hair behind my ear.

"Great dinner," he said.

I slid my palms around his hips and brushed against his waistband. They settled on his warm back. "I know it was a small step. But it was a big step too." I pulled him closer and fully relaxed for the first time that day. He kissed the top of my head and I pressed my cheek into his chest. The thought of getting busted by one of the girls for our open display of affection jabbed my gut.

"Come on," I said. "I'll do the dishes later."

In the living room, Carly had set up the video games and Shae begged for a turn to dance. Had there not been guests, my girls would have finished in tears and insults but, instead, they both agreed to let Nate have a chance at whatever he wanted first. Ben and I kept a respectable distance on the couch, occasionally exchanging smiles when one of the kids did something funny.

At nine o'clock, Ben and Nate got up to leave. Nate thanked me for a nice time and walked down the lit front path. He hopped into Ben's truck and waited.

"When can I see you again?" I asked.

"Maybe next Friday. I'll call you. Night." With the girls on both sides of me, Ben didn't lean in for a hug or a kiss. Instead, he waved and left to join Nate.

They pulled away, the light rumble of the engine fading with each second. I closed the door behind me and directed the girls to the stairs.

"I'll just do the dishes and be up to tuck you in. No story tonight, you had enough with the games."

They groaned but climbed the stairs and the floor squeaked above my head. I stretched my arms and walked through the kitchen to the dining room. While the family date had been a huge success in my book, I was missing the kiss, the curling up in those strong arms, nuzzling into Ben's broad shoulders, inhaling his warmth, kissing so I could work out a little of the sexual tension. Lordy, when he'd rubbed up against me before dinner I could have pushed him into the pantry and yelled at the kids to order a pizza. That man needed to give me some kind of release or I would explode.

I smiled, stacked my plate into the empty salad bowl and reached for Ben's. I grabbed the napkin first and it revealed a full plate of Carbonara. He hadn't touched his pasta.

Chapter Ten

Beef

Ben

I plopped the grocery bags down on the beige counter and Kim eyed me from the table. Her blotchy skin drooped off her cheekbones and she sipped her coffee out of a faded mug advertising an insurance company that had closed their doors years prior. I tried to picture her with Nate's dad, how happy she'd once been. Maybe my support was making her weak. She hadn't started the drinking until the responsibility of Nate had become shared, when she was sure I would cover for her. I sent her a tight smile.

"Morning." I unpacked the chicken breast and gave it a new home in the fridge.

She cleared her throat and pulled her light blue bathrobe tighter. "Turns out we have something in common."

We both loved Nate and we both ensured Teddy got enough to eat, but apart from that and some DNA, she was crazy to think we had anything in common. As she sat in front of me, anyway. Before? Yes. Our parents had been close, and I'd even been in her wedding. But I didn't want to rock the boat, so I played along. "Oh yeah? What's that?"

"We both had dates last night."

Nate must have spilled the beans. Being mad at Little Man was emotionally impossible for me, but Kim wasn't going to get any dirt on my personal life.

"That's great, Kim. Glad you're putting yourself out there." The tins of tuna clinked as I stacked them in the cupboard. I folded the paper bag and stored it under the sink.

"Yeah." She sniffed and stretched her arms over her head. "I'd forgotten what it was like to have a real man's attention."

Ew.

She needed to stop there. Images of her private moments with a man would be worse than those fucked-up scary clowns that Trev messaged me at Halloween. *Shit, that horrible holiday is right around the corner.*

"Well, that's great. I hope he's a good guy." I walked toward the door that led to the basement, the sole of my sneakers squeaking on the linoleum. My hand was on the knob and I was almost free.

"Ben?"

I glanced over my shoulder and raised my eyebrows.

"I was thinking I could take Nate to the mall. I think he needs some shirts or something then maybe get something for me. I haven't bought new underwear…"

"Stop." I raised my hand and shuddered. *Cars. Think about cars. Anything, just not Kim buying underwear.*

Nate hugged the doorframe at the opposite end of the kitchen. *Stalker.* His little lip twitched. He still hadn't fessed up to his mom that he didn't want to go to the mall with her. And was Kim so out of it that she didn't know he'd already gotten his school shirts? I was willing to make a lot of exceptions for my female cousin, but she'd done the laundry, for Christ's sake. Had she really not noticed his new shirts? Or had Little Man done the laundry?

I shook my head. "You can't take an eight-year-old boy to buy that kind of shit. Besides, we were going to hang. And now we have to do something extra manly. Right, Little Man?" I walked over to him and put my hand on his shoulders.

"Really? That would be great." Her eyes lit up and she stood. "I mean, I'll miss you," she said with her crooked grin to Nate. "Just tell me where to get the shirts."

"I got the shirts two weeks ago. He needed them for the first day of school." I tried to keep my tone casual. I didn't want to make Nate uncomfortable for going behind Kim's back.

"You should have told me, buddy." Her eyebrows scrunched together and her new wrinkles deepened.

Right. As if he would have dared. I didn't need to see him to know his lip was twitching again.

"It was no big deal. I was going to the mall anyway," I lied. Because that was what we'd done with Kim for the last three months. We pretended she was a decent mother so that Nate could feel somewhat normal. I gave his shoulders another squeeze and headed to the door that lead down to my room.

"Oh, this means I can't drive my dad to the airport. Maybe you and Nate can take him? Like a road trip."

I closed my eyes and pressed the tip of my tongue into my teeth. "No problem." A blue-light Kim special. She skipped two responsibilities for the price of one. She'd agreed with enthusiasm three days earlier to drive her dad to kick off his retired boys' week doing something none of us wanted to know about.

Nate thundered up the stairs, and I was almost safe to descend mine when she called my name.

"Benji? I'm gonna try and be better. I am. I promise."

"Okay." What else could I say? That I'd heard that before?

"Seriously." She crossed her arms and nodded. "I like this guy and I know I need to do better for Nate. I just assumed they gave him the shirts at school. Thanks for handling it."

I'd believed her too many times before. But for Nate's sake I still held a shred of hope that it was true. He deserved more than what she was serving.

Later that night, with Nate asleep in his room and his mom watching a horrible reality show in the living room—at least she *was* home—I secluded myself down in the basement and my pathetic den. I plugged in my phone and raked my fingers through my hair.

Spaghetti. I tried not to take it as a dig, but she *knew* I had one cheat day. She *knew* it was Friday. Amee had even asked me what I ate on my non-cheat days. She'd said she was going to court me, but she hadn't even thought about what would make me happy. I shook my head and grabbed my textbook. My first big test was in ten days and I was fourteen kinds of screwed. I flipped the pages to where I'd left off in chapter two.

Gibberish. Every single word.

* * * *

The click of the overhead loudspeaker caught my ear. "Ben, you have a call on line three. Ben, line three, please."

My chest tightened. No one ever called me at work. In fact, the only time I'd used the number was on the emergency contact sheet for Nate. *Shit.* I secured the wheel in front of me, wiped my hands on the rag from my back pocket and walked over to the phone on the wall next to the steel work bench.

If Nate had finally kicked some bully's ass, I hoped he'd gotten in a square shot to the jaw.

I punched the flashing red light on the base of the phone.

"This is Ben."

"Hi, Mr. Mathis? This is Sandy Pritchard from St. Regis School. I'm sorry to disturb you at work." Rich people. Always so polite. *Hop to the point, lady.* Was Nate bleeding or in trouble?

She continued, "I did try Nate's mother, but there doesn't seem to be any answer on her mobile or at home."

"Right. Is Nate okay?"

"Oh, yes. My apologies. He's fine. But he missed the bus."

I dropped my head back and rolled my neck. I still had two hours of work. *Where the hell is Kim?* "So, I need to come and get him?"

"Well, Carly Benton's aunt is here and says she can drop him at home. But we don't have anything in our files that the Bentons are on Nate's back-up drop-off list..."

Back-up drop-off list? Is this woman serious?

"Is Jude there with you now?"

"She is." Sandy Pritchard's tone made me want to chuckle. I could only imagine the hard time Amee's sister had given her.

"May I speak with her, please?"

The receiver of the phone scratched, and Jude's familiar voice said, "Hey. I can drop him, no problem."

"Thank you. Can you just make sure his mom is there? I'm not sure why she's not answering." I hated the idea of Kim mixing with my life or being drunk in the afternoon and embarrassing Nate, but with Teddy out of town, I couldn't let him be home alone.

"Yep, no problem. And if she's not, he can hang with us. Does he know your number?"

"Yeah, text me with whatever happens. And thanks again, Jude."

"It's not a problem at all. Can you just tell Mrs. Sandy Pritchard that I'm now on your *back-up drop-off* list?" Poor Sandy Pritchard. She didn't stand a chance against Jude. *Who does, really?*

"With pleasure."

I had a text from Jude thirty minutes later saying Nate was home with his mom. I called him myself before class to check in and he explained Kim was 'just sleeping'. I wasn't sure how that was her doing better, but at least she'd been home.

In the parking lot of the community college, I shoved down my slices of roast beef and raw peppers. I had almost hoped that Kim wouldn't have been home — that way I could have legitimately skipped class. I grumbled between bites. What was the point of these stupid accounting courses? I could barely pay for groceries. How the hell would I get enough money to start my own business? A stupid idea for a stupid man.

If I hadn't been trying to set a good example for Nate, I would have quit that shit after the first week.

The fluorescent lights hummed overhead and the teacher babbled on about balance sheets. His muffin tops had seen too many muffins — or cupcakes. *Not my Cupcake*. Mr. Balding Accounting man with his thick rubber-soled shoes would never know the likes of Amee Benton. I remembered that subtle shimmy she did when I passed by and intentionally bumped into her before dinner. My Cupcake smelled sweeter than frosting. So what if she'd made me spaghetti? Being mad was stupid. The woman had more problems than my diet. I'd call her the next day.

When the two painful hours were thankfully at their end, I gathered my books from the white Formica table and piled them into my backpack.

"Hey," said the brunette who always sat in the front. She was around my age and her light blue sweater hugged her curves. "You want to get together and study? Someone once told me the best way to learn things is to explain them."

"Yeah, sure." I needed all the help I could get.

We exchanged numbers on the way to our cars and said goodbye.

When I pulled up to Teddy's house, a black Cayenne was waiting for me on the street. Jude hadn't wasted any time giving Amee my address.

I got out of my truck and hiked my bag over a shoulder. Amee hopped out of her SUV. She approached with her hands in her back pockets and a tentative look on her face. An oversized cream sweater hung off her shoulders and dipped in a long V on her chest.

"I didn't peg you as the stalker type."

She took her hands from her pockets and scrubbed her face. "I served you carbs. Strike two for the Douche Queen."

"You could have called." I wasn't exactly jumping for joy at the thought of her seeing how we lived. It was a stark contrast to her lap of luxury.

"I didn't think you'd answer." Her sad gaze met mine.

I scratched the scruff on my cheeks and stopped at the base of my neck. "I would have answered. And I was going to call you tomorrow."

"Can I come in?" She stepped closer and I caught a whiff of her sweetness. "Please?"

"It's...not very impressive."

Visions of Kim's gossip magazines and dirty dishes flooded my head. With Teddy gone, there was no one to impress, and she could do a lot of damage in an entire day on her own.

Amee inched closer and placed her hands on my chest. "I don't care about that shit. I need to make us right." Her warm breath lingered on my neck. Everything inside me screamed to kiss her, but it sounded like she wanted to talk. I let out a forceful exhale and moved away from the temptation.

"Let's go around. Nate's mom is, well..." *Complicated, at the moment.*

"Jude mentioned."

To my surprise, the kitchen was as clean as it could get. The backsplash tile and countertops were still dated and cheap, but there were no dishes in the sink. *Probably Nate.* The television barked a testimonial of a woman's voice from the living room and I ushered Amee through the kitchen and to the basement door. At least I could count on my own tidiness to not embarrass me with piles of sweaty clothes or empty water bottles.

I flipped the light on inside the door and we descended as the wooden steps creaked with our weight. At the bottom, I dropped my bag onto the end of my bed and switched on a lamp.

Her eyes dropped to my backpack. "Where were you, anyway?"

"How long have you been sitting out there?"

"Oh my God, Ben. Seriously? Do you do that on purpose?"

I bit my bottom lip. Feisty Amee was too much fun. I had to tease her. "Do I do what on purpose?"

"Stop it." She shook her head.

"Or else what? You're going to…?" I shrugged. Maybe it was wrong to tease her when she'd come to chat, but she was cute when she was flustered. And selfishly, it helped me gain the upper hand.

"Can we just talk for a minute?" She sat on the edge of my bed with a sunken posture. "I need you to communicate with me. You should have said, 'Amee, I don't eat pasta on Saturdays.' I felt like shit after you left. Then you didn't call me." She shifted so that one of her knees made an angle and the sole of her black ballerina flat pushed into the inner thigh of her dark jeans. "I want to make you happy, too. And I could use a little feedback." She wrung her hands in her lap and looked away.

Bless her. She was trying and probably more honest than any woman had ever been with me. Whatever was happening between us was no game to Amee Benton. She wanted and deserved more. I bet she didn't think that her little monologue was sexy, but to me it was everything. She was ready to try to make us work for real. I walked over to stand in front of her. It was my turn.

"I was at night school. I'm taking an accounting class and I'm pretty sure I'm going to fail because I suck at it." I ran my fingers through her soft hair.

"Thank you." Her eyelids fluttered, and she let out a little sigh. The tension faded, and I was reminded of our solitude. I bent down and let one of my knees rest between her legs. Amee pushed her cheek into my palm.

I leaned in and whispered, "You know what sucks about family dates?"

The bed dipped with all my weight and a little moan escaped her throat. She wrapped her arms around my waist and pulled me close. I leaned into her and she lay back on the navy spread of my bed. I kissed down her sweet silky neck, my hunger for her mouth increasing with every breath. She arched under me, and I reached for a lock of her hair and I tugged.

"Holy fuck..." Her words were barely audible and feathered with her desire.

I smiled a little, pleased by her shock. The pulse in her neck throbbed against my cheek and I returned to her ear.

"Not kissing you. That's what sucks about family dates." I hovered my lips over hers and she whimpered. My sweet Cupcake actually whimpered. I pushed my mouth onto hers and she opened for the full kiss. Our movements turned frantic, as if we'd both realized what we'd missed and suddenly couldn't get enough. Every sense buzzed its overload and she dug her nails into my back.

We rocked against each other as we kissed, moaned and nibbled. I squeezed her ass and she reached down between my legs.

She rubbed me through my jeans, the friction pleasure and the confinement pain. "I want this," she said between kisses, "so fucking bad."

Amee flipped me. After a whip of her hair, she pushed into my belly and glided her hips over my erection. She crossed her arms and lifted her sweater over her head. With lazy eyes and a sexy smile, she dropped it on the floor. Her breasts hid behind one layer of cream lace and their small pink middles called me. They were everything I loved — not too big and with the promise of soft femininity. She reached behind her back and the flimsy lace fell on my stomach.

Mercy.

I reached up to her heavenly chest and brushed my thumbs over the stiff centers. Her head fell back as I slowly squeezed. Her silhouette glowed in the warm light from my lamp, highlighting her natural beauty. A small shiver brought her eyes to mine and she said, "Your turn, big boy."

Her confidence led her hands to my stomach and I propped up on my elbows. With a little awkward maneuvering, I managed to pull my shirt off and lie back down. She pressed closer and the skin-to-skin contact made my dick ache for its own warm connection.

She kissed around my beard with a little giggle then down my chest. "You're fucking gorgeous, Ben."

My already hot face burned with her compliment and she trailed her tongue to my pecs. *Shouldn't I be the one commenting on the radiant woman on top of me?* I tucked my chin. When she got to my nipple, she glanced up. Wet warmth spun around the edge, then she caught the small pebble in her mouth. With the same grin from before — the one I was sure was my new favorite thing to see in the world — she bit down.

"Fuck..." The word was more breath than speech and I twirled her soft hair in my fingers.

She reached for the button on my jeans and the relief of the small opening increased my need for more freedom. Still working my stomach with her mouth, tongue and little scrapes of her teeth, she opened the fly of my jeans.

Quiet moans from both of us matched her heavenly massage. Only the thin cotton layer of my boxer briefs stood in the way of more pleasure.

"Amee... I... We..."

"Let me do this. I want to." Her breath heated my stomach and her fingers dug into the waist of my boxers, scratching me with her nails on the way.

All my self-lectures about taking it slow went out of the window. Her doing dirty things to me with her dirty mouth won — no questions asked.

I lifted my hips. I should have stopped, been the sensible one, but I couldn't. Her instincts were magical. The teasing duet of pain and tenderness were too much pleasure to deny.

My dick had barely sprung free before she had it in her warm hands and circled the tip with her tongue. She ran it up and down the shaft then around my balls. She opened her warm mouth and took one inside. She pestered and pulled it at the same time, all the while stroking.

Mercy. Fucking mer-cy. And ho-ly shit.

I peeked down, and she moved back to my main event. Her dark blonde head bobbed, each movement tightly coiling the energy that begged its release inside me. The spontaneity of the moment mixed with the fact that it'd been months since anyone had been in the room with me and an erection, and I crept closer to my edge. I grabbed the covers below and prayed I could savor her skill. But the steady suction from her warm mouth and her own hums of pleasure had me clenching my jaw. I squeezed my eyes shut. Maybe if I stopped watching I would last. My muscles tensed as a final barrier, but when her free hand cupped my balls and squeezed, I was a goner. The combination of the suck, pump and tug was too much, not to mention the internal boasting of my ego that the beautiful Amee Benton had wanted to pleasure me, Benji Mathis—a stupid mechanic who lived in his uncle's basement.

Through gritted teeth, I whispered, "Slow. Slow. Super slow."

Her lazy pace was my final undoing and I threw a pillow over my mouth to contain my deep groan. Fireworks erupted behind my eyes and bliss shot through my veins while Cupcake swallowed me down. Aftershocks rippled through my muscles and I twitched like I'd been electrocuted.

"Holy shit, woman," I said with an airy laugh once I could form words again.

Amee shimmied up and kissed my neck then laid her head on my shoulder. "I like doing that." She trailed her fingers in a random path on my abs while I tried to catch my breath.

"Now who's the fucking unicorn?"

Chapter Eleven

Cornflakes

Amee

The leftover granulated sugar from Carly's cinnamon toast sparkled on the countertop. I shooed the girls out of the kitchen to brush their teeth and stirred milk into my third cup of coffee.

"You made up with your unicorn?" Jude grabbed a green apple from the large wooden bowl on the island and bit into it with a juicy crunch.

I smiled, remembering my full-mouthed apology from the night before, tapped the spoon on the rim of my cup and tossed it into the sink next to Shae's half-eaten bowl of cereal.

Jude chewed like a horse gnawing hay, and she stared me down. After swallowing she asked, "Did you get laid?"

"Shh!" I checked around the corner to make sure small ears weren't lurking. "No! We..."

The bracelets on Jude's arm rattled as she raised her apple-free hand for me to stop. "No details." She whipped the other wrist up and presented the apple. "I'm eating."

"You asked."

I sipped my brain-starting liquid then cradled the warm cup in my hands. "Can I just say how fucking amazing it was to be held intimately?"

Jude smiled softly.

"Just that precious moment where no one needs to speak. I could have listened to his heartbeat the entire night. I had to pry myself away."

"I'm happy for you. I am. But you may want to save it for the weekends. You look like shit. Don't you have that huge new pre-nup client today?"

"Yes. I know. But I suddenly understand addiction for the first time in my life. God, Jude, he has these ridiculous wrap-around tats on his arms. And his biceps are like tree trunks." I set my cup down on the counter and overly exaggerated the circumference of his arms with my hands. "The naked unicorn did not disappoint." And just because Jude had a particular horror of certain male body parts, I added, "In any way."

After she cringed and gagged, which made me giggle, she lobbed the apple over in my direction and I caught it at stomach level.

"Blah. You have to finish that now." Her body wiggled like she was shaking off a hundred spiders as she walked out of the kitchen and called to the girls to hurry up, their chauffeur was waiting.

I dug my teeth into the cool, sweet fruit and leaned back against the counter. Yep, I was addicted to Ben's arms and how he mindlessly ran his fingers through my hair, not to mention the random kisses on the top of my head. Plus, he had more than toned muscles. The strength beating from his chest was hypnotic. The rhythm had lulled me to a secret state of euphoria I'd known existed but hadn't dared to believe I deserved. Hell, I was addicted to every damn inch of that man. I swallowed the bite. *And inches there are.*

My happy cloud and internal buzz carried me through the sleek marbled floor and windowed walls at Morrison, Hunt and Perdue. I'd been working at the law firm for the last five years, and with the upswing of my high-profile cases, had been on target to make partner. Then Pete had happened. Even though the huge red splotch that was his accident and the subsequent sentence had been brushed under the rug by another firm, the ordeal had left a dent in my attorney armor. At least we had already been divorced when he'd fucked up.

The new client for the prenuptial agreement was a referral. In fact, since I had settled a bitter and potentially career-damaging divorce for a professional basketball player the year before, I was now the go-to girl for marital affairs of local wealthy athletes. And their frequency in our modern halls was helping to erase the scandal of my past. Brock Jenssen, rookie pitcher and Southern heart-throb, was my ten o'clock.

Right on time, a receptionist ushered him in to my sunlight office, and after formalities, he sat down in the dark leather armchair opposite my lavish wooden desk.

"Thank you for coming without your fiancée, Mr. Jenssen." I smoothed the back of my black pants as I lowered into my chair. "As I mentioned on the phone, I only represent one party, not the couple as a whole."

He crossed a foot over the opposite knee and tugged his jeans closer to the heel of his cowboy boot. "I'm not even sure why I'm here. Ever since I got moved up from the minors, it feels like all I do is talk about paperwork." His innocent draw was no doubt a huge part of his charm, and the dark curled eyelashes around his chocolate eyes weren't hurting him either.

"Mr. Jenssen, I'm sure sudden fame is overwhelming." I delivered my words with my best sympathetic eyes.

"That's the other thing. You're gonna have to call me Brock or I'll be lookin' over my shoulder for my daddy." He mimicked the move and behind him a gaggle of legal administrators spread from the visible hallway like frightened birds.

"I'll work on it." I shot him a tight smile and interlaced my fingers on the desk. "So…you're getting married. Congratulations."

I spent the following half an hour explaining to him how money will change people—how fame could become a jealous mistress, how the stress of the game could lead to arguments among couples, how having finances clear from the beginning saved a mess later and that I'd seen divorce for more reasons that he could imagine. I tried to be as gentle as I could. No one wanted to think their future spouse would steal their money, but I'd seen some strong evidence to the contrary. When I'd finished my sales pitch on why he absolutely needed a document before his marriage, he leaned into his chair and scratched his head beneath the loose, dark curls.

"Yeah, but I'm not lookin' to get divorced. If you could just meet my girl, you'd see we don't need anything like this."

Ah, the stupid fool. Young, dumb and full of hope.

"I'm sure that's the case," I lied. "And you are by no means obligated to use my services. But as with every contract, you should know all your options and weigh the risks."

"I'm makin' a promise in the eyes of the Lord, not a contract." Brock dipped his chin and crossed his arms, pulling his black dress shirt tighter down his chest.

"It will be a beautiful moment, I'm sure. And since your love is solidified with your faith, asking her to sign an agreement will be easy." It was an old sales pitch, but usually successful.

"Are you married, Ms. Benton?"

"Not currently."

"Did you have a pre-nup?" His foot bobbed on his knee.

"I did not. But I also didn't have a multi-million-dollar signing bonus, nor did my ex-husband."

"I tell you what. You come to the game this weekend and meet my girl. You'll see how special she is. Then you can call my manager and explain to him that I don't need her to sign anything."

Like hell I will. That poor, sweet, innocent, optimistic boy would be taken to the cleaners. Lord, he'd probably already given her his credit card. Brock Jenssen needed me. The professional athlete divorce rate was astonishing.

"I'd be delighted to meet your fiancée. She's one lucky girl."

He blushed. The naïve babe blushed, right there in front of me. I rose and extended my hand for the shake. There was no way I would let Brock Jenssen not be my client. Securing his assets was my newest priority.

"So, you'll come to the game?" He pushed into his knees to stand.

"Wouldn't miss it for the world."

I held the glass door open for him, once again scattering the oglers on the other side.

Brock stopped walking halfway through the threshold and turned back. "You sure do fit your nickname."

"I wasn't aware I had one." I raised an eyebrow.

"Yeah, they call you the Nice-queen. You know, on the count of you being so polite. But one of my teammates told me there's still ice in nice."

"I assume you're referring to a certain center fielder whose wife changed teams, so to speak."

"That's the one. I'll get someone to send you the tickets."

I nodded my final goodbye and closed the door behind me. At my computer, I clicked on the web browser to search Brock Jenssen. There were no pictures of the girlfriend and no mention of her name on the gossip sites or team homepage. But social media was made for stalkers. I found Jenni Lynn Banks in two minutes and spent the next hour getting to know my new roadblock.

I ate my lunch alone at my desk and sent a text to Ben, asking him to call me when he was on break. When my mobile rang, I checked the number and my heart fell into my stomach, souring all the food I'd just swallowed.

Pete's attorney's name flashed on the screen, which meant Pete was either hurt or had gotten a bumped-up parole hearing. White upper-class men were always the first inmates to be released as soon as a facility started getting crowded. *Is it wrong to wish a shanking on the father of your children?*

My nose turned up and I swiped to answer. "This is Amee."

"Hey, it's Dave. They're releasing him on Friday."

* * * *

Light rain covered my windshield and I reversed into the free parking spot next to Ben's truck. I didn't know where else to go. I wasn't ready to face the girls. I needed to be happy for them, not gutted for myself.

Pete being present would change everything. He would need a car, a place to live and gainful employment. And he would be all up in my business about Ben. There was no way he would take my new relationship lying down. In fact, the scheming prick had probably already dreamed up ways to turn the girls against me.

A little after six, Ben strolled out as he zipped his hoodie. His brow was scrunched, but soon a warm smile lifted his cheeks. He dug his hands into his front pockets and tilted his head in question. I motioned for him to hop into the passenger side of the car, and once the door was closed, he leaned over for a kiss like it was the most natural thing in the world.

"I called you back. You didn't answer." He scratched his light beard and yawned. Then he looked over at me and his face fell. "Are you okay?"

"No." My chest deflated. "I'm not."

"Shit. I'm sorry, Amee. I let things go too far." He wiped down his cheeks, mimicking the drops on the glass in front of us.

I shifted in my seat to face him then rolled my neck against the leather headrest. "That's not it. I don't regret one second of last night." I reached for his hand and threaded my fingers through it. His warm touch seeped into my skin and wandered to my heart.

"You sure?"

He was too much. A definite fucking unicorn. I climbed over the center console and into his lap. "I'm sure."

With his free hand, he brushed through my hair and he narrowed his blue eyes. "So, what's wrong, Cupcake?"

I nuzzled into his shoulder, enjoying the tickle of his whiskers but dreading the words I had to speak. "My ex is getting released at the end of the week."

His hand stayed still for a few breaths before he said, "That sounds like a good thing to me. The girls will be happy."

"They will be." I closed my eyes. "I should be."

He kissed the top of my head and held his lips to my hair.

My quiet confession continued. "I hate him. I didn't love him at the end of our marriage. He'd changed so much. I loathed him for making our divorce so difficult. And I hate him for what he did — not just the fact that he took a life but for scarring the girls. I hate him."

Six months prior, I might have cried with such brutal honesty. But over time, the rage against Pete had flourished — every time the girls needed something and I was the only one around, trying to juggle schedules and keep a positive attitude, holding my daughters as they sobbed for the consequences of their father. I hated Pete more than I'd ever hated anything or anyone. And apart from Jude, I'd never spoken the harsh truth before, not even to the therapist.

Ben let out a low mumble of understanding and stroked my hair again.

"He wants to move in. Live in my fucking guest room."

"I get it. It's a hard balance between your happiness and the girls." He kissed me again and I sunk deeper into his lap. "You want to take a break? Start back up when things settle?"

My heart stopped. Hell no, *I* didn't. "That's the exact opposite of what I want to do." I tensed, preparing myself for what I needed to say next. "But if that's what you want, if I'm too complicated, there are no hard feelings." I braced for the blow of rejection.

"Amee" — he lifted my chin so our eyes met — "I knew your situation within ten minutes of meeting you. The only way I'm going anywhere is if you ask me to. Or if you ignore me again." He stared into my eyes then his face softened into a faint smile.

I blinked a few times as the understanding seeped in. He wasn't leaving. My cheek met his shoulder, the hoodie slightly damp from the rain. The roughness of his fingers tickled my neck as he gently played with my hair.

"What can I do to help?" he finally asked.

"This. This is perfect." His embrace was indeed my newfound sanctuary. Pete and I had been in love when we'd gotten married, but it hadn't ever been like that when he'd held me — the feeling of safe, of escaping, of security. It was new…and it was wonderful.

I was pushing the clock, sure to be late for dinner and bedtime would be rushed, but I needed a few more minutes. Maybe the filling of my heart would help my compassion for Pete.

"Cupcake?" Ben whispered into my ear.

I purred my response, letting him know I was listening but not moving.

"I need to go. I'm studying with someone from class." He kissed the top of my head and pulled away. "Do you want me to call you later?"

"Can I come over again?"

The dimples buttoned on his cheeks. It was a clear non-verbal cue asking me if I thought it was *really* a good idea.

"Okay. Okay." I lifted my hands to surrender. "But I can't guarantee I won't be thinking about you." I readjusted on his lap and trailed kisses at the base of his beard to that spot before his ear that made him shudder. "You know...in my bed." I nipped his lobe and pulled down harder than I should've with my teeth. "Alone," I whispered. "In my pajama pants."

Ben let out a light chuckle — either in response to my joke or the tickle — and turned to face me. He brushed his lips over mine and ran his hands down my back. That kiss would never do. I leaned in and deepened it. He responded by upping his own passion. He dug his fingers into the flesh of my hips and encouraged me to grind.

Abruptly, he pulled away and let out a throaty groan. "Sorry. I really do have to go. Is there anything I can do besides letting you worm your way back into my bed?"

"Yes, actually. Can you move your cheat day to Saturday? I have tickets to the baseball game." I pecked his lips again, their smooth plump irresistible. "I'm still courting you. Box seats." I waggled my eyebrows.

"That I can do. I'm a sucker for a cold beer on a warm fall day."

I glanced over my shoulder at the storm outside. "If they call it off for rain, we're playing spin the bottle in your basement."

He smacked my ass and motioned for me to get into the driver's seat.

"You feeling better?"

I nodded. I'd found a happy place and was ready to use it to mask my dread when I told the girls about Pete.

Ben leaned over. "Good," he said and followed it with a peck on my cheek. "I'll call you if it's not too late when I finish."

He hopped out of the car and jogged over to his own through the wind and rain. After an adorable wink, he started his truck and pulled away.

Chapter Twelve

Carrot Sticks

Ben

On the way over to Jemina's, Amee was heavy on my mind. I congratulated myself for doing the right thing and not letting her come over later. Since I'd had a taste of what that hot mama was capable of, resisting would be impossible. And it was no time for us to consummate our relationship. She was emotionally fragile, and I didn't want to take advantage of that. It would be hard, literally, but I could wait. *Mercy, that woman's mouth is a treasure chest of sin.*

I pulled my truck into the visitor's spot in front of the address my study partner had given me, told myself to focus on math for two hours and grabbed my backpack.

After two rounds of security buzzing and climbing one flight of stairs, I knocked on Jemina's door. When she opened, a pungent blast of artificial sugary candy — like one of those horrible soap stores at the mall — hit me. She was more casual than in class, in black yoga pants and a deep-cut long-sleeve lavender T-shirt. Her long dark hair was in a tight ponytail and edges of her brown eyes wrinkled with her smile.

"Right on time." Jemina held the door open.

Her apartment was small — a simple open kitchen with light gray countertops and a red futon facing a small flat screen. Separating the two areas was a cheap wooden table with two mismatched chairs. Beyond the table was a hallway, probably leading to the bedroom and bathroom.

I stood still when the door closed, chewing my bottom lip and waiting for her cue.

"It's not much." She shrugged. "But it's all mine. Have a seat."

I dipped my shoulder to let the backpack slide off and walked over to the table. I fished out our text book, my beat-up notebook and my erasable pen and set them all on the table.

In the kitchen, Jemina opened the cream door of the fridge and pulled out a plate of raw cut vegetables. She hip-bumped it shut, scooped up her books from the counter with her free hand and came over to join me.

"I've never had a study date before, but I heard that snacks are essential."

Did she just say date? My brain tilted like the head of a confused dog. Maybe it was just a generic term.

"You don't seem like the kinda guy who eats junk food. I hope this is okay." She placed the tray on the table and we both sat. "Anyway, I'm on a diet. My last boyfriend broke up with me because I'm fat."

Oh, God. No. Not the 'f' word. Handling women's body issues was a time bomb. If I told her she looked great, which she did, it was a compliment. If I said nothing, I was as bad as the original dick who said it.

"Your ex sounds like a douche." I hoped that was enough.

"Yeah, I always fall for the wrong guy." She rolled her eyes.

I chomped down on a carrot stick. I wasn't going to touch that one either.

A beat passed, and she said, "Anyway, let's get started."

We opened our books and she walked me through the first part of the chapter on budgeting. She had a way of explaining that finally made sense to my normally stuttering brain. I wrote down occasional notes with her tricks and tips on how to remember details and formulas. And she didn't laugh when I asked what were probably stupid questions. Instead, she would say things like, "that stumped me too" or "I'm not sure. Let's see if we can figure it out."

When the water bottle I'd brought along was empty, I asked if I could refill it.

"I'll do it." She took the bottle, and on her way to stand, her chest brushed against my forearm. It didn't seem intentional, but it definitely didn't go unnoticed either. I darted my eyes back to the pages in front of me and I told myself there was nothing to it. The little break gave me a reason to stretch and I flipped over my phone to check the time.

Shit. It was already past eleven. I piled my things into my bag.

"Sorry," I said when she returned with the full bottle. "I didn't realize how late it was. I need to get going."

"Oh. Right." She checked the thin watch on her wrist. "Time flies. But we didn't finish. I have a family thing Friday but I'm free Saturday night if you want to go through the rest."

I had made so much progress in the hours we'd studied, her explaining the rest would be incredibly helpful, but I couldn't risk her thinking a study date translated into a *date* date, however nice she was.

"Sunday?" I tried.

"Lemme check." She walked across the room and bent down to fish her phone out of her purse. Her yoga pants left zero to the imagination as the fabric stretched around her butt. I didn't need to know she wasn't wearing underwear but I did. I turned around and re-zipped my bag three or four times until she was back at the table and swiping her phone.

"I have a baby shower in the afternoon. I could do Sunday night." She looked up with arched eyebrows.

Meeting her at night again might risk the wrong idea, but there was no other time. And I needed her or I would surely fail the first test. "Perfect." I hiked the backpack over my shoulder and headed for the door.

Jemina unlocked the deadbolts and panic struck me. *How the hell does one say good night to a study partner? Quickly,* I decided. *Very quickly.*

She propped the door open by leaning against it and the stale un-candied air from the hall immediately relieved the sugar-brain haze from her apartment. I saluted her, said thanks again and briskly shot down the hall to the stairway. Her eyes burned a hole in my backside until I was sure I was out of sight.

* * * *

Over the next few days, Amee and I sent texts but didn't talk. Holding off on my cheat day made me cranky, and Friday night Trev took a massive beating from me. He called me 'hangry' and made me promise never to move cheat days again.

But it wasn't just the lack of sugar pissing me off. It was Amee's ex, Pete. With nowhere else to go — apparently all his relatives were in other states and his friend bridges had been burned — he would be spending the night on my girlfriend's couch.

My girlfriend. If Cupcake was going to court me, snuggle into me and give me amazing head, she was my girlfriend. Except I wasn't the one sleeping in the same house as she was. Ass Clown was. So yeah, Trev's face might have turned into the picture I'd seen of Ass Clown and I may have hit a little harder than usual.

And it turned out, Pete wasn't my only unwanted male guest. When I got home from the gym, instead of Kim rushing to get out the door, she was in the kitchen behind a mountain of dishes. My mouth watered as the very distinct savory smell of roasted pork filled the room.

"You're making dinner?" My keys clanked on the one spot of open surface I found.

"Yes. Your favorite. And we have guests." She dumped a huge pot of boiled potatoes through the metal strainer in the sink and steam engulfed her. She looked odd. She was dressed in new clothes, she'd had her hair cut and dyed to an acceptable shade of brown and her makeup was simple. She even seemed rested. *Holy shit.* She was almost pretty. Maybe she really had just been sleeping the other day.

Nate came in, gave me a huge smile and dug out the silverware from the drawer. "Mom's new boyfriend and his son are coming for dinner. It was my idea."

I shook my head once quickly. I was in the fucking Twilight Zone.

"Nate said it was really cool when you took him to what's her name's. So, I invited Rob and his son. Nate wants you to join. You can, right?" She dumped the yellow floury crumbles into their original pot and headed to the fridge. With a stick of butter in hand, she said, "Cheat day, right? I even made chocolate cheesecake."

"Cheat day cake!" Nate chanted, raised his hands over head, then did a little dance. The utensil drawer rattled shut and he left the kitchen.

Kim did a lot of things wrong, but one thing that woman could do was a roast, mashed potatoes, gravy and dessert. *Damn her.* My 'hangry' transformed into whatever hungry and depressed was. *Dungry?*

"I moved my cheat day. It's tomorrow." I walked over to the sink, flipped on the faucet and soaped the sponge.

"Well, move it back. Rob wants to meet you, and Nate is so excited."

The warm water trickled over my hands as I scrubbed the mixing bowl from her dessert, its evil chocolaty cheese mocking me with every stroke of the sponge. I rinsed it clean and set it over in the drying rack.

Nate came in from the dining room and asked, "I don't need to put glitter and stuff like Amee, right? The only girl is Mom."

"He changed his cheat day." Kim shook her head.

Even in the middle of doing something nice, she couldn't help but throw me under the bus. Nate's face fell, and the lip twitch started.

"Relax. I'll eat the meat and veg. And you better save me a piece of that cake. It's gonna be my breakfast."

The doorbell chimed, and Kim froze mid mash.

"Oh my God." Her nostrils flared, and the color erased from her face. "I'm not ready. Benji! Go! Answer!"

I dried my hands on the way down the foyer and flung the stained dishtowel into the laundry basket on the stairs as I passed. Nate hovered in the dining room doorway behind me and I reached for the knob.

On our front step was my definition of a mall dad, complete with mobile phone on his belt. His shirt was tucked in, revealing an either dessert- or beer-loving belly. The pleats in his khaki pants pointed right at me and stopped above generic white tennis shoes. His hair was thinning but still styled into place. *Christ, he's normal. Like, totally normal.* A far cry from the beefed-up soldier Nate had for a dad, but normal nonetheless.

I extended my hand and appreciated the firm handshake that returned.

"I'm Ben. Come on in."

"This is my son Devon." Rob pointed his thumb over his shoulder. "He likes video games and dirty magazines."

"Oh my God." Devon's head dropped back, revealing even more acne on his skinny neck, and his hands pushed deeper into the pouch of his gray hoodie.

I couldn't help but smile and wondered how Nate's and my relationship would change as he got older.

I held the door open wider. Once inside, I led them to the living room. Devon found a distant corner of the couch and Rob sat right in the middle. "Can I get you something to drink? I don't think we have any soda, but there should be a beer…"

"No alcohol for me when I drive. And I'm good for now, thanks."

Nate slid next to me and said, "Mom bought a two liter of Coke. She said Devon and I could have some." He peered up at me. I'd told him time and time again never to drink soda. He obviously didn't want me to judge him.

"Well, you guys are lucky then," I said with a wink.

Nate let out the tension in his shoulders with a happy sigh and smiled. "I'll get them. Devon, you like ice in yours?"

"Yes, please." The scrawny bean shifted and created a little breathing room between himself and the armrest.

I went over to Teddy's recliner and sat down with my elbows on my knees. The three of us waited in the hollow air of forced acquaintance. I studied the not-so-odd couple in front of me. Devon had manners. Rob, as far as I could tell, was just another man in the world trying to make it.

Kim's husband had been exceptional—an Army green beret who loved his family and his country. She had always known the risks of him being on the battlefields but had refused to believe it could happen to her, to them. The little he'd seen Nate, he'd loved him. I'd tried to replace Nate's dad the best I could, but Kim deserved someone too. Rob couldn't hold a candle to Kim's high school sweetheart, but it didn't matter. It was someone, not just a random guy at the bar.

I gave Rob my mental blessing and brought up sports, the even field of man chat. We talked well into the meal, and I enjoyed myself. Even with that damn gravy and its evil counterpart mashed potatoes taunting me from the other side of the table.

When the dishes were cleared and the boys were playing an age-appropriate video game, I volunteered to clean up and gave Kim and Rob their privacy.

When I was finished, I filled my water bottle and crept down the stairs to my dungeon of a room. I crashed onto my bed and pulled up my covers, sure Amee's perfume still lingered in the cotton. Was I like Rob? Just some dude coming into her life after she'd already had her one huge love?

My phone pinged, and I rolled over and grabbed it off my thick accounting textbook. Instead of typing a response, I called back.

"Hey," she answered. Her voice was quiet, tired.

"You okay?"

"Yes... No." Her breath crackled into my ear. "Fighting the urge to be stalkery and drive over."

A twitch below my boxers begged me to ask her over. "If it makes you feel less obsessive, I was just trying to convince myself that my bed still smelled like you."

"You were not." A lightness returned to her voice.

"I was. Breathing you in is better than cupcakes." I wedged the phone between my shoulder and ear and unbuttoned my fly. "And now I'm taking my pants off because that little smile in your voice makes me horny."

She giggled.

"Stop it. You're killing me." I stood, let the jeans fall down and kicked them off, leaving them bunched up on the floor.

"I have the cure for your problem," she teased. "Your *big* problem."

I shook my head and laid back down. A scratch to my beard reminded me to trim it in the morning. "As much as I want that, tonight it's the wrong move."

"Why are you always so good?"

Pouting... I was sure she was pouting on the other end.

"I'm just trying not to be a douchebag."

"Mission more than accomplished. Are you sure I can't come over? Now I've gone from sad to horny."

The image of her on top of me half naked was more tempting than the chocolate madness waiting for me in the fridge upstairs and I moaned. Restraint all around. Damn, I was boring.

"I could get used to the sound of that," she said, bringing the flirtatious tone of her voice back. "I do like it when you moan."

"Every single part of my body wants you in my bed, Amee. Make no mistake about it. But tonight, the timing's off. Your girls need you."

That was it. My dick hated me.

"Tomorrow after the game. We're going back to your place. You can't say no."

"I can't say no?" I grinned. *God bless her boldness.*

"I need some things from you — and your body."

Mercy, the woman is brilliant. "Deal. I'll pick you up around two," I said.

"Oh. I, uh..."

"You thought I wasn't going to come and get you?"

"Well, Pete will be here..."

"Amee Benton, if you think for one second that I will not pick you up, you're crazy. I'm going to pull up in your driveway, get out of my car and ring your doorbell. When he answers, I will shake his hand and introduce myself, because I'm a man — a man whose girlfriend is taking him to a baseball game. And he should know that."

"I..." Her voice shrunk.

"The girls already know, so there's no point hiding it."

"But—"

"No buts about it," I said, hoping my confidence would rub off on her.

"You called me your girlfriend." It was hard to tell if she was asking or stating.

"Did you want to be something else?"

"Nope," she answered quickly.

Chapter Thirteen

Bacon and Eggs

Amee

Shae's glitter-painted toes dangled from the edge of my bed and I nuzzled her closer. Her head still smelled like it did when she'd been a baby. I wasn't sure what time she'd padded into my room and crawled into my side, but I did remember making a little spot for her and lifting the duvet. It wasn't something she did very often, and with the light from the windows bouncing off her blonde hair, I decided to take full cuddle advantage of powered-down daughter number two.

She really was a beautiful little creature, my Shae, with her turned-up nose, long eyelashes and round head. Funny, because she'd been by far the ugliest baby I'd ever seen. She'd been early, probably a product of me working too much and smoothing over the fact that Pete had opened a bottle of wine every night. When she'd come out, she'd had skinny little frog legs. Her huge eyes had resembled more an alien than a baby, and her fingers had been freakishly long.

And, Jesus, Mary and Joseph, could that tiny baby wail. She'd slept in two-hour intervals for what seemed like the first three years of her life. When she'd wanted food, attention or a diaper change, there had never been a doubt. I chose to believe she was made out of love, but between feedings, laundry and pots of coffee, I honestly couldn't remember the moment I stopped caring about Pete.

Pete, who was downstairs. Pete, who was out of the correctional facility. Pete, who would be sure to find another way to fuck up my life.

Shae stirred, and I kissed her hot head. She squeezed her eyes shut and stiffened her body into a morning stretch.

"Hey there, Squirt. How'd you get into my bed?" I wiped a lock of hair away from her eyes.

"My babies were so loud. I couldn't sleep." Shae glanced over to the sunbeams sneaking in from the shades and popped up. "It's sunny?"

I nodded my obvious yes.

"Is it gonna be sunny all day?" She ran over to the window and pulled the drapes open, letting in a full bath of golden rays.

"I hope so. I'm going to the game with Ben, remember?"

Shae looked over her shoulder with wide eyes. "Can he come over early?" Her hands clapped in overdrive as a plea for a yes.

"Why?" I rose from the bed and reached for a long sweater. From the nightstand, I grabbed a hair tie and made a quick bun on the top of my head.

"I want to learn to ride a bike. Ben said he would teach me. It's not raining. Today is perfect."

I squished the skin on my face up with my fingertips then dug in and smoothed it down. Shae Benton had shitty timing. Really, shitty timing.

"I'm not sure Daddy..."

She flared her nostrils. Uh, oh — pissed-off Shae on a Saturday morning. And I hadn't even had caffeine.

"I don't care about Daddy." She crossed her arms in front of her Superwoman nightgown. "He spends all his time with Carly. Ben said he would teach me, and I know he will." She scowled and stomped out of the room.

Well, fuck.

A door slammed — confirming the tantrum — and I was almost jealous of her ability to express her anger. I wouldn't have minded banging a few things around the house, throwing a vase or kicking my ex and his sorry ass all the way down to the curb. But I wouldn't do that because the girls needed their rock. I would never take that away from them.

When I reached the top of the stairs, the aroma of fresh life source and its roasted beans lured me down to the kitchen. I passed Carly in the family room, giggling at the television, and met Pete, who was leaning over a plate that likely contained the rest of the eggs and bacon from my fridge.

He cut the egg white with the side of his fork, stuck it and said, "Morning."

I forced down a shudder. Pete had rummaged through his storage boxes in my basement and was still in the sweats he'd found and put on after his thirty-minute shower when we'd gotten home the night before.

"Real coffee." He held up his mug. "Real eggs. You can't even imagine, Ame."

I reached for my favorite mug in the cupboard and had just set the coffee back on its round hotplate when a door slammed from upstairs.

"Saturday morning tantrum?" he asked.

"Yep…" I dumped the remains of the milk into my coffee and sipped.

Carly, because she had some kind of weird-ass child radar that said, 'come closer when adults needed her to be miles away,' walked into the kitchen. She stole a piece of bacon off her dad's plate and sat down next to him at the island.

"So, what are we going to do today?" My daughter's simple smile and bright eyes rang of hope and happy times.

"Well…" I glanced over to Pete's now-empty plate, foresaw my next coffee without any dairy products and said, "I need to hit the grocery store."

Another door slammed, followed by child-sized stomps down the stairs. Shae entered the kitchen in a fluorescent yellow vest with silver reflective stripes. She had pants on —which was rare—her dark pink-and-black tennis shoes and held a hair tie out like it was a wafer for communion.

"I need a low braid so my hair doesn't hurt under the helmet." She stared me down and flicked her wrist just enough as the rubber band reached closer to me.

"Where you off to, Squirt?" Pete asked with an innocent, stupid smile.

I leaned back on the counter and crossed my legs. Pete had never sparred with six-year-old Shae. It was sure to be a show. I took another drink of my coffee then cradled the mug in my hands.

"I'm going to learn how to ride a bike." Her cranky face turned into a smile and she walked over to stand in front of me — waiting for her braid.

I set the cup on the counter and separated her hair into three parts. I caught a glimpse of Carly out of the corner of my eye, completely confused.

"Did you call him, Mommy?" Shae asked as threaded her locks.

"Not yet, baby."

"Who?" Pete stood and brought his dishes to the sink next to us.

"Ben," Shae answered, turning her head to Pete and throwing off my symmetry.

"*Boyfriend* Ben?" Pete's tone switched from amused to annoyed.

"That's a great nickname for him, Daddy! Imma start calling him that."

I tapped Shae's shoulder, my signal it was time for the hair-tie, and she obliged. When my duties as hairdresser were complete, I found Carly and Pete staring at me.

"Not my idea." My hands shot up in the surrender position. I reached for my coffee again and shrugged over to Carly. Pete was on his own. He could ruin Little Miss Sunshine's day all he wanted. I didn't need to be a part of it.

He knelt to be face-to-face with Shae. "What if *I* want to teach you how to ride a bike, baby?"

"No thanks." She turned, walked out of the kitchen and exited the house through the door leading to the garage.

Pete pushed against his knees and stood. "Carly, could you go brush your teeth please?" His crooked face lacked conviction.

She rolled her eyes but got up. The dragging of her feet matched her sunken posture and Pete waited until we heard her on the stairs before saying, "Nice, Amee. Fucking nice. I'm home one goddamn day, not even, and you're already throwing your boyfriend in my face."

I would have liked to throw the rest of my fucking coffee in his face. But my words would be enough. "You're so fucking blind, Pete. I didn't have anything to do with this. *She* asked for Ben. And you know why?" I placed my cup in the sink, hoping my calm action would rub off on my emotions. "Because she wants some fucking attention. You spent your whole night with Carly. It's no wonder she rejects you. You give her nothing but reasons to."

I spun around to leave but turned back when he said, "We need to talk about when Jude is going to move out so I can have the guest room." His hands were perched on his hips like he had any leverage, any authority. *Fool.*

"Jude is free to come and go as she pleases. You, however, will find a furnished apartment on Monday and move out of here no later than Friday." I straightened my spine and took a step in his direction. "You will then get gainful employment, report to your parole officer, and, with any luck, maybe you can get your driver's license back."

He swallowed and shifted his jaw from left to right.

I continued, "Whatever little fantasy you had about playing house under my roof is a fucking pipe dream, Pete. You and I are divorced. We will remain divorced for as long as I live, and you will give me the space I fucking deserve after all the shit I've cleaned up for you."

"I—"

I raised my hand. "I'm giving you one week on that couch, because I love our daughters."

I stomped up the stairs, not unlike Shae would have done. In my room, I closed the door and leaned against it. It was a mystery to me how I always managed to come across as the bad guy when my only crime had been to dare to chase a deeper happiness. Come to think of it, maybe my baby girl had the same goal.

After I'd showered, dressed and was ready to get the hell out of Dodge, I found Shae on our front steps. I could have told her she'd hurt Pete's feelings. I could have insisted she put on a brave face. But there was no malice in her heart. She simply wanted Ben to teach her to ride a bike. I sat down next to her and pulled my phone out of my bag.

"Do you want me to ask him or do you want to do it yourself?"

Her eyes turned sweet like a doe and she pushed her lips together tight to contain her smile. "I can talk to him? On the phone?"

"Yes. But it's possible he might be busy." I unlocked the phone and scrolled down to U. His phone rang four times before he picked up.

"Hey, Cupcake."

I smiled to Shae but said into the phone, "Hey. Did I catch you at a bad time?"

"I'm getting my hair cut, you okay?"

My grin grew. He was making himself handsome for our date.

"I'm fine. It's Shae..."

"What happened? Is she okay?"

I smiled over to my baby. "She'd like to talk to you."

Shae's fingers were already trying to magically manipulate the phone out of my hand and Ben said, "Well, then you should put her on."

"Hello?" Shae's excited voice was uncontainable. He must have said something adorable, because Mini Me giggled and brought her free hand to her mouth. Then the precocious little monkey stood, wandered to the other side of the front porch and had a conversation with my boyfriend entirely on her own. She hung up the phone like a boss and handed it back to me like she'd been doing it her whole life.

"He says he'll come an hour early, if it's okay with you. If not, text him and he'll be here like he said."

"Did you just make a date with my boyfriend?" I winked, so she knew I was kidding.

"Mommy, Boyfriend Ben likes me too."

* * * *

Right on time, the bell rang, and chaos broke out inside. Shae screamed, "It's for me!" and flew down the stairs, cut me off in the entryway and swung the huge door open. Ben, with shorter hair and a neatly trimmed beard, pursed his lips for a smile and revealed his heavenly dimples.

Carly and Pete, who had been drawing together in the dining room and listening to some old horrible jazz albums Pete liked, emerged behind us. Ben and Carly exchanged simple waves and Pete cleared his throat.

"Daddy, this is Ben. Ben, this is my dad, Peter Benton."

I wanted to take Shae to the mall and buy her every damn doll I could find. She'd just diffused a sure-to-be awkward moment that I'd been dreading for half a day.

The men shook hands and Ben turned his attention back to Shae.

"You ready?" he asked.

"Yes! My bike is outside." Shae grabbed his hand and pulled him down the front steps. Over his shoulder, he waved to Carly, nodded to Pete as if he were wearing a cowboy hat and managed a grin to me before being whisked away.

"Carly, you can put your music on now. I'll join you in a minute." Pete faked a smile to our daughter and watched her mumble her way to the dining room. Whispering to me, he said, "*That's* your fucking boyfriend? Jesus, Amee, is he even out of college?"

"Jude'll be home soon. She was planning on watching the girls for me tonight. She'll be around if anything happens." I walked toward the stairs and placed my foot on the first step.

"You don't trust me to be alone with our kids?"

I continued my slow climb and my words matched my pace. "You can't drive, and you don't have a phone. You have no friends. You have no resources. I'm a responsible parent who leaves my children with a responsible adult. Until you prove to me otherwise, you will not be alone with our children."

He scoffed. "Are you even happy I got out?"

My reply warranted me to spin around. I needed him to feel as unwelcome as I could. "No. I'm not."

I finished getting ready and popped my makeup into my bag. I grabbed my favorite burgundy and cream scarf and looped it around my neck and over my camel blazer.

From the window, I watched Ben with Shae. The handlebars wobbled, and he held on to the seat while jogging on the sidewalk behind her. He stayed with her halfway down the block and they stopped. With her feet on the ground, she straddled the bike and awkwardly turned it back in the direction of our house. Ben bent down, pointed and gave her the thumbs-up. They repeated their path several times and he never left her side.

He was a natural teacher. Pete understood Carly because they shared a talent. Starting from nothing took patience, encouragement. Part of me had pitied Pete when Shae had said no to him. But Shae must have known that Ben would get her up on that bike. Her will and his coaching were a scary combination. She was already less wobbly than when she'd started.

Jude's light blue Prius pulled into the driveway and she went over to say hello. She kissed Ben on the cheek, a gesture she had never once extended to Pete. Ben and Shae took off again with him still tailing her. They flipped around at the end of the block, he said something to her again and she gave him an enthusiastic thumbs-up. That time, halfway, he let go and stayed standing.

"Oh my God! Oh My God! She's doing it!" I ran down the hall and jogged down the stairs. When I got to the front door, Pete was in the living room, spying from behind the drapes. He blinked several times then turned away.

At the edge of the lawn, Shae was in a full-on victory dance with Jude. I ran down, scooped her up and spun her around.

"I told you he could teach me, Mommy!"

"There was never a doubt in my mind." I smiled to Ben and said, "Hey," to Jude.

Jude flipped her wrist and checked her watch. "You guys need to go."

I went back to the door, leaned in and called goodbye to Carly. Shae decided to practice her newfound skill outside and she and Jude waved to us as we pulled away.

On the way to the stadium, I thanked Ben profusely and hinted at promises of my gratitude. We parked the car and while we walked to the gates, I interlaced my fingers in his. The emotional lows of my day were washed away with the buzz of our contact and easy energy.

In the box, we were seated next to the one and only Jenni Lynn Banks. Her freshly dyed hair and long fake nails reeked of potential high maintenance. She wore Brock's jersey with tight, super-short cut-offs. If she hadn't tied the jersey's front, one would never know she had pants on at all.

I couldn't keep my identity secret, so I introduced myself. She shrugged me off. I assumed she thought it was no big deal. Ben and I ate hotdogs, drank ridiculously expensive beer and shared an ice cream. By the bottom of the seventh inning, I was more ready for a nap than anything else. I excused myself to use the restroom, and when I returned, Ben and Jenni Lynn had struck up a conversation.

"Hey," Ben said as I shuffled to my seat, "her boyfriend's buying her a new car." He pointed to Jenni Lynn's phone, which had square pictures of luxury cars on it. "I was giving her some advice."

"Fiancé," she corrected with a small clearing of her throat.

I faked my smile. "When's the big date?"

I'd never been more sorry to have asked a question. Jenni Lynn started a dissertation about wedding ideas. From vacation destination to trying to get a ballroom downtown, she was in full planning mode with all Brock Jenssen's money to burn.

"Your fiancé must be very excited to help plan," I said.

"Brock? Goodness no!" Her phone vibrated, and she excused herself to answer.

I burrowed into Ben and tried to hush the divorce rate calculations racing through my mind. Brock Jenssen needed a prenuptial agreement in the worst way. I would call him on Monday. And Jenni Lynn might be just a little bit pissed if she ever saw my face again.

By the time the game was over, the sun had set but it was still early. We walked to the car in silence, holding hands. When we found his truck, he followed me to the passenger side. I stopped his hand from opening the door and spun around.

"Ben," I said and pulled him into me. "I had a really fucking shitty twenty-four hours at home." I moved closer and let his beard tickle my cheek. "You've made it better." Slowly, I dragged my bottom lip along his jaw and I whispered, "I want to get lost in you. Please take me to your place."

He let out some kind of grumble mixed with a moan. He looked away then focused back on me. "You really think you're ready for that?" He brushed my cheek with his thumb and I pressed my head into the truck.

"I'm a grown woman, Ben. I have needs."

While he studied me, heat spread up my neck. What if he said no? Lord, the rejection was all I needed after a horrible day with Pete. He had to say yes. We were two consenting adults. I was his girlfriend, damn it.

"All right, Cupcake."

Chapter Fourteen

Chocolate

Ben

She climbed into the cab of my truck and I swung the door shut. I walked around the back, giving myself two extra seconds of composure. When I got to the bumper, the grin couldn't have been wiped off my face. I just hoped I was doing the right thing. But her, naked in my bed? Hell, that was worth singing about. And that woman was dead wrong if she thought it was going to happen quickly.

I climbed in, winked and cranked the engine. Once we were out of the parking lot, I reached for her hand and kissed her knuckles. The tension in the air was thick enough to pass for conversation. But after ten minutes of me driving five miles under the speed limit and being passed by a fourth car, she leaned over to look at the odometer.

"Are you driving slow on purpose?" I caught Amee's eyes narrowing in on me when I glanced over.

"Impatient?" I raised an eyebrow. Fluorescent lights of a pharmacy beckoned from a strip mall ahead and I tapped the blinker to turn in.

"Why are we stopping?"

"Cheat day. I'm craving chocolate," I fibbed and threw the truck into park and killed the engine. "You want anything?"

She rolled her eyes. "We're going to have sex and you're stopping for chocolate. You can't be serious."

I pecked her on the cheek, grinned, and said, "Be right back."

From the sliding glass doors, I waved and seriously thought about browsing every aisle to kill more time and work her into a frenzy. But I was anxious too and went straight over to pick out my favorite brand of condoms. I snagged two packs—a man could hope—and went to the counter where the impressive candy display awaited. *When did there get to be so many types of M&Ms?* I found the orange and brown package I craved and put all the items on the counter.

The elderly man behind the cash register scanned my merchandise and said, "Wish I was having your Saturday night." He opened a thin plastic bag and packed my three items.

"No need for that." I punched in my code and decided to really sell the drama to Amee. The two little shiny boxes found homes in my back pockets and I unwrapped the candy right away.

I was halfway through by the time I slid into the driver's seat.

"Mercy. I do love chocolate and peanut butter. You sure you don't want one?" I offered her the package.

Amee's face scrunched, and she leaned into the passenger side door. "Are you fucking kidding me?"

I knew what she meant but decided to play dumb to rile her up. "No. Scout's honor." I crossed my heart. "My favorite." I shook the package for the added drama.

"Your girlfriend asks you for sex, you agree, then you drive slower than my dead grandmother and stop to buy chocolate?"

Her blue eyes searched my face for an answer and I smiled. "And condoms."

"Oh." She pursed her lips, turned forward and sat on her hands.

Maybe reality had set in, maybe she was changing her mind — but she didn't speak for the rest of the ride. When we pulled up to my place, the driveway was taken with Rob's sedan.

"Looks like Kim has company. You sure you want to go in? I can take you home."

She peered over at me. "Oh no. We have condoms. We're having sex, Ben. In your bed. Don't try and wiggle your way out of this. You said, 'All right, Cupcake.' We're doing this."

Her door creaked open and slammed shut before I had my fingers on my handle. She marched up to the front porch and waited. The only thing missing was a tapping foot.

I snickered and got out then did my best impression of a man walking in slow motion. When I finally reached her, there was a sexy little snarl on her face. "You're going to pay for that, Unicorn."

"I doubt it," I said and kissed her quickly on the lips before opening the door. I ushered her in and we passed Teddy asleep in his recliner, the television shooting off images and the volume low.

Beeps and laughter came from the kitchen and we found Nate and Devon on phones at the dining room table.

"Hey, Little Man. You remember Amee." They waved, and I introduced her to Devon. "Where's your mom and Rob?"

"They went upstairs to talk," Devon said, air quoting the last word, and I rushed to erase any visuals from my brain. I had my own little dirty blonde to focus on.

"What are you guys doing here?" Nate asked with a smile.

"Uh…" I fumbled for a better explanation than Kim and Rob had offered. "We're going downstairs to study. I have that huge test Monday night."

Devon rolled his eyes. His fifteen years were wiser than Nate's eight.

"I thought you were going to do that with the Jemina woman tomorrow?" Nate scratched his head.

"I'm gonna do both. See you guys later."

Locking the door to the basement behind me, I followed Amee down the steps, but instead of sitting on my bed and flashing me the sultry eyes I was craving, she stayed standing with a sour look on face.

"Who's Jemina?"

Bless her wounded heart. Amee Benton was jealous.

"She's the very voluptuous, single woman from class. She loves to study with me." I teased and slowly stalked closer to the only woman I wanted.

"Excuse me?" Amee stumbled backward as I pressed forward.

"She helps me study," I said in her ear. "Do you think it's weird she rubs her boobs on me?"

"What?"

I smiled and bit my bottom lip as her knees buckled on the side of the bed.

"What the fuck, Ben?"

"Mmm...there's that dirty mouth." I pressed my lips to hers and she fell to her back with the weight of me. She surrendered to my kiss and I reached under her sweater and found her cool stomach.

"Wait." She turned her head away and I sat up. With a push from my knees, I stood and reached for her sexy little ankle boot to unzip it.

"Are you seeing that chick from class too?"

I threw her boot over my shoulder then pulled off her sock.

"It's downright fucking adorable that you're jealous, but I was messing with you. Yes, I study with a woman from class." I kissed her precious ankle. "But you're all I think about." I licked my lips. "All I want." I held the gaze to sear in my words. "Besides," I said and motioned for the other foot, "she smells like the fucking mall." I unzipped the boot and pulled off the sock then kicked off my own boots.

"What do you mean she smells like the mall?" Amee unwrapped her scarf and shrugged off her blazer.

"You know, that disgusting store with all the fake soap smells." I shivered.

"And you don't like that?" She pulled her sweater overhead and tossed it on the floor, revealing a cream lace bra that barely hid her breasts.

"I do not." My shirt met her sweater and I unbuttoned her jeans. In a *whoosh*, I whipped them off, revealing more cream lace and a sorry excuse for underwear. "But I do like that." I pulled off the rest of my clothes, leaving just my boxers to hide my erection. "You're beautiful, Cupcake."

I slithered over her, not fighting the urge to rub against her, and I found her sweet mouth. "You sure you're ready for this?"

"So. Fucking. Ready."

"All right. But if you change your mind, just say." I kissed down her jawline and nibbled her earlobe. I whispered, "Try not to scream. There are children in the house."

I brushed my lips down her collarbone and landed in the center of her chest. I pulled out each breast and reminded myself to be gentle. Although rough and vocal was my preference, it wasn't the time or place. After a squeeze of the soft flesh, I circled my tongue around the nipple on my left.

She played with the hair at the back of my neck and let out a soft moan. Lost in the heat, I bit gently on the nipple and she whimpered. It had been too long since the goddess before me had been worshipped. I found her mouth again and she dug her nails into the soft part of my neck. An impatient man would have already been inside her. Her beauty and need were intoxicating.

I slipped my right hand down the front of her panties and discovered how ready she was. With my middle finger, I gathered her slickness and found her clit. Amee arched her back below me when I circled around it, causing her to moan again.

"Fuuucck." Her voice was breathy like a ghost and warm on my cheek. I debated asking her how she wanted to come—like we were or with my mouth—then decided she'd have both. I quickened my finger tease and her body stiffened under me. She was close.

"Yes. There. *Fuck*."

Adding my ring finger was all it took and I could practically feel the waves of energy bursting at her spine. I kissed her deeply as she shook and trembled below me. She squeezed my wrist and I started peppering her lovely neck with small kisses.

"Holy fuck, Ben."

I didn't want to move my hand. I loved the intimacy of finally touching her in her sweet spot. "You still okay?"

Amee grazed her cheek against my beard and sighed. "Way fucking better than okay," she said between kisses.

"Let me know when you're ready for more. I'm a three-for-one guy."

"A what?" Amee pulled her chin in slightly, so we could look each other in the eyes.

"You get three and I get one."

"You really are a fucking unicorn."

"Maybe…" I moved down her body, disposed of her bra and bit a little harder on her perfect pink nipples. Her flimsy little excuse for underwear hit the floor too, and my tongue met its new favorite plaything. As soon as her whimpers and moans deepened, I backed off a little, letting her climax build. She swore, bucked against my face and pulled my hair, begging me for her next release. When her talk changed to my cock inside her, she won, and I watched her quake through number two.

I went to fish the condoms out of my pocket, and when I stood over her to check in, she was staring blankly at the wall.

"We don't have to go further," I said.

"It's just that…" She dropped her head onto the bed. "It's been a while."

"No shit."

Amee shot up on her elbows. "What do you mean, no shit?"

"I mean, I have skills, but you're a live wire. Jesus, you should consider masturbation." My eyes popped.

"I masturbate."

"I'd really, really like to hear more about that." Truly I would, and I wouldn't forget about it. "But right now, I need to know if you're okay to keep going."

Her expression softened, and she let out a slow breath. "I haven't been this okay in a very, very long time."

"We'll go slow." I put the condom on, hovered over her and she nodded as I searched for permission. One of her hands flew up to my chest.

"Slow," I reminded her as I pushed in a little more, giving myself a glimpse of the bliss awaiting me. She fit around me perfectly and I kept repeating 'slow' in my head, a message for my body not to betray either one of us.

Once she'd relaxed, I closed my eyes and allowed my own pleasure to wash through me. I stayed upright at first, taking in all her beautiful reactions. We locked eyes, but I needed more. I bent over her, hungry for her kiss to confirm the sacred moment from her end. She ran her nails the length of my back, teasing me, and I pumped into her a little harder, a little faster. She crossed her cool heels over my ass and encouraged me to thrust deeper.

I put all my body weight on my left hand and moved my right between her legs. When she finally dug in with her nails, my hand and pace reached their pinnacle.

"Fuck!" she cried.

Her scream, the perfect pain and the undeniable bliss, overloaded my senses. I came hard inside her with my own thunderous groan. *Mercy.* How had I forgotten how fucking great sex was? Especially with an emotional connection.

A pearl of sweat dripped off my nose, landing on her neck, and I kissed it away.

"Fucking A, Ben. Three for one is the greatest deal of all time."

We eventually caught our breath and I rolled onto my back. She tiptoed to my makeshift bathroom and I let her have her privacy. When she finished, I took my turn and returned to find her under my covers.

I pulled on some boxers to cover my now-limp dick and propped my hands on my hips.

"Can you take me home at the crack of dawn?" She did her best sad puppy impression.

"You got it, Cupcake." I crawled in next to her and an unfamiliar mint flavor touched my lips when I kissed her. "Did you pack a toothbrush?"

"Yep," she said, and pushed her little ass into my stomach.

"You are presumptuous."

"Determined." She kissed above my wrist and laid her head on my arm.

"Thanks for the game, by the way." I pecked the top of her blonde head. "Awesome seats. I can't believe we were next to Jenssen's girlfriend."

"That's how I got them. He's a potential client." She nuzzled into the crook of my elbow. *Potential client?* The guy wasn't even married yet. Or maybe he was already married?

"I thought you were a divorce attorney?" I ran a hand over my beard and smiled, thinking about how I could tease her next time — because that was going to be very soon if her naked body kept wiggling toward me.

"Yeah, but I do prenups too. And, boy, does he ever need one."

"I thought she was nice."

Amee's eyes closed and her mouth stretched into a full-on yawn. "Nice has nothing to do with it."

* * * *

After dropping Amee off — and with no reason to go back to bed — I downed a shake and went out to the garage in my sweats. With the clean mat on the cold concrete floor, I dropped to the ground and began my push-ups.

Despite the urge, round two had never happened. Amee's blissful slumber had stopped me from waking her. I wished I'd slept half as much as she had. In fact, my body and mind had been at war the entire night. *What the hell did she mean, Jenssen needs a prenup?* That little country girl was nice. *'Nice has nothing to do with it.'* Her words rang in my ears.

True, I wasn't the sharpest tool in the shed, so maybe she saw something that I'd missed. But what really ate at me was her dismissiveness about their relationship. Amee had barely said two words to that girl. Was she that much of a cynic?

I finished my reps and added a hundred more. I needed to put all that shit out of my mind and focus on my test the next night. The routine calmed me and two hours later, I went back in the kitchen to find Teddy drinking his coffee, faded bathrobe open and brown socks on his feet.

"Busy night in here." He hacked a few times and took a sip.

"You need anything from the store? Other than new underwear?" Focusing on the sink, and what I hoped wasn't flesh from his inner thigh, I filled my water bottle.

"Nah. Gave my list to Kimberly yesterday. Think she got it covered." Another cough followed, and he pounded at his chest with his fist.

"How many cigars did you smoke with your buddies last week?"

He shrugged, and I left him to his tobacco consequences.

Later that night, when I'd escaped the artificial fruit haze of Jemina's with a better understanding of accounting than I'd ever had, I stared at my phone. A simple text from Amee said 'thank you', with a yellow round head sending a kiss and a missed call an hour after. I tossed the phone onto the passenger seat and drove home.

Chapter Fifteen

Chicken

Amee

As much as I hated to admit it, Pete's extra set of hands in the morning were helpful, even with Jude scowling at him every time he turned around. Maybe my little fire under his ass had worked. The girls were dressed, bags organized, fed and had clean teeth five minutes before they needed to leave. I had forgotten that one thing he did right, even when he was hungover, was send the girls out of the door.

We kissed them goodbye and watched them file into Jude's car with waves and smiles. Pete and I walked back to the kitchen — which he'd already cleaned — and I headed to fill up my portable mug for my drive to work.

Leaning against the island, he ran a hand through his hair and said, "I looked online, but all the furnished apartments are across town. Since I don't know when I'm getting my license, I was hoping for something closer."

I wanted to tell him that across town was closer than the correctional facility, but I decided not to pick a fight. At least he'd started searching. I snapped the lid shut to my coffee and unplugged my phone from the charger. Still no texts from Ben.

"Can we just talk for a minute, since there are no little ears around?" Pete took a step toward me and I recoiled. "Jesus, I can't even touch you?" He backed away, hands in full-on surrender mode.

I checked the digital timer on the oven and said, "I have ten minutes. But then I have meetings all day."

"Okay, I'll be quick. I have a lot of logistical things to do today, too. Do you know if my bank cards still work?"

"I assume your account is still active. I've been paying your alimony every month."

His eyebrows raised. "Seriously? That's…"

Stupid? Generous? More than he deserves?

"Congratulations. You have a cushion," I said with regret.

Between my salary and the money I'd inherited from my parents early on in our marriage, I was an official sugar mama. And when I'd filed for divorce, I'd done what all rich spouses do when they wanted something over quick. I'd thrown money at my problem. I'd wanted Pete out of my house and he'd gotten a sweet settlement for it. It was a tactic I'd used with many clients, but their payoffs usually included a gag order from the former spouse. I remembered what my attorney had said to me after it was all over *'Sometimes the worst players make the best coaches.'* I was a horrible divorcée but a great divorce lawyer.

"When can we talk custody of the girls?"

"Pete," — my eagle eyes bored into his — "you need a job. You need to report to your parole officer. You need a place to live. Until you have those things, I retain sole custody. There is nothing negotiable about that."

He walked over to a barstool and slid in. Pete dropped his head into his hands and hunched over the counter. "And you can just parade your young boyfriend around in front of them as long as you wish? I heard you sneak in Sunday morning. You think sleeping around is a good idea right now?"

"Fuck you." *So much for me not fighting.* "And don't pretend to know anything about my personal life or the man I'm dating." I reached for my bag. The conversation was over.

"I know you're rich and he's not. I know he's young. What do you think he's doing with a divorced mom of two, Amee? What is he getting out of being with you? Open your fucking eyes."

"I repeat... Fuck you." I stormed out of the kitchen and slammed the garage door behind me.

At work, my heavy and determined steps echoed through the halls. When I got to my desk, I found the number of my favorite private investigator who answered on the second ring. "I'm emailing you a name and file. Find out everything and make this your top priority."

That afternoon, I had a painfully tedious meeting to divide assets. My client, on his third divorce, continued to assert that his soon-to-be-ex-wife had known the risks when they'd married and therefore did not deserve what she was asking for financially. Her attorney had prepared a list of items from the kitchen — complete with mixing bowls — that she planned on taking. He decided to object to almost everything, and by the end of the meeting, I didn't know who I wanted to throw out of the window first, him or myself.

When I finally got in my car, there was still no word from Ben. Lord, I had slept well in his arms. And getting back into the saddle had been better than I'd dreamed. I already craved more. He had his test, so I decided not to bother him.

At home, rosemary and garlic led me to the kitchen and I found Pete over the stove tossing green beans in a skillet. Carly sat at the island, her photo-copied spelling list for the week in front of her, and a smile on her face.

"Hey." I walked over and kissed my daughter's head. "What's happening here?"

"Daddy's making his roasted chicken."

"Smells great. Where's Shae?" I asked.

"With Jude. They're reading upstairs," Pete said from over his shoulder. He opened the oven, releasing both heat and more mouthwatering fumes, and the memories of so many other similar nights flooded my senses. I stumbled and excused myself to change.

Later, after an admittedly delicious meal without fighting and the girls were in bed, I knocked on Jude's door. Her textbooks were spread out around her on her quilted duvet and she had one knee bent into the opposite thigh.

"Can I talk to you?" I pressed my lips together and waited for the okay.

"If you mean, can I listen to you, then yes." She winked and cleared me a spot.

I wrapped my sweater a little tighter, walked over and curled up next to her. I laid my head in the crook of her hip and stared at the closed door before asking, "Do you think he's doing it on purpose?"

"Pete? I don't know. I mean, don't get me wrong, I'm not signing up to lead his fan club. But I assume he's just trying to find any grain of normalcy he can." Jude found a lock of my hair and she twirled it like I did to Carly.

"He thinks Ben is a gold digger." I closed my eyes to the rhythm of her soft twist and pull.

"He would. He's jealous. Even I can see that Ben is hot."

"I had sex with him." I opened my eyes and looked up to find her grinning.

"About fucking time. Literally."

I sat up and crossed my legs in front of her. "It was so much better than sex with Pete. I had three orgasms. *Three.*"

Jude flashed her hand between us. "You can stop there. I don't want any dick details."

I fought a small smile and lay down again, hoping she would continue to play with my hair.

"Ben hasn't called me since."

"Maybe you suck in bed, Amee."

I could feel the grin in her words. "I don't suck in bed, asshole. Well, I suck…"

"Stop."

I nuzzled my head into her leg, and she continued her calming twists and twirls.

"Give him time. You're complicated. And you probably said something to fuck shit up. You do that sometimes."

With my eyes closed, I thought back to my night with Ben. Jude was wrong. I hadn't said anything to mess it up with him. We'd cuddled, and I'd fallen asleep right after. Although he had said something about me being presumptuous.

No, he'd laughed. But she was right about one thing. My situation was hella complicated. I was sure that Pete being under the same roof was not easy for Ben. I'd give my boyfriend a little more space. Besides, his week nights were busy with school. And to the boob-rubbing study partner—whoever she was—she'd better back the fuck off my man. There was no way I was letting Ben Mathis go.

* * * *

I lasted until Wednesday night. He hadn't called or texted and my cool, calm, give-him-some-space morphed into find-him-at-night-school. I knew what community college he went to. I'd snooped through his textbooks when he'd showered Saturday night. Then, really, it had only been a matter of checking classes online and driving through a few parking lots before I found his truck. *Maybe I need to cut down my time spent with private investigators.*

I parked near it and surveyed the various orange lamp-lit sidewalks that led from the lot. At a quarter after nine, he swaggered down one of the paths. The curvy bouncing brunette at his side could only be the study partner. She clapped her hands together twice, gave him a fast hug and skipped away. He watched her go then hiked his backpack over his shoulder and came walking toward his truck.

I waited for him to see me, and when he did, he squinted before shaking his head. *Uh-oh.* I may have been a shade too dark into stalker mode again. *Crap.* I had been so pleased with myself as a P.I.

He walked over to my side of the car and I rolled down the window.

"You never returned my call." I shrugged, hoping it would excuse my behavior.

"Seems I don't need to." Ben raised his eyebrows and kept them up while he stared at me.

"I'd really like to talk to you. Will you get in?"

He walked around the front of the car, opened the passenger door and slid his bag onto the floor in front of him. Once he'd settled, he turned to me and said, "You're right. I didn't call you back — and not just because I was busy."

Holy shit. My face fell and the confidence drained out of my body. He was breaking up with me. I was too needy, too complicated and probably did suck in bed. At least Pete was wrong. Ben wasn't after my money.

"It's just…" He closed his eyes briefly then glanced forward, watching a sedan leave the dark lot. "I'm not really into being used." He turned to me with an expression that crushed my soul and heart with one glance — distance. Adding insult to injury, he continued, "I think we want different things."

We'd never discussed what we wanted, so I interjected before he could get me wrong. "How can you be so sure?"

"You said it. You said, 'nice has nothing to do with it.' Well, nice is about all I have to offer, Amee. I don't have money or a house. Fuck, I barely get by."

Shit. Two points for Jude. I'd said something stupid.

"Then you sent me a text saying thanks, like I was just… I don't know. A one-night stand."

I hid my face. I really was a colossal fuck up. "I'm so sorry, Ben. I don't know how to date. I don't even know what you saw in me to begin with."

"I saw — see — a beautiful woman who is a great mom. And that's what I want." He shook his head and made eye contact again, even though I was peeking out of my fingers. "I want a family. Sounds stupid, I know, but I didn't have a dad growing up and my mom did the best she could. When she died, I went to live with Teddy because I like the idea of support and unconditional love. Then Kim and Nate came and, well…"

I slid my hands down from my face. His words, his truth, his biggest desire were laid out in front of me. And I realized I had been so busy trying to make sure *I* was okay with him, I'd never thought about what I could do *for* him. I reached out for his hand and when he didn't pull away, I said, "I want all that too. And you may think I already have it, but I don't. I want a man who loves me like I know I deserve. I'm not sure where this is going, but I can assure you, my goal is the same."

I rubbed my thumb over his strong knuckles. "But if you want to make this work, you have to talk to me. You have to call me on my shit. And I promise I want to see where this goes, Ben. Nothing about me wants to be done with anything about you. You are the farthest thing from a one-night stand. I swear."

With his free hand, he scratched his beard and neck. He wedged his elbow in the window crook and he stared forward. After what seemed like too long, he finally looked at me and said, "You haven't even asked me how my test went."

Fuck. He was right. I had blown it all. My unicorn was going to ride off into the forest and remain a memory of what could have been if I hadn't been a selfish, thoughtless idiot. I pulled my hand away, breaking the warm connection I had obviously read wrong. The emptiness of no longer touching him smacked me in the head and tears puddled in the corners of my eyes. I didn't deserve him.

"I'm sorry." I blinked several times. "Thank you for talking to me. You probably should go." I straightened my posture and tried to hold it together until at least he got into his own car. Then I could sob and scream at myself for being selfish.

"Wait... What?"

"I loved spending time with you. And damn it, I loved kissing you." My lip quivered and a stupid lone tear fell. "I want to say thank you, but I know that sounds empty now." I quickly wiped away the tear in hopes he wouldn't notice it had been there. He grinned, showing deep dimples, and I'd never not wanted to see them more. "Why are you smiling?"

"You said I needed to call you on your shit. That was me calling you on your shit."

The tears in my eyes didn't know which way to go, they were as confused as my brain. "What are you saying?"

"I'm saying you're being a shitty girlfriend at the moment and you should ask me how I did on my test."

He said girlfriend. At the moment. "Does that mean I still am?"

"What? Shitty? Yes."

"No...girlfriend."

"Not if you don't ask me about my test." A little smile came back to his gorgeous rough face.

"How did you do on your test?" The realization that I may still have a unicorn for my very own creeped into my body and flushed my skin.

"Thanks for asking, Cupcake. I got an eighty-three."

I beamed. "That's awesome!"

"Thank you. It was Jemina. She explained it all," he said in a dismissive tone.

"I don't believe that for a minute. You worked hard. You deserve a good grade." *Holy crap, please let the previous half hour be behind us.*

"She aced it. Maybe some of her understanding rubbed off on me." The leather seat creaked below him as he shifted toward me for the first time that night. "You know, with all her boobs."

That was it. I was claiming Ben back for myself. I climbed over the armrest and straddled him in the confined space of my car, letting my wrists balance on his wide shoulders. "Really? You're going to tease me? After all that?"

Ben slid his hands into the opening of my sweater at my waist. He brushed his thumbs against my stomach. "I'm sorry I didn't talk to you."

The air grew still, and I looked down into his blue eyes. "I'm sorry I'm an asshole."

"Can we kiss and make up?" His whispered words sutured my fragile soul.

I was too tired and too hazy to find a witty comeback. Not to mention too transfixed by that damn mouth. I leaned down and kissed my boyfriend once, twice, three times. He ran his hand up my spine and pulled me closer. I grinded against him and he rubbed his beard into my neck. Ben slinked a hand around to my front, slipped it under my bra and squeezed my breast. When he pinched my nipple and bit my earlobe at the same time, a rush of wanting shot between my legs.

"Follow me home." His warm breath hit my neck and sent blissful shivers down my spine.

Chapter Sixteen

Pancakes

Ben

Amee kissed me goodbye for the fourth time and hobbled down the driveway in the first light of the day. When she sat down in the driver's seat and winced, I wondered if I might have been a tad too rough with her. But then again, she had panted and cried out, 'fuck yes!' most of the night. At one point, when I'd had to cover her mouth for fear of waking up everyone in the house, she'd bit my finger. I bet Daddy-O-Douchebag never got those kind of moans, bites and blissful scratches. *No way.*

Her black Cayenne hummed away, and for the first time since I could remember, I skipped my workout and went back to bed. Spooning the pillow she hadn't really slept on, I let go of all the bullshit around her and focused on the woman that she was. Driven, smart and sexy as hell, she was everything I'd always thought girls should aspire to be. I liked her. And after the previous night where I'd let loose and she'd proven responsive, I liked her a lot. I grinned into the used cotton and took in the subtle sweetness she'd left behind one more time. I had no idea what a bum like me had done to deserve her, but I was officially under her spell.

* * * *

Friday morning, I walked into the kitchen and found Kim. She was dressed, ready for the day and at the stove flipping pancakes. The microwaved dinged and she pulled out the tray of sizzling bacon.

"Please don't tell me you moved your cheat day again?" She opened the grease-stained paper towels and placed the steaming bacon on an empty plate with metal tongs.

"Are those buttermilk?" I pointed to the pan on the stove and resisted the urge to steal a piece of burnt pig fat in front of me.

"Homemade." She beamed. "Nate! Breakfast's ready!"

Thunderous footsteps hauled down the stairs and Nate rushed into the kitchen. He quickly found his place at the table, propped up his fork and knife and stared at his mother with hunger and delight.

I joined him, poured both of us some orange juice from the carton and smiled as he licked his lips.

Kim set the plate of bacon between us and positioned the maple syrup and butter closer to the edge to make room. She winked at Nate and returned to get the skillet.

Her game was obvious. It was the only one she had. Bribe Benji with food. But then again, it rarely failed. She was a good cook — something she shared with my mom—and I was a sucker for company around the table, especially with my favorite Little Man.

Nate had an unusual way of eating his stack of pancakes. He slid the bacon between layers and drowned it all with the syrup. His eyes lit up after the first bite. He was in his own little breakfast heaven.

Kim poured herself a cup of coffee and came back to the table. It was odd to see her so alert, such a functioning mother, but it was a step in the right direction, so I offered her a tight smile when she sat down.

She held the steaming cup in her hands and watched us eat. Between bites, we complimented her breakfast, and when Little Man finished and went up to brush his teeth, I finally asked.

"What do you need?" I wiped the corner of my mouth with my tongue to catch the last bit of maple-flavored stickiness and reached for Nate's empty plate to stack on mine.

Kim held up a hand. "Leave it. I'll do it when you're gone."

She was really digging deep into her bribery bag if she was volunteering to do the clean-up. I braced myself for how much the delicious breakfast was going to cost my bank account.

"So… Dad has something at the Legion's Club tonight." There was a small squeak in her voice.

I narrowed my eyes. Breakfast, dishes *and* the squeak? I was in for it.

"And due to recent events"—she cleared her throat and looked down her nose—"Rob and I feel it may be best to have a little privacy. Which, I can attest to, this house does not offer." Her nostrils flared and the message was well received.

"Sorry about that. It didn't wake up Nate, did it?" I cringed then sank deep into my chair.

"No. But it did get me thinking that we should maybe watch that shit around him."

I don't know what kind of voodoo Rob had or where it came from, but it was seriously working. In the month that Kim had been dating him, she'd shaped up. Her nights at random bars had ended and she was finally showing interest in Nate's wellbeing. I didn't know if it would last, but I had to give her credit for trying.

"So, I talked to Rob and we were wondering if you could watch the boys here tonight. Devon can sleep on the couch."

"You want me to babysit so you can get laid?"

She sipped her coffee and put the mug down before saying, "Basically...yes."

I clenched my jaw and released it several times as I mulled over the implications and bit back any imagery of her kissing a mall dad.

"You owe me, Benji. I listened to that woman all night."

Well played, Kim.

"Fine. But they're going to the gym with me. Tell Devon to bring workout clothes."

Nate lingered in the doorway with his school bag hitched on his shoulder and I glanced at the round plastic rooster clock on opposite wall.

"I can take him," I said to Kim as I stood up and wiped off my black workpants.

"Really?" Nate's voice practically cracked with excitement.

"Just let me brush my teeth before they rot." I winked at Nate and jogged down the steps to my not-so-soundproof lair.

A short while later, I pulled up to the drop-off line, my older model Chevy pick-up an eyesore among the Audis, BMWs and Lexus SUVs. Kids in burgundy Polos filed out of the cars, some waving to their drivers, some never looking back.

"Aww, man." Nate glanced out the window at three boys who were loitering near the empty bike rack.

"Who's that?"

"Logan Simmons and his idiot friends."

I zoned in on the boys, hoping my eyes cut like lasers into their skin and burned like the emotional wounds Nate came home with.

"He's having a huge party for Halloween and invited, like…everybody but me. Even Carly got invited and she's the quietest girl in our glass."

"Sounds like a douche." We inched forward one car-length.

"Yeah, he is. But I still wish I could go. I overheard a girl saying he had a home cinema where you can play video games. Sounds awesome. And if they could just see that I do that too, maybe I wouldn't be such a dork." He let out a small sigh and reached for the handle. "Thanks for the ride. Oh, can we have those super sloppy burgers tonight?"

"You know it, Little Man."

At lunch, I sent a text to Amee that tonight was a no-go, and she replied with a picture of her hipbone and the freckle I adored peeking out of band of black lace.

The message after it said, *Pity*.

The newer side of Amee, the playful one, that had been brought out after our nocturnal activities, was a happy surprise. With a shit-eating grin on my face, I finished my chicken salad sandwich in the break room at work. Even the bookkeeper and the receptionist babbling rumors about other co-workers couldn't faze me.

Until one of them said, "Take Ben, for example." She pointed her plastic fork over at me. "Put him in a nice suit with a decent haircut. He could flutter those baby blues at any divorced woman in this city and they would buy a car from him. Sales is more flirting than anything else." She picked at her salad and sighed. "God, I hope I get promoted soon."

Backhanded compliments weren't my thing, so I scooted my chair away from the table and gathered up my mess. "Enjoy your meal, ladies," I said with a simple nod.

"Hey, we're going out for happy hour across the street. You should come," the bookkeeper said with a warm smile.

I rose, horrified at the idea of having a beer with half of the people who worked with me. Stories of sales, bragging about vacations or complaints about customers flooded my head and I hid my shiver. "Can't. Sorry. I'm babysitting."

"Babysitting? Aren't you a little old for that?" The receptionist tucked her chin and raised her eyebrows. It was another reminder of how different I was from girls my own age. Most of them I'd met were just like the woman in front of me. They wanted to go out. Socialize. Party. Then they'd go home with whoever and either fuck them once or for a couple weeks. I didn't judge it, but I didn't admire it either. It wasn't what I wanted, and all seemed so empty and pointless.

"Have a good time." I flashed a fake smile, tossed my empty plastic bag into the trash along the wall and left the fluorescently lit room.

Over my shoulder, I heard the bookkeeper say, "He could babysit me."

* * * *

A disgruntled Devon and a bouncing-with-excitement Nate—my yin and yang dates for Friday night—walked into the warehouse converted to a boxing gym. They widened their eyes, taking in the evidence of lingering sweat and testosterone. We walked past the two blue sparring rings, their ropes tattered and used, and to the back office where the owner, Craig, hunched over his Sudoku puzzle book.

The frosted glass on his office door rattled when I knocked. With bifocals at the end of his nose and untamed, coarse gray eyebrows curled in all directions, Craig checked out the two scrawny kids to my left and said, "Fresh meat?"

"Yup. Gonna need some gloves."

"Might want to start with weights." He grumbled, put down his pen and his old metal office chair squeaked its resistance as he turned around. From below a dusty bookshelf, he reached into a cardboard box. He pulled out two pairs of gloves, just as dated as his horrible green wool sweater, and turned around.

One by one, Craig threw them at the boys, who were both equally surprised by his precision and speed.

I nodded my thanks and we headed to the benches. With the hook and jab pads on my hands, I took turns with each kid. Devon was skinny but quick and Nate had surprising power. *Maybe it was all that built-up nerd rage.*

After an hour and with their arms resembling more wet spaghetti than limbs, I sent them over to do crunches. *Is it wrong that I'm getting personal pleasure from working them to the bone?*

Trev clasped my shoulder and he let out a chuckle. "Who's the skinny dweeb next to Little Man?"

"Devon. Kim's boyfriend's son."

"Dude, don't even tell me you're babysitting for that woman."

"Nope. I'm kicking their little asses and having a blast. But you would be surprised at her these days."

Trev leaned back and slightly turned his head.

"She's changed. Seriously. She even made me breakfast."

"Trev!" Nate walked over and the two slapped and bumped the secret handshake they'd made up when Nate's dad, a high school buddy of Trev's, had died.

"I missed you, Little Man." Trev ruffled Nate's dark hair.

"Can you come for burgers after? We're going to the Beef Barn."

"You know it."

The frays of the rope tickled my lower back as I slid into the ring. Trev waited in the center, jogging in place and tapping his gloves in front of his torso.

"How you feelin' today? Tired, sad?" He faked a frown and continued his taunting, "I'm feelin' good. Real good. Like I'mma 'bout to whoop your ass good." He popped in his mouthguard and cracked his neck.

"I had to cancel my date to watch Tweedle Dee and Tweedle Dum complain about being more out of shape than your momma. I got some pent-up energy, and it's all for you, big boy." I cracked my own neck and grinned over to him.

Nate and Devon, who had long given up on strengthening their bodies, were joined by Craig and a couple of other stragglers on the wooden benches on the side of the ring. Trev and I sparred for forty-five minutes, breaking only for a shot of water either in the mouth or over the head.

When our time was up, we tapped gloves, climbed out of the ring and ripped off our head gear and mitts on the open bench in front of our small crowd. Craig's knees cracked behind me and he walked down the tiny bleachers.

"Your uppercut sucks, Dr. Doolittle," Craig said to Trev. When I snickered, to me he added, "And your footwork is a disgrace. You wearing irons for shoes?" He checked out my feet, as if his question were real. "Good thing you never went pro, Benji. You'd be easier to hit than a lamppost."

We let the old man have his insults and give a show to the younger crowd. Two more boxers slipped into the ring and Trev and I headed off to shower, leaving Craig and the boys behind.

I sat on the bench in the locker room with a towel on my waist and my hair dripping clean. Hunching over my bag on the floor, I searched it for my boxers.

"Holy shit, man. You got a tiger at home?" Trev stood behind me with his eyebrows raised. "Those are some serious claw marks."

Fuck. I had completely forgotten the physical reminder Amee had left on my back.

"You like that kinda shit?" Trev moved over to his own bag and plopped it down on the bench next to me.

I shrugged. "I like getting that level of a reaction out of a woman."

He threaded his arms through his white T-shirt. "Go no further."

"You asked." I dressed from the waist down and turned around.

"But next time, have her put some cream on that shit before she leaves. There's no need for you to be scarred for life."

"Awe. You takin' care of me, Dr. Doolittle?" I faked a frown.

"Somebody's got to."

Chapter Seventeen

Funnel Cakes

Amee

Cool air touched the small of my back and warm breath hit my shoulder. I cracked an eyelid and the orange hue of dawn snuck through my windows.

"Mommy?" Shae whispered as she snuggled into me and pulled the blanket from over my hips.

"Mmmh?" *Too early. Way too early for Saturday morning.* I shut my eye and pressed my cheek harder into my pillow.

"Mommy?" Her whisper was more insistent, and I rolled over to face her but kept my eyes closed.

The heavy lull of slumber begged me to return into its arms and I was just about to give in when she said it again.

"Mommy!" I startled awake and found her round hazel eyes staring at me. "It's date day. Wake up. Is it going to be warm enough for shorts? Will you braid my hair? Can I take Miss Funnel Cake? She's never been to an outdoor concert. Will you make me a dippy egg?"

I kissed her babbling cheek and looped my arm around her chest then pulled her close. To the top of her head I said, "We're not getting Ben until after lunch. We have plenty of time. Let Mommy sleep a little more."

She fiddled with my fingers and stayed quiet for as long as I suspected she could. There was never a chance of getting Shae back to sleep after she'd woken up, even though I'd lied to myself there was almost every Saturday morning since her birth.

"What's Boyfriend Ben's favorite color?" she whispered.

She was trying to be quiet, but I'd be up and boiling her an egg in ten minutes. I released her from the cuddle and rolled over for a full-body stretch.

"I don't know, baby. Maybe blue?"

"What do mean you don't know? He's your boyfriend, Mommy. That's like the first thing you ask people."

Her simplicity brought a smile to my tired face. "We can ask him. Go get my phone from the charger."

Shae dutifully hopped out of the bed, happy with a task and now having my full attention. She skipped back over and handed me the phone. I pulled up Ben's and my chat, thankful the pics I'd sent were too far up in the feed for my daughter to see.

"Can I write it? Can it be from me?" She beamed.

It was impossible to say no to her without coffee and I secretly delighted that she was looking forward to the day as much as I was, I helped her type her message to Ben complete with emojis for bikes, music and candy.

To my surprise and Shae's thrill, he replied almost right away. *Green.* His favorite color was green, and he'd added all the emojis with the color to prove it. Tiny avocados, cucumbers, tennis balls, a truck, a battery and a green squirt gun filled his message bubble.

When I returned from the bathroom, Shae still held my phone on the bed, but her face had dropped.

"What's wrong?"

She placed the phone on the pillow next to her. "I don't have anything green to wear and neither does Miss Funnel Cake."

"Well, only three hours till the mall opens."

"Really?" Her grin grew, and her hands clasped together in front of her.

"Come on. I'll make your egg."

"And the strips of toast with butter—but not too much butter?"

"Yep." I threaded my arms through my long gray cardigan that also doubled as a robe. I followed Shae out the door of my bedroom and peeked in on Carly, who was sound asleep with her mouth open, flat on her stomach.

At the banister, the snores hit me like a baseball bat in the face. *Pete.* Pete was still on my couch, in my house. With a finger at my lips to signal our silent descent, Shae and I snuck down the stairs and tiptoed past the living room.

Once her breakfast order had been filled, Shae scooped out her egg at the counter with a small spoon and I sipped my coffee to restart my brain. Barefoot and in the Halloween pajamas I'd bought for him years prior, Pete stumbled into the kitchen as he scratched his belly under his black T-shirt.

"You two are up early." He made his way around me and to the coffee pot.

"It's date day. We're going to the outdoor concert at the downtown mall." Shae popped her last piece of toast into her mouth and slipped off the barstool. "I'm going to tell Miss Funnel Cake. Can she come with us to the mall and pick out her outfit herself?"

"Sure, baby," I said with a wink.

"Hey! No morning hug and kiss for me?" Pete faked a frown to Shae and perched his hands on his hips.

"Sorry, Daddy." She ran over and hugged his belly. "I'm just so excited." She released her grip and skipped out of the room.

I watched her happiness, eager to hold on to it and anticipating the shit I was about to get.

"Date day? Really?" Pete crossed his arms.

I decided to ignore him. Any answer would have been unacceptable to him, no matter how I sliced it. With my coffee in hand, I moved over to the glass double doors leading to the backyard and wondered how warm or cold the fall day would be.

But the temptation of us being alone must have been too great, because Pete followed and stood next to me.

"I'm going to check out the house I told you about today. Carly said she wanted to go with me. She's trying to be excited about it."

I turned and narrowed my brow. "Carly is supposed to come with us today. We already talked about this."

"Yeah, well, she changed her mind." He shrugged and drank his coffee.

"When, exactly?" We had discussed our plans at an awkward family dinner the night before. *What the hell is he trying to do?*

He continued to stare at the trampoline with its drooping nets littered with orange and yellow leaves. "Last night...when I tucked her in."

"You can't do that. You can't disrupt my plans. Now I'm the bad guy if I make her come with me and she'll sulk the entire time." I reminded myself that throwing scalding coffee in my ex's face was the wrong thing to do. But him going behind my back was such a typical Pete move. It had been invented and repeated since the day Carly had learned how to ask for something she wanted. I would say no, then later he would say yes.

It had been a recurring fight throughout our marriage and I had no intention of rehashing it again. He wouldn't change. There was no point. My best plan was to talk to Carly later and explain that she would need to spend time with both of us and her not respecting our agreed-to plans was not acceptable. Once again, I would be left to adult while Pete played his fucking games.

"Sorry." Again, he shrugged as if he was really trying to sell his apology.

"Fuck off." I stomped over to the sink and dumped out the remainder of my coffee. But before I could leave the kitchen, I needed to let him know where he stood. "You've already over-stayed your welcome, Pete. If you continue to pull shit like this, don't think for one fucking minute I won't make it hard as hell for you to get joint custody. You're not the only one who knows how to work a system."

* * * *

With braids in her hair and a smile on her face, my errand partner Shae and I had done more before eleven a.m. than most people would do all day. *Thank the Lord above for drive-thru coffee.* When we got back home, she ran upstairs to her room with her doll and new clothes. I lugged the food bags in from the car and deposited them on the counter. Jude must have heard the ruckus and came out of her room to help.

We loaded the fridge, cabinets and pantry in silence. After months of sharing the task, it was almost meditative. When the canvas bags were folded and stored, she finally spoke.

"I'm going out tonight. I hope that's not a problem." She pressed her lips together in a familiar gesture we'd both inherited from our mother.

"Not at all. You do so much already. Have fun."

"I wish I were having fun, but it's a huge study group for midterms. There's even a cowboy. You know how I feel about cowboys." A tiny shudder, which was fake, shook her shoulders.

"Jude Saint Prude, we've been over this. Cowboys are people too. Many people, of both sexes, find them downright sexy." Fighting my smile was hard, but I needed the straight face to keep up our banter.

"Jude Saint Prude?" She raised an eyebrow. "You're going old school with your insults, Amee, I-once-kissed-a-girl-named-Jamie." She grabbed a bottle of water from the fridge. "And cowboys are weird, especially if they don't own a horse or a farm."

"Wanna-be cowboys."

"Precisely." She pointed in my direction then headed back to her room.

I managed to avoid Pete for the rest of the morning. He was still rummaging through his boxes in the basement, which allowed me to have a calm conversation with Carly alone in her room. We said goodbye on a civil note and I was out of the door without any more drama.

As Shae hummed behind me in the car, my talk with Carly played through my mind. She had understood that it wasn't right that she and Pete had changed plans without consulting me, but what was more worrisome was her reasoning. She didn't want her dad to be alone. In her mind, he'd been separated from his family long enough, and now that he was back — and had paid his dues — she intended to spend as much time with him as possible. She'd even asked about how he and I would break up custody. Would she have one week with him and one with me? Or would it only be weekends?

But what I couldn't and would never say to Carly was that I didn't trust Pete with her or her sister yet. Any remaining confidence I'd had in him as a man and father had evaporated with one call from the police months prior.

It wasn't that I didn't want them spending time with Pete. It was that I had become one fierce mama bear when he'd turned our lives upside down. Our girls had been through enough. Carly was trying to make up for lost time, but her father had a lot to prove before I would let that door swing open.

When we pulled up to Ben's, Nate and Devon were shooting hoops in the driveway. I smiled at the thought of Nate having a friend. Ben had told me it wasn't easy for him. I'd even offered to talk to Michelle Simmons to get her son to lighten up, but Ben had insisted that Nate make his own way.

Shae's seatbelt clicked its release and the car door slammed before I'd fully shifted into Park. She ran up to the boys and I didn't need to hear her to know she was asking one of them to teach her how to make a basket.

I climbed out of the car and smiled at the trio as I passed them on my way to the front door. Ben leaned into the frame with his arms crossed and a dimpled smile on his face.

"Hello, beautiful."

Every ounce of tension melted with his words and sparkling eyes. My stressful work week, my shitty morning and the worry of Carly, gone. And selfish me already needed more. I stepped closer and he unfolded his arms and wrapped them around my back. I nuzzled into his strong chest and breathed in his clean, earthy scent.

Ben brushed his beard across my forehead then kissed the top of my head. "I missed you, Cupcake."

I snaked my arms up his shirt and around to his shoulder blades. "Not as much as I missed you." I tilted my head, stretched on my tiptoes and found his soft, sweet lips. Yes, there was electricity and excitement, but there was also an underlying current of comfort — a calm that mended a broken piece of my heart that had remained forgotten for years.

"I definitely think I missed you more," he said when we broke from the embrace.

Shae ran up to us and I took an unwanted step away from Ben and his heavenly arms.

"What?" he asked with big eyes. "You're wearing green? For me?" Ben bent down to be at eye level with Shae, who grinned from ear to ear. Quieter, he added, "That was very thoughtful. Thank you."

"You're welcome, BB." She smoothed out her green cardigan and flopped her braids over her shoulders.

One of Ben's eyes closed, and he studied her with the other. "Did you just call me BB?"

"Yeah. It's Miss Funnel Cake's name for you. BB. You know, for Boyfriend Ben. My daddy said you can't be my boyfriend and that I had to stop calling you that.

But Miss Funnel Cake is smart. She found a way around it." Shae beamed with pride.

Ben pushed on his jean-clad knees and stood up. He held out his hand and said with a smile, "BB wants to drive."

When we got to the massive lawn, small tents with food and random unneeded souvenirs flanked both sides all the way down to the center stage. Shae insisted on holding both our hands and I couldn't get over how goddamn sexy Ben was with her sparkled fingernails against his worn knuckles. The entire afternoon was a blur of bliss. Ben hoisted Shae onto his shoulders so she could get a better view of the concert and gave her a piggyback ride all the way to the car when her little legs gave out on her.

Contented snores from the back seat were the soundtrack to our ride home. In his driveway, he killed the engine.

"Feels wrong to make out with you when she's so close," he said with squinted eyes and a scrunched face. "But I want to. I really want to."

"Not as much as I do." My unicorn was magical. I'd never imagined him going on a family date would make him more attractive, but it had. Any kiss he'd given me in public had been on my cheek, hand or head. He'd glided into Shae's world but never forced his presence. He was balance, perfect balance.

I leaned over, and he met me in the middle. We ended our date the same way we'd started it, with one simple lingering kiss that meant more than anything else we'd ever done.

Chapter Eighteen

Leftovers

Ben

Hitting the bag at the boxing gym only fractionally helped with my frustration.

I'd tossed and turned the entire night. The day date with Amee and Shae warmed my heart and tore at my brain. Shae was an awesome little girl. In fact, I couldn't have designed one better myself, but she wasn't mine, just like Nate wasn't mine either. And Carly was most definitely not mine, a point she'd proven by not even wanting to spend the day with us.

What am I doing? Am I forcing myself on her family? Maybe it was too soon. Maybe the timing was shit. Pete sounded like an asshole royale, but he was still their dad.

I hit the dead weight harder and a bead of sweat followed the jab. Again and again I punched, trying to figure out my next move. I liked Amee a lot, but I didn't want to get in the way of those girls and their dad. Even

Deana Birch

if there wouldn't be a reconciliation between the parents, maybe I was an unnecessary roadblock.

My stomach voiced its anger at my mere protein shake for energy, and I went over to sit down on the bench and take off my gloves.

Craig was there waiting for me, a cup of his not-to-be-touched potent coffee steaming in his hand. "Good therapy, that ol' bag."

"Don't talk about your wife like that." I winked and ripped the Velcro apart at my wrists.

Craig grinned and nodded to the hanging bag in front of us. "She's a cheating sack a shit. Lets anyone hit it."

I chuckled. "Hit it? You been hangin' out with the younger crowd?"

He leaned back and let out a sigh that filled the air with coffee breath and old man stink. "Unfortunately for me, everyone who comes in here is the younger crowd. But they don't stay. I need to update the equipment, but I can barely afford the rent." He stood, stared at the bag, scratched his flat ass and added, "She's terrible in bed too. Just flops around like a dead fish."

* * * *

Nate and Uncle Teddy were perched in front of the TV watching pro-wrestling when I got home. I nodded my hello and dumped my gym bag next to the door leading down to my room. In the kitchen, I found Kim.

"Hey!" She popped up from her seat at the table. "Can I make you some eggs?"

197

"Uh… sure." I tossed my keys onto the side counter and walked over to the table to sit. I rubbed my beard and she pulled out the frying pan.

"Oh. Also, there are tons of leftovers from last night." She kept her eyes on the task of cracking eggs and tossing the shells into the sink. "I made some carb-free lunches for you and put your name on them if you're interested."

She and Rob must have been planning a vacation. She was going to ask me to watch Nate for a week while she gambled on a riverboat in Louisiana or something.

"The pork was really lean, so you don't have to worry about it being fatty. I know that bugs you."

The egg mix sizzled into the pan and she stirred it with a wooden spoon.

Shit. She was going to ask for me to watch Devon, too. And here I'd thought Rob had been a good influence on her, that she was going to finally put her son before herself. Hell, those two boys actually got along. They even had a shot of making it as a family. But it seemed old habits of selfishness were dying hard.

"Water?" she asked.

"Sure." She filled a glass from the tap and brought it over with the cutlery before returning to the stove. A plate clanked against the others as she pulled it out of the cupboard. She loaded it up with eggs and brought it over. My breakfast steamed in front of me and even though I was starving, I couldn't take it anymore.

"Just ask. You don't have to butter me up with food every time you need something."

Kim chewed on her bottom lip. She looked down the hall, maybe checking to make sure our conversation would be private, then back to me.

"You're right. I have something to ask you."

I cut off a bit of the eggs with the edge of my fork, gave it a little blow and took the bite. Why her eggs always tasted better than mine was a universal mystery, but they did. I raised my eyebrows, encouraging her to continue.

"So…" She let out a long breath and paused. I speared another bite and waited. "Well, Rob and I have been talking. The boys are really getting along well and he's good to me. Like, better than I thought I deserved. And he makes me want to be better."

I brought the water glass to my lips and took a drink. "That's great, Kim. I'm happy for Little Man." I placed the glass next to the chipped plate. "And for you." A forced smile tugged at my cheeks.

"You know, the shirts thing did a number on me. And when I met Rob, I knew I needed to stop wallowing in my shit."

"Your husband died, Kim. You were mourning." They were the same lines I'd repeated for months.

She nodded slowly, and when my plate was almost finished, she said, "The thing is, Devon's school isn't that far from here…"

I could practically hear the Hawaiian music and see her lying on a beach. *Fine, the woman deserves a vacation.*

"And it's really not fair to make him sleep on the couch all the time."

I tucked my chin. Why would she care if he was on the couch while she sipped drinks with fake fruit in them? He could always sleep in her bed.

"And I know you've done so much for us and my dad. So, this is really hard to ask you." She swallowed. *Wait, what?*

"It's just that… Well, I thought maybe it would give you some privacy. You know, now that you're dating again. And it doesn't make sense for Rob to pay rent anymore since we've decided to live together."

Whoa. Whoa. Whoa.

Holy shit on every shingle. She was kicking me out.

"Devon can have my room and Rob and I will move into yours. They can help with Dad and you'll get your freedom from us."

And she thought she was doing me a favor, as if my connection to Nate was nothing, like I only took care of him out of obligation. I stared down at my half-eaten plate. I'd been used in the past, but this was a whole new level of rejection. All along I'd thought I was part of the family—a key part, a fucking responsible part. But no. I was a means to an end. Money for food and a default babysitter. I would have preferred a slap in the face.

"I thought you'd be happy to be rid of us." Kim shrugged.

Nate bounced into the kitchen with Teddy's favorite worn coffee mug in his hand. "Grandpa wants a refill."

Kim smiled and pushed into the table to stand. "I'll get that for you, buddy. I know just the right amount of vanilla creamer he likes."

She completed her task, and when Nate was out of earshot, I asked, "When do you want me out?"

"Well, I mean, I don't think you'll find anything in the next couple of days, but the sooner you can let us know when you've found something, the better."

"Right." I stood.

"I'll do your dishes," she said with her sickening sweet smile.

Normally I would have objected. She'd cooked, after all. But she could wash my fucking plate. She'd just ripped the one place I had been sure I belonged out from under my feet. I grabbed my gym bag and closed the door to the basement behind me.

On my bed, I tried to study, tried to think of anything else but the fact that I was a square peg forcing myself into a round hole. Nate needed a true family and I had to give him that chance. It would have been much easier to fight Kim if Rob and Devon were dicks—but they weren't. Rob was responsible, and Devon and Nate got along like wildfire. I couldn't take that away from Little Man. But that didn't mean I was going to disappear from his life.

I changed out of my sweats and climbed my stairs two at a time. Nate sat cross-legged on the carpet next to Teddy's worn-out recliner. He was still in his pajamas.

"Come on, Little Man. Let's go get muddy."

A grin filled his young face and he hopped up. "Bye, Grandpa." Nate rushed past me, ran upstairs and was dressed and in the passenger side of my truck before I'd secured our dirt bikes in the back.

I let him choose the radio station as we drove out to the place where I'd taken Amee to our night picnic. We pumped our pedals up the hills and Nate even caught a little air on a jump as we charged down. Next to a particularly well-rounded and not-too-steep bump, we stopped, and I showed him a couple of tricks he could add when he rode. I reclined on the dirt as he walked his bike up and rode down what must have been a hundred times before he'd mastered it.

I bought him some crappy fast food for lunch while I had a salad and what I was sure was fake chicken. When he finished his fries, I finally breached the subject. "You excited about Devon moving in?"

Nate looked down and smoothed the empty, grease-stained package.

I pressed my knuckles into my chin and waited.

He hesitated before saying, "I am. But where are you gonna go? I mean, what if my mom gets…"

"Tired again?" Drunk and depressed, while closer to the truth, was still too much to hear about your mom at that age. I always went with 'tired'. After all, she'd been that too. "I may not be able to live with you anymore, but you're a part of me forever. You got that?"

And he would be. In my eyes, our bond was just as strong as if he were my nephew. I didn't want to get in the way of someone else stepping in to be his dad, but my commitment to Nate was the most solid relationship in my life.

He nodded. "Devon and I want to box more. Can we come twice a week? I told Devon he would probably have to promise to get his homework done and he groaned, but I think my mom would be okay with it. Plus, I'm gonna miss you."

"You're not going to miss me when I start making you jump rope and do a hundred push-ups before you get into the ring."

"Even then."

* * * *

With my backpack over my shoulder, I knocked on Jemina's door. When she opened it, instead of the normal nauseating mall smell that meant she had over-body-sprayed or had lit an obnoxious pink candle somewhere, I was hit with warm South American spices and fresh coriander.

She welcomed me in, her long, dark hair in its signature ponytail, and she wore yoga clothes I was sure had never stretched in a class. I eyeballed the crockpot on her kitchen counter as I went over to her table where I dropped my bag on the tan carpeted floor.

"That smells amazing."

She smiled. "Thanks. Brazilian jerk chicken. I'm making it for my grandfather."

My sense of smell hadn't prepared itself to enjoy being at Jemina's, and with the other distractions of the day, studying became almost impossible. Finally, I closed the textbook and gave up.

"You okay?" she asked with small wrinkles around her dark eyes.

"Can I ask you a personal question?" I scratched my beard.

"Sure." The wrinkles disappeared as her eyes opened wide.

"How much do you pay in rent for a place like this?"

A shot of disappointment flashed on her face before she said, "Rent here is twelve hundred a month. You looking to move?"

I thought she'd asked me a question, but I hadn't gotten past her twelve hundred a month. After taxes, that was half my take-home. I paid Teddy five hundred and bought groceries. But if I doubled that, I would be completely strapped. *Shit.*

"My sister works in a rental office. She could help you." Jemina stood up and walked to her counter, where she picked up her glitter-cased phone. "I can send you her number. She only works mornings 'cuz she has her kids in the afternoon, but she's available some nights and the weekends when her husband's around."

It was a start, at least. I'd probably end up downtown in a warehouse next to junkies and their spoons. It was a good thing I could throw a mean punch. And there was no way I would be able to afford any more night classes. I'd most likely need a second job.

"Yeah, sure. Send me her number. Thanks." I dropped my book into my bag and zipped it up. "Sorry. I'm a bit distracted tonight. I should go."

"You sure? We didn't even finish the second half of that chapter."

I pulled on my hoodie and her eyes drifted to my midsection when my arms were overhead.

Not for all the jerk chicken in the world, baby.

I liked Jemina. She was nice, and I loved the way she got me to understand our class work. But that girl was not my type. I forced a smile, thanked her again and walked through the crisp night air to my truck.

As I let it heat up, I called Amee.

"Hey, BB," she answered in a sleepy voice.

"Any chance you can come over? I need to talk." I tested the air in front of a vent to see if it had turned warm.

She cleared her throat and asked, "You okay?"

"I'd be better with you by my side." The last thing I wanted to do was to come off weak or burden Amee with my shit. But I needed to feel better and her blonde head on my chest — even for one hour — would do that.

"There's no way I can argue with that. Plus, I'm wearing your favorite pajamas."

A quick, airy laugh escaped me. She thought it was a booty call. I wished it was. But if I couldn't even afford rent and a car payment, Amee Benton was the Sears Tower of beyond reach. I had to break up with her. I would hold her in my arms one last time, savor the treasure I'd found then let her go. I was no match for a woman like Amee Benton.

"So, you can come?"

"Yeah, lemme just tell Jude. Thirty minutes, okay?"

"See you then." I hung up and tossed my phone into the passenger seat, where it bounced next to a bit of dried dirt left behind from Nate.

Chapter Nineteen

Roasted Marshmallows

Amee

I pulled up on the dark street. Ben sat in his truck with his head down. It was unlike him to beckon me to come over, and his slumped posture blew away my high hopes for a quiet quickie with the dry leaves tumbling in his yard.

Hugging my sweater tight, and regretting I'd skipped a warmer coat, I clicked the lock on my car and walked over to his. He startled when I knocked on the glass then gave me a smile that didn't reach his normally warm eyes. I stepped back for him to open and stretched up on my tiptoes for a kiss. It was over too soon, and he motioned to the side door of his uncle's house.

"Let's go inside," he said with a sigh.

I wrapped my arms tighter under my breasts and told myself not to worry that he hadn't reached for my hand. Maybe he'd lost his job or someone was ill. Although, I couldn't imagine discovering either of those things on a Sunday night. I'd just seen him the day before and, apart from Carly not being there, I couldn't have invented a better day.

Shit. Fuck.

Shit and fuck.

Maybe it was about Pete. He still wasn't out of my house, and I could only imagine how I would feel if an ex-anything of his was living under the same roof as my precious unicorn.

He held the door open for me and, without asking where we were going, I moved to the steps in the kitchen leading down to his room. Ben flipped a switch and a dim light fluttered on next to a beat-up tan couch opposite his bed. We descended the stairs, the only hint of life the creaks from the boards. I went to the edge of his bed and sat. Ben unzipped his black hoodie and sank into the couch across from me. Being at a loss for words wasn't really my style, and a thousand thoughts begged their release from my sealed lips.

Holy shit. He was going to break up with me. I had too much baggage, too many issues. My chest tightened as I waited for the blow of the inevitable words to rip my heart out, and my eyelids tensed to hold back the tears.

Ben looked over to me and rubbed his neck. "I like you so much…"

Fuck. The tension in my chest crawled up my shoulders and clawed into the base of my brain.

He paused for a long blink and continued, "And I know things aren't perfect with Carly, but I want you to know I adore those girls. So, whatever you might think later, it's not them…"

If he was about to try and sell me a 'It's not you, it's me' line, he would lose. He had better say that he hated me — my cooking, my job, my breath, anything. Because if he thought for one second I would let him walk out of my life, he was wrong. I would go back home and kick Pete out that very minute if that was what it took. I deserved my fucking unicorn. I'd waited, suffered and lived in lonely misery for too long.

I set my shoulders and blinked away the threatening tears. Ben Mathis would not break up with me. No way.

"Don't say it." I unhooked my leg free from under my butt and stood. Shaking my head, I walked over and knelt between his legs. "I don't know what brought this on, but we are not ending this."

Ben dropped his head back into the sofa. He closed his eyes, avoiding my own pleading ones from below, and softened his posture.

As if he was tasting his words before spitting them out, he rolled his tongue behind closed lips. "I have to find a new place to live. Kim's boyfriend and his son are moving in, and that makes too many people and not enough beds."

"Okay..." How on earth that meant he couldn't see me anymore was beyond comprehension, but he'd said he wanted to talk, so I would listen. Unless he went down break-up lane. Then I would talk, and he would hear me.

He clenched his jaw, which deepened his adorable dimples. "You're very distracting on your knees."

The tension in my shoulders escaped but my heart remained on high alert.

Ben reached up and scrubbed his beautiful face. "Amee... Cupcake..."

I crawled into his lap and let my ass fall over the side of his strong thigh. I dropped my head into his chest and couldn't be stopped from sneaking a hand inside his shirt and touching the firm, soft skin of his stomach. He let out a long breath and played with my hair.

In a low voice, he said, "Maybe I'm making the situation harder for your girls. They need their dad. And I don't want to fuck that up for them."

The soft, barely there, fuzz around his navel tickled my wrist. My brain screamed for me to object to his argument, but he wasn't finished.

"And now that I have to pay more rent, I just don't see how I can—"

The lawyer in me won the battle and I pulled back then hooked my legs over his hips to straddle him. He met my stare with mild amusement, but I was stone-cold serious.

"No. Just... No. The first time we met, you asked me who takes care of me. And up until we started dating, no one did. So...no. You don't get to walk away from me because you're feeling insecure."

Ben closed his eyes and hid the sea of blue behind them.

I nuzzled into his heavenly scratchy neck and whispered, "Come away with me. One night. Just us. For me. For us." I placed a soft, delicate kiss below his ear and he brushed his hands up my thighs and around my waist. Ben drew me in tighter and we stayed like that for longer than I wanted him to take to answer.

When I was on the verge of sleep, he said, "I'm not good enough for you."

I'd wondered if that would come up again after my fuck up at the Fall Fest. But the balance of his bank account was of no interest to me. I needed him, his arms. Ben Mathis was slowly repairing my heart and making my life whole. Hell, I was pretty sure I was falling in love with him.

"I'll be the judge of that."

The remainder of our tension dissipated, and he carried me over to his bed. I crawled in, and he stripped down to his T-shirt and boxers then pulled on a pair of sweatpants. He set the alarm on his phone and joined me. With my ear on his chest, I focused on the rhythm of his heart and squeezed him as tight as I could. There was no way I was letting him go.

* * * *

I tossed my lipstick-stained paper coffee cup into the trash under my desk and tightened the silk bow at the side of my neck that was attached to my cream blouse. I stacked all pertinent files for my next client and slid them into the upper right-hand drawer of my desk. I was going to try to get my point across the old-fashioned way…with reason.

As he entered the glass door of my office, Brock Jenssen flashed me his All-American smile, the kind of grin that could probably diffuse any situation with ladies. But not me… I wasn't interested in the baseball star for his handsome face. I was there to protect his assets from the woman he was about to make his wife and add another all-star client to my roster.

I rose, greeted him with my sturdiest handshake and invited him to sit, which he only did after I'd done so myself.

With my fingers crossed in front of me, I said, "It's nice to see you again. I do hope you've given more thought to securing your financials before that ring goes on your finger."

He let out a full-on country-boy sigh and followed it with a tight shrug. "Not really, Ms. Benton. I mean, I know I was supposed to, but I just don't see how my little sweetheart could ever go after my money."

I hated his naiveté but had to admit I admired his innocence. After all, my usual client athletes had gone through the ranks of big man on campus and racked up notches in their bedposts. But not Brock… He'd only had two years at a state university on a scholarship before he had been lured into the minor leagues. And he was a good boy. He probably called his mama every Sunday night.

Two years ago and a different client, I would have already shown him the hot mess the investigator had discovered in the manila folder burning a hole in my top drawer. In fact, my hand itched to reach for it and the USB card holding the pictures of Jenni Lynn and another athlete.

According to a friend of the guy who'd flapped his jaw with pride for discovering she was a gold digger, Jenni Lynn had bragged to someone he knew about how she would be set for life by just marrying an idiot with a paycheck. Then they'd tricked her after a couple of drinks in Miami, where they'd all been staying for spring training, and filmed her repeating the same thing. The video had never been made public. There had been no need once the former boyfriend had broken off their relationship.

Until my private investigator had found it—and paid the friend for a copy. It had cost less than the shoes on my feet.

I tapped my nails in a pensive rhythm on my spotless desk. I had three moves. Show him the file and ruin two lives, let my whopper of a client walk out the door or meet with Jenni Lynn. And I needed Brock Jenssen. *Damn it.*

"You know," I said with a smile, "I didn't really get to speak to her at the game. Before I send you two on your way to what's sure to be marital bliss, I would feel a lot better talking to her. She'd need a lawyer present, but I'd really feel so much better seeing her in a formal setting."

Brock drew his bushy eyebrows together. Bless his sweet heart, he was trying to figure me out. It wouldn't work. I conjured up an image of Jude flipping off Pete behind his back and my grin widened to bliss.

"Well, I don't see the trouble in that." He adjusted in the leather chair and pushed his dark jeans down with his massive hands.

"Wonderful." I stood and strode over to him. "I'll tell my secretary to fit her in as soon as possible, then we can put this entire fuss behind you, and you can focus on your curve ball."

Brock nodded. "Sounds good to me. Then you'll tell my manager to stop buggin' me about this?"

"Absolutely." *Not.* I would never do that.

I ushered him out of the door, ready to start my weekend. I grabbed my bag from behind my desk, changed into my jeans and oversized sweater in the bathroom and was on my way to fetch my boyfriend in record time.

After thinking about having Ben to myself, I'd realized I needed two nights, not just one. I'd insisted that we leave Friday after he'd finished the boxing lessons with Nate and Devon. Gone were the days of putting everything and everyone before my own needs. And as I watched him in the ring, instructing Nate how to throw an uppercut, I had some serious needs.

"He's great with him."

A middle-aged man stood next to me in full-on dad gear. His dark gray fleece covered a light Polo underneath, and where his round belly met his khaki pants, a phone was clipped to his belt.

"You must be Amee. Nate's told me about you. I'm Rob."

We shook hands and I turned back to the fine specimen that was my boyfriend. Ben sat on the bottom rope and let Nate crawl out then helped him with his gloves. Nate walked over to Devon—who had been trying his best to hit a bag—then the trio came to meet us.

"You guys all set?" Rob asked and hoisted their bags over his shoulder. "Kim's ordering pizza."

I gave Nate a compliment about his skills and watched them exit. Ben's heat steamed against my back and I tilted my head to give him access to kiss, lick, bite, maim, whatever.

"You gonna tell me where we're going yet?" He kissed my cheek and stepped to the side as I spun around.

"If I said the back seat of my car, would you think I was cheap?"

"I'd think you were horny. And rightfully so. I missed you this week." A small smile brought out his dimples.

Puddle. I was a damn puddle. He gave me another quick peck and walked backward two steps. "Give me five to shower."

I didn't think it was wrong that I loved Ben always insisted on driving. In fact, something about it made me more attracted to him, and I was sure that wasn't even possible. I kept the GPS on my phone and guided him the hour north it would take to get to the cabin I'd rented for us.

When I'd started planning our getaway Monday night with a glass of wine and my laptop, Jude had peered over my shoulder and laughed.

'You're going to take him to a fucking five-star hotel, Mom-fail?'

I'd snapped the computer shut and mulled over her words in a stare down she'd eventually won, then asked why.

'Because your unicorn belongs in a forest, shit-for-brains.' Jude had rolled her knowing eyes and walked away.

I hated it when my sister was right, and she'd been *so* right.

Per my instructions, Ben turned down a dirt road and stopped in front of the old-fashioned blue lamp post.

I unclicked my seatbelt, flashed a smile and told him I'd be back in a minute.

As I pushed open the wooden door, bells chimed overhead. The dark orange wood glowed behind the lamp-lit walls, and a roaring fire danced in the salon to my left. A rail-thin older lady, whose skin said she'd smoked too much to live in a log cabin, stood behind the reception desk and greeted me with a smile. I gave her my name, and she assured me that our accommodations had every detail I'd instructed. She'd even sent someone to light the fire for us fifteen minutes prior. I thanked her and grabbed the key. The weekend could officially begin.

I hopped into the car and we drove farther down the path until the warm lights of our private abode flickered beyond a yellow lamppost.

"This is it." I dangled the key from its banana keychain, let out a happy breath and got out of the car. Ben followed with the bags and a twinkle in his baby blues.

I unlocked the door and the heat from the fire took the chill from my arms. The little cabin had a small kitchen, a leather sofa that faced a massive stone chimney and a loft with a huge bed — complete with patchwork bedspread.

A thud behind me made me jump a little and reminded me that I had drunk an entire liter of water on our drive up.

"Just gonna freshen up. There should be beer in the fridge, and I'd love a glass of wine."

Ben grumbled as I walked away, and I glanced over my shoulder.

"Are you checking out my ass?"

"Damn skippy, I am." He winked and bit his bottom lip. "I told you that I've been thinking about you all damn week, Cupcake."

If a squirrel and I didn't share the same size bladder, I would have been on top of that man right there in the entry way. But I also needed to freshen up all my bits up. I wanted to come out of the bathroom a little more confident than how I'd gone in.

I unzipped my boots and scrunched off my socks to reveal my green-painted toes. Next came my jeans and sweater, until I stood in front of the mirror in just my hunter-green silk underwear. *Thank God the malls push Christmas early.* I spun to check out my over-thirty but acceptable ass and cupped my hand to check my breath. From my purse, I grabbed a condom and hid it down the front of my panties. My last task was folding my clothes, and from the other side of the door, the unmistakable pop of a cork rang out.

I took another breath. I shouldn't have been nervous. Ben had seen every inch of me before. But the solitude and lack of need to rush made the time special. It meant more.

From the dark brown couch, his gaze found mine the second I opened the door. He wet his lips as he watched me walk over to him and the flames from the fire warmed the back of my thighs when I stopped in front of him.

"Green underwear and a log cabin?" He set his beer down on the wood floor. "Are you trying to make me fall in love with you?" His follow-up was a wink, but it had me at a loss.

Is he joking? Should I laugh? Maybe a scoff to prove how cool I was. Or just be fucking honest.

I swallowed and moved one step closer. "Yes."

His gaze fell to my body, I hoped because he liked what I'd put on display. He widened his stance and signaled for my approach. When I reached him, he interlaced his rough fingers in mine with one hand and let the other trail over my stomach. The need for his mouth on my body eclipsed all else, and I knelt onto his lap. He pushed into the leather behind him and he let out a contented sigh before he kissed my collar bone.

I tilted my head, and the tips of my hair tickled my shoulder blades. Ben moved his skillful mouth and soft lips up my jaw and his scruff sent a shiver down my spine.

"It's working," he whispered in my ear.

Chapter Twenty

Toad in the Hole

Ben

A contented murmur woke me and I pulled Amee's naked body closer. We had nowhere to be, no responsibilities. A very big part of me wanted to get out of bed and work out, and another part of me hollered that my location and the mix of soon-to-be sweat was a very suitable form of exercise.

She pushed her cheek harder into my stomach and I glanced down at her mess of hair. *Mercy*. With her flawless skin, turned-up nose and contented smile, she was beautiful — and she was mine. The night before on the couch had been different. She'd laid out the weighted feelings, and her gamble had paid off. Yes, I was absolutely falling for her, and everything that came with it. I smoothed her tangles down and kissed the top of her head.

I allowed myself a few minutes of potential thoughts about how the two of us could work and got good and mentally high on them. Her ex would move out, maybe have the kids from time to time, and Amee and I would build more of these quiet moments. Maybe once I'd found a place to live, she could even spend the night once a week.

After a small groan, the woman who was latched onto my midsection rolled to the other side and stretched.

"Morning." Her eyes twinkled through their wake-up fog and she smiled. "I slept ridiculously well."

She scooted to the side of the bed, stood in all her nude glory and walked over to the bathroom. The swivel of her hips and lack of shame in her exposed body sent a twitch below the sheets. The previous night had been heady, intense and I already needed her again.

When I heard the spray of the shower, I didn't wait for the written invitation.

I rapped my knuckles lightly on the door and she opened. White toothpaste foam bubbled from her mouth as she repeated her wrist's circular cleaning motions.

She spat into the sink and must have caught a glimpse of my erection, because she looked up with big eyes. "We are totally having shower sex. I don't care how bad it is for the environment."

As I took care of my own dental hygiene, she skipped back to the bed, grabbed the condoms and was under the water within seconds.

From the increasingly steamy mirror, I watched her close her eyes and melt under the hot, pelting liquid pressure. Just when I thought she couldn't be more enticing, she was.

I stepped into the warm vapor and she moved to me like a magnet. Amee draped her arms over my shoulders and she wrapped a lock of my hair in her fingers. I half expected her to say something, but the mood in her eyes had changed from playfulness to desire.

If it hadn't been for the need for a condom, I would have taken her right then. Instead, I squeezed her ass and bent down to kiss her below the ear. Her smooth neck led to her sharp collarbone, which led to her lovely breasts. I cupped one and twirled my tongue around the other's nipple before taking that tiny bite she craved. I ached to reach between her legs and intensify her pleasure but I told myself to be patient. I moved to her other perfectly rounded breast and repeated the slow tease.

Amee stroked me, and as much as I loved her hand on my dick, I wanted to watch her explode on my face.

A trail of kisses mixed with the tiny streams of water down her stomach like heavenly rivers. I spun her so her back was against the wall, and I dropped to my knees. She draped a leg over my shoulder and I held her hips steady.

One slow, long lick from my greedy tongue, followed by a quick tease at her center, was all it took for her to say a throaty, "Fuck."

I grinned and repeated the same exquisite path. Amee raked her fingers through my dripping hair and when I glanced up, I caught her staring down. My dick throbbed with her voyeuristic admission. With my thumb and middle finger, I opened her and started the fantastic process of torturing her to bliss.

After whimpers, pleading and even some begging, I finally sucked the sensitive spot and she screamed her release. And fucking hell, I was beyond ready for mine.

I reached for the condom, putting it on faster than a quick draw in a spaghetti western, and thrust inside her. I pounded her drenched body against the tile while I reclaimed her mouth. Between kisses — and with only the forest animals to complain — Cupcake unleashed her volume and slew of profanities. I grabbed her wrists with one hand and pinned them over her head. With the other, I coaxed her to another climax. The muscles of her inner walls throbbed against my dick, and as much as I loved it and it shot pleasure to the root of my being, I needed more. I was addicted, greedy and quite possibly falling in love. But I was most certainly not done.

I pulled out, flipped her around and took her from behind. As I quickened my thrusts, her voice quieted to heavy breathing. God bless that perfect woman, through the smacks of our wet skin, she managed to secure one arm against the shower wall and reach through her legs to cup my balls with the other. The squeeze and tug, combined with the view and friction, were enough to put me over the edge. After one final deep effort, I growled as a lightning bolt burst at my base and shot into my girlfriend.

We stayed there panting while Amee released her grip and flung her hand to the tile for support. My heart rate settled, and I pulled out. Still using the wall to stay upright — her head must have been spinning as fast as mine — she slowly faced me.

After a gently kiss, she said, "You owe me one."

I quirked an eyebrow then understood. "You want number three now or later?"

She gave me another peck and pushed by me to the warm stream. "Later. Definitely later."

I met her downstairs in the small L-shaped kitchen where she stood in oversized socks, form-fitting skinny jeans and a light gray deep V sweater. Her wet hair was piled on top of her head and she cracked an egg into a hollowed-out piece of bread in the frying pan. *How does she make simple so stunning?*

After breakfast, which had already creeped closer to lunch, we went for a long hike in the woods. She had really planned the weekend to perfection—a rugged yet calm escape that we both could appreciate. Back at the cabin, I made a fire in the outdoor pit and we roasted our hotdogs on sticks left behind by previous occupants.

When we were finished, I added another log to the fire and sat behind her so she could lean her petite frame into my chest.

"If I didn't love my girls so much, I would ask you to keep me prisoner here forever." Amee pushed harder into me and tilted her head, a gesture I understood as a command to kiss her delicate neck.

I nibbled it instead and sent her into a fit of giggles. We eventually stilled, the cracking fire and singing birds our soundtrack to paradise.

"Did you have any luck finding a place this week?"

No. I hadn't. Everything had been out of my price range and I'd had to lower my expectations about what my 'new' apartment was going to be. I would be lucky to get a studio that would fit my bed and a folding table. And I had no idea what I was going to do with my gym equipment.

"I'm meeting with a broker Tuesday. Hopefully, there'll be some better options." I didn't want to drag down our mood with my financial woes, so I asked,

"What about you? Did you get that baseball player to sign his agreement?"

"Ugh." Her blonde head dropped into the padding of my coat. "No. He's ridiculously lovesick and naïve. God, especially after what I found out about that country bumpkin girlfriend of his."

I knew better than to ask, and quite frankly, from the sound of her voice, I didn't want to know. But what I did want was to smash the disdain laced in her voice and throw it into the fire pit at our feet.

I hadn't imagined her as judgmental, but I guessed that was part of her job. And her career and brains were not something I could compete with on any level. Maybe she did what she had to do. She was the one supporting an entire family, after all. I let it slide. There was no reason to put a damper on our weekend. Plus, I had a score to settle.

My hand wandered — aimlessly and of its own accord, no message from my dirty mind at all — up under her coat to her warm stomach and found her lace bra.

"You ready for number three?" I kissed her temple and let my thumb rub across her hardened nipple.

"You better fucking believe it." Amee lay back in the dirt and dead leaves around us. "Right here. Right now."

* * * *

I swung her overnight bag into her SUV and pressed the automatic button to close the hatch. As I walked to the driver's side door, I shook my head and hated the cowardly knot growing in my stomach. In the car, I tried to cover it up with a wink and a smile, but her tilted head told me I was a shitty liar and she sensed my unease.

"What is it?" Amee let go of the seatbelt she was about to buckle, and it slid back into place. "Is this about my ex? Trust me, Ben. I want him out more than anybody."

I chewed my bottom lip. Admitting weakness was definitely not my strong suit. And fifty percent of me would have preferred to bury the subject in a deep grave beneath the colored leaves and autumn forest's floor surrounding us. But I hated being a chickenshit more than being vulnerable, so I spat it out. "I can't afford to pay you half of the cost of the weekend yet." I stared at the dashboard in hopes it had a button for courage. "In fact, I don't know when I can."

Amee held my gaze until she said, "I don't want you to pay for this weekend. It was my idea. I'm covering it."

I scratched my growing beard, afraid of tasting the can of worms I'd just opened.

She continued, "I have money. And I understand that you probably have less. But that seems like a really shitty reason for this to get weird."

"It's just that..." God, I hated myself for being that much of a pussy about her lifestyle. I knew guys who would be jumping for joy to find a rich girlfriend. "I need you to know that's absolutely not why I'm with you."

"Oh, yeah?" Amee crawled to my side of the car and straddled me in the confined space. She brushed a piece of hair from my forehead and smiled down. "Why are you with me then?"

I slid my hands over her hips and grabbed her ass. "When I first met you, yeah, I thought you were hot, except for your hideous shoes..."

She quirked an eyebrow and feigned hurt.

I continued, "And maybe a little sad."

"Oh my God. You thought I was *sad*?"

"Let me finish, woman." I reached up and palmed her cheek. "But when I saw you playing with Carly's hair in front of us at that uniform store, I knew you were beautiful."

Amee widened her eyes then blinked several times, a softness coming over her face.

"It's true. You're the most beautiful woman I've ever seen."

She pressed her silky cheek into my hand and closed her eyes. A second later, she looked up with wide eyes and said, "Are you trying to make me fall in love with you?"

I swallowed my fear. "Maybe."

She laid her head on my shoulder and her fingers twisted the string of my hoodie. "It's working."

On the way home, we couldn't stop touching each other. The perfect weekend had given us a glimpse of hope—a still frame of what could be the movie of our future and, I dare say, a goal of what had become apparent that we both wanted. I hated leaving her at the gym. Our cloud of happiness floated off as we put our feet back on the cracked cement of the parking lot.

Amee stopped my hand from pulling my duffle bag out of her trunk. "Hey, I was thinking a little. And you can tell me to suck it—which I gladly will," she said with an innuendo waggle of her eyebrows. "But why don't you give some boxing classes to kids here? I bet I could get some of the moms from school to sign up their boys. God knows they need less screen time and more exercise. Again, sorry if this is out of line. I just…"

I exhaled and let the lack of air deflate me. "Thank you for trying to find solutions. I actually thought about that too. But this place is a dump. None of the rich kids from Nate's school will want to slum it here, and the owner already told me he can barely afford rent. So, I don't think he'll want to pay me." I grabbed the bag, secured it over my shoulder and motioned for her to step aside so the hatch didn't close on top of her.

She followed me over to my truck with her hands on her hips. "I can put together a fundraiser. Jude will bake, and we'll get money for him to buy new equipment and pay his rent. Is he there?"

I searched the lot for Craig's rusted green Ford and found it parked close to the entry to the gym. *How many times have I fixed that clunker in exchange for gym time?* My bank account and right hook were thankful his car was a 'fix or repair daily'.

"Yeah, he's here." I fought back a grin. I'd never seen Amee like that. Determination poured out of her, then it hit me. She was Shae. Or Shae was her…whichever.

"Great. I'm gonna go talk with him. I can probably get it all organized for mid-January."

She walked off and I wondered if I was supposed to go with her. It didn't matter. Adult Shae and crusty Craig together was a sight I wouldn't miss.

Chapter Twenty-One

Meatballs

Amee

The second I cradled the receiver of my phone back into its place on my desk, my assistant rapped his knuckles on my glass door. I smiled and motioned for him to enter, the high of Ben's goodbye kiss from the night before still heavy on my mind.

Bradley walked in and closed the door behind him. His perfectly knotted dark tie poked out from his form-fitting gray V-neck. The girl gaggle of his co-workers probably mopped up their drool when he passed by. *Poor kid.*

"She's here. And you're going to love who she's with." He walked over to my desk and bit his bottom lip.

I slid open my top drawer, took out a mint from its metal container and popped it into my mouth. "Fuck. Don't even tell me Brock Jenssen is with her."

"Worse. Her lawyer, Chad McFarlen."

Oh, that was far from worse. In fact, that was a million times better. Chad McFarlen liked to think he was hot shit, but he had no idea. I'd gone up against him the previous year when I'd been distracted. He'd sparred with Amee Light. Amee Full-On-There-Is-No-Fucking-Way-I-Am-Losing-A-Client's-Assets had showed up for work today. *Sorry, Chad.*

"Send them in." I closed out my email draft to former clients asking them their availability for an autograph signing in January and chewed the mint.

Bradley escorted the casually dressed Jenni Lynn Banks, with her spirally curled hair and her bland attorney, into my office.

"Miss Banks" — I extended my hand and stood — "it's a pleasure to see you again." I glanced over to the man in the double-breasted gray suit. "Chad."

Jenni Lynn Banks sat down — without being asked — in the chocolate leather chair opposite my desk and I tried to hide the swagger in my step as I took my own seat. Chad unbuttoned the jacket of his ugly suit and humphed into the open seat next to Jenni.

"Ms. Benton, forgive me for stating the obvious, but I'm representing Miss Banks."

"Wonderful." I faked my best sugary grin. "I'll assume that means she's agreed to sign the paper-work."

Jenni Lynn's eyes bulged before they shot over to her lawyer. *Yeah, not sorry.* Amee Bold had also showed up to play.

I continued, "It's the standard agreement for spouses of professional athletes. Wait…" I puffed my chest out and savored the moment. "You probably haven't seen one of those before, Mr. McFarlen."

Chad's nostrils flared. "Miss Banks has no intention of signing a standard agreement."

Oh, Chad. You silly fool.

I opened my second drawer and pulled out the top folder. There would be no need for the one below it. It almost made me sad how easy it was going to be. From the unlabeled generic sleeve, I handed an 'unprepared' document over to Chad. The second it was in his greedy hands, his gaze danced over the page.

"Take your time. I'm headed to Miami for a few days. We can talk when I get back next week."

Chad continued his skim and I locked eyes with the future Mrs. Brock Jenssen. With a millimeter tilt of my head, I asked, "Have *you* ever been to Miami?"

Poor, sweet, money-hungry Jenni Lynn. She blinked a few times at the floor until Chad's voice revived her.

"This is ridiculous. Her fiancé just signed a multi-million-dollar deal." He flipped through the pages. "This says they will split their assets from the day they met. No one in their right mind would sign this." The document flew from his hands and landed on my desk.

"I'll sign whatever." Jenni Lynn's voice broke as she stared at the open file.

"What? Miss Banks, this is not what we discussed in my office." Chad swiveled in his chair and begged her attention, which she did not give.

"Fantastic. I'll draw up the formal papers and have them sent over to your office. Are you still above that grocery store?" I asked.

"I never…" Chad McFarlen studied his client then me. He was slow on the uptake but not stupid. Behind his gray eyes, I could practically see the tape rewinding the conversation and him listening to it over and over.

I sent Jenni Lynn a small smile. "Miss Banks, I do think it would be wonderful if you gave the news to Brock yourself. You know, reassure him that you don't love him for his money. In my vast experience with these issues, professional athletes need that comfort. And the fact that you came to the decision on your own will only solidify the bond you're about to make in marriage." I tidied up the papers on my desk and stored the folder back in my drawer.

Jenni Lynn stood, crossed her arms and frowned to Chad.

"It was lovely seeing you, Miss Banks." I rose and walked over to my door. "I wish you and Mr. Jenssen nothing but happiness." It was true. She may not have believed me, but I spoke the truth.

She shot me a dirty look and stomped over the open threshold. Chad followed, squinting at her designer-clad shoulders.

Fifteen minutes later, Bradley came in with a coffee in my favorite cup. "Mr. McFarlen wanted me to tell you he's never had an office above a grocery store."

I brought the mug to my lips and blew a bit of steam in his direction. "I know."

Bradley grinned and asked, "Does this mean you won the Brock Jenssen account?"

"Not until she signs on the dotted line. But I am going to have a glass of wine with dinner." I nodded for his departure and sipped my coffee. If I could get Brock to come to the gym's fundraiser, it would draw a huge crowd.

* * * *

The cork squeaked out of the bottle as Pete served the girls their spaghetti and meatballs. They sat at the counter and Shae happily clapped her hands together, waiting for her favorite meal.

With me out of the way for the weekend, Pete had scored some major points with the girls. They had done a huge arts-and-crafts project with wood and paint, the colorful totem pole with wings adorning our entryway as proof.

I poured myself a glass of wine and eyed Pete. As far as I'd been aware, he hadn't had a drink since he'd been let out, and I hoped for the girls' sakes he would never start again.

Shae speared a meatball and Carly wound her spaghetti into a large spoon. I took my glass to Jude's room, where I knocked on the door and entered with the all clear.

My sister came out of her en-suite bathroom, clocked the wine and asked, "Is that the Oregon Pinot Noir?"

I grinned. "So good."

"Hand it over. I'm trying to cope with Assface having some real value. I prefer him as a douchebag." She signaled for the glass, which I gave up, and moaned after her sip.

"Seems like Shae is defrosting..." I said.

"Yeah, well, he was a pretty good dad this weekend." She drank again. "I hate that they need him around, but he had all their homework done before the movie on Friday night and played endless board games with them on Saturday. By the way, never let Shae be the bank. Last night, they built the atrocity in the foyer."

"Must be nice to swoop in and be the good guy." I reached out for the wine and she handed it back. "What am I gonna do when he settles into his job and place?"

Jude crossed over to her desk, swiveled the chair and sat. She pressed her lips together, her sister code detecting the rhetorical question.

"I don't want to keep them from him, but I don't trust him. Christ, he can't even drive."

She leveled her blue eyes. "There are plenty of parents who don't drive. Think of it as one less thing to worry about."

I groaned. Her logic was right, but it didn't make me like it.

"Don't become one of those assholes who punishes the kids by not letting them see their dad. You chose to breed with that fucker. You have to own that."

I leaned back. She was in a mood. "If I give you more wine, will you play nice with me?"

She shrugged and stuck out her bottom lip. "Maybe."

Jude and I giggled our way to the kitchen where the girls were finishing their dinner.

Pete clapped his hands together from behind the sink. "Oh good. Everybody's here."

Jude pulled down a wine glass from the cupboard, refilled my glass and poured her own. I hoped with all my might that the rental application he'd submitted had gone through. He needed to be out of my house. Pronto.

"I got the house!"

Thank you, sweet baby Jesus. Finally. Jude and I clanked our glasses together and the sarcasm was lost on the girls.

"Congratulations, Daddy." Shae smiled, slid off the barstool and collected her plate.

"Yeah, and I'm moving in with him." Carly beamed a quick smile before her face fell to worry.

"Excuse me?" I set the wineglass on the counter and crossed my arms. My gaze darted between my elder daughter and her father.

Crash!

Shae's tomato-sauce stained plate shattered on the tile floor in front of her and she glared at her sister. "I hate you, Carly. And I hate you, too, Daddy." She served her father more contempt than she had her sister. "First, you ruin this family. And now you do it again. Nobody ever wants *me*! Nobody ever thinks about *me*!"

She ran out of the kitchen. From the entryway we heard a loud bang—no doubt their art project—then small feet stomping up the stairs and the loud slam of her door.

"I'll go," Jude said as she shook her head.

But it wasn't Jude's job. It was mine. Pete's and my parenting was much like the broken dish on the floor. He made the mess and I cleaned it up.

"No," I said to Jude. "*I'll* go." Showing Carly how much I wanted to murder her father would only add fuel to his guilt blaze, so I looked at her instead of him. "This is far from over or decided."

Upstairs, I found my baby girl sobbing into her green polka-dot pillow. I sat down on the bed and rubbed her back. There was one thing I knew about Shae to be sure and true. When she was upset, letting her cry it out was the best thing possible. Once she was calm, she would talk and listen. But in the heat of the moment, she needed to get it out.

Shae turned her tear-stained and swollen face to me and my heart broke yet again for my baby girl. She paused for a second as if searching my eyes for an answer. When it came up empty, she threw her arms around my neck and buried herself in my shoulder.

I continued the slow circles and she eventually caught her breath. I maneuvered myself against her headboard and played with her blonde hair.

"Why, Mommy? Why? Why do they always leave me out?"

"I don't know, baby girl. But I'm gonna try and fix it. I promise." Even as I spoke the words, I knew they were hopeless. Pete had ripped out his youngest daughter's heart too many times. There would be no recovery. She was too old. She would remember. She would know for a fact that Carly was always his first choice.

I cursed knowledge and the loss of Shae's innocence, but mostly I cursed Pete. He'd fucked up one too many times. And when I got done putting Band-Aids on the soul of my baby, I would have to walk down the steps and break my other daughter's heart. There was no way she was going to live with her father. I would pull every damn string in family court that I could to ensure it.

Chapter Twenty-Two

Pizza

Ben

I'd never been one to use my strength in anger, but after I'd hung up with Amee and she'd told me about her night, I wanted to kick the ever-living shit out of her ex. Unfortunately, that would make it worse and set the wrong example.

Still. What a self-serving prick. I'd never felt more useless in my life. And as much as I wanted to swoop down and save the day for Amee and the absolutely brilliant little Shae, it was not my place.

They had their family dynamic to work through and none of that included the new boyfriend. And it shouldn't have. I kept telling myself that as I set my alarm early so I could get up and make it to the boxing gym before work. I knew just the punching bag to picture Daddy Douchebag's face on.

At lunch, I met Jemina's sister to check out a studio apartment not far from work. Weather-stained shingles lined the second floor on top of a red brick foundation.

An iron staircase led up to a cheap wooden door and the number seven hung sideways. I finally understood snobs.

When she opened the door, I was expecting blood stains on clumpy green carpet and rust around the faucets, but it was surprisingly clean. Well, clean-ish.

The hardwood floors bore several scratches, but the narrow walls had been refreshed with a coat of white paint. Immediately to the left of the entryway was a bathroom with a tub and more space than the makeshift corner of the basement I'd been using for the last few years. The kitchen was dinky, with a cooktop and fridge half the size of Teddy's. And while the narrow white fridge wouldn't hold much, at least it had been cleaned out.

But that was it. The bathroom, a kitchen with just enough counter space to hold a drying rack, and an open room.

"I know it's not very interesting, but it's clean. And you know, simple is good." Jemina's sister held her clipboard tight to her chest and leaned against the wall.

I rubbed the back of my neck. The place was the first I'd seen in my actual price range. I wouldn't be eating organic free-range chicken anytime soon, but by not taking the night school classes again, I wouldn't starve by living here either.

"How soon can I move in?"

She smiled and revealed the same eye glimmer as her sister. "Well, we already checked your credit and verified employment. I'm sure I could get them to prorate the rent for the rest of the month."

I looked around the empty space one more time. It wasn't as if it was my first apartment. It was just my first apartment alone.

Before my mom had died, I'd moved in with my girlfriend from high school at an age when neither of us had had any business being in a committed relationship—a fact that I'd unfortunately proved to her after she'd accused me of cheating for the hundredth time. Stupid and young, I'd thought I'd might as well assume the guilty behavior if she wasn't going to believe me.

We'd lived together in all our drama for almost two years until I finally decided to make a change and Teddy had offered me his basement. When Nate's dad got killed in Iraq and they moved in, I wasn't disappointed with the company. I liked the idea of having a family, of not being by myself. Which, other than Teddy, Kim and Nate, I was.

And Nate deserved that same feeling of comfort in a unit. Rob and Devon were a real future for him. My stand-in days were over.

"All right. Let's do it," I said with a nod.

* * * *

Friday after work, I picked up Nate and Devon and we headed for our workout. Craig grumbled his hello from his squeaky chair and returned to his crossword as we passed by the office. I had them both skipping rope and complaining within minutes.

Trev waited for me in the center ring, clueless that I was about to replace his handsome face with the one of the asshole who'd been on my mind all week. We tapped gloves and gave each other a small lift of the chin to say hello.

To my surprise and competitive delight, Trev hadn't come to play. He matched my intensity blow for blow and we started to draw a crowd. I caught Nate and Devon watching us out of the corner of my eye and it was just enough of a distraction for Trev to land an effective right hook to my chin. *Fucker.*

I shook it off, the sweat spreading with my recovery, and I narrowed my eyes. With my jaw set, I threw several jabs and backed him against the ropes. The success of the attack had me a little lighter in my feet, and I jogged away to give him some space.

But homeboy must have been having a messed-up week too, because he came back with just as much vigor. At some point, Craig snaked through the ropes and separated us.

"What the hell has gotten into you two bums?" The old man widened his eyes.

Both panting and trying to catch our breath, we popped out our mouthguards and grinned from ear to ear. We met in the middle of the ring, bromanced our hug and laughed.

"Thanks, man," Trev said and exhaled forcefully from his mouth. "I needed that."

My heart settled, but my lungs still searched for oxygen. I dropped to my knees and sprawled out belly-up in the ring. I closed my eyes and let the tension of my week melt into the mat. Two minutes of nothing sounded perfect. Craig muttered a trail of disapproval farther and farther away and the rip of Velcro from Trev's gloves meant he was abandoning me too. I lay there dripping and physically spent. With my eyes still closed, I floated away on my post-workout high.

Some point later, a cool small hand touched my sweaty forehead and the sweetest voice I'd ever heard asked, "Are you okay?"

The smile on my cheeks was the easiest thing I'd done in days. I tilted my head in the direction of happiness and opened my eyes. "I'm fine, baby girl. How are you? I missed you this week."

Shae kneeled next to me in a green sweater, her blonde hair tied back in pigtails. She flattened her lips then leaned down to my ear. "I had a shitty week."

My laugh turned into a cough, no doubt from the cheap shot Trev had taken to my kidneys. I propped myself up on my elbows and regained control of my breathing.

Amee stood outside of the ring with her hands in her pockets and her mouth in a tight line. I shot her a quick wink and the worry in her forehead softened.

"You ready for pizza?" I asked the tiny nurse at my side.

"Not before you shower. You're gross."

How could Pete — or any man, for that matter — leave out that sweet, sassy little mama? I scoffed my fake hurt. "Gross? I thought you liked gross things? Your mom told me you like pineapple and cream cheese on your pizza. Now *that's* gross."

Shae crossed her arms and closed one eye. "Ever tried it?"

"Nope."

"You'll see. Come on, BB. Carly's hungry."

I scanned the gym for signs of her older sister and found her at the entryway reading in a chipped plastic chair. I'd been thinking all week about how to win her over without forcing my hand. Because, for Amee and I to work, both her girls would need to be on board, not just the glitter addict to my left.

I pushed to my knees and walked over to the edge of the ring, where Shae slid on her tummy down to the ground. With a duck and a bob, I was on the wooden steps and in front of my girlfriend within seconds.

"Hey, gorgeous." I gave her a simple peck on the cheek, heeding Shae's observation of my less-than-presentable state. I was indeed a pile of perspiration.

"Quite the show," Amee said, her tone flat.

I pulled off my gloves and raised an eyebrow.

"Shae, go sit with Carly. Ben will be ready in five minutes."

Shae obeyed without question and skipped to the entrance where she plopped down next to her sister.

"You mad?" I asked.

Amee rolled her eyes then smiled. "Frustrated. That was sexy as fuck and I have no idea when I'll be alone with you again. But in general, I don't like seeing you get hurt."

I stole a quick kiss from her soft lips. "Back in five."

"No worries. I need to talk to Craig about the fundraiser anyway."

Nate and Devon passed by in their street clothes as I entered the changing room. They had the positive sign of wet hair, but had there been soap included in their rinse off?

Steam hovered out of the showers and hung like a cloud over Trev's shoulders. He sat on the bench in the middle of the locker room with his head in his hands.

"Thanks for letting me kick your ass." I propped my foot next to him and untied my shoe.

His head jolted up. "I kicked *your* ass. You were the one laid out like a granny."

"A draw." I moved to the other shoe.

"No. Not a draw. A Trevor Franklin ass whooping — by one Trevor Franklin to one Benji Mathis."

My ribs lodged a formal complaint as I chuckled. "What's eating you, anyway?"

Trev stood and packed his wet towel into his duffle bag. "Lost a kid during my surgery rotation today."

Fuck. It was one thing to lose a patient, another to have to tell parents they didn't have a child anymore. I regretted not letting him win but was grateful he could take his shit out on me.

"You want to come out for pizza?" I wrapped my towel around my waist and headed to the showers.

"Nah. I'm gonna go hang with Mama. I'll see you tomorrow for the move."

"All right. Thanks for the Trevor Franklin ass draw."

I had a quick shower and was following Amee's car to our group outing within minutes.

We'd decided to take one for the team and go to the noisiest pizza joint in the city. Video games and carnival stands chirped from the perimeter, and the six of us found a picnic-style table in the middle of chaos. It was an even tie with the mall for hell on earth.

But even the normally stoic Carly was smiling, and after the pizza crusts had piled up on the paper plates, she led her little sister with a handful of tokens to the games. Devon and Nate went in their own direction, which left me on the most unromantic date of my life.

Amee cleared away the empty plates and instead of returning to sit opposite me, she shimmied next to my side. Her arm linked into mine and she rested her head on my shoulder.

I inhaled her sweet scent and kissed her temple. "How did it go this week with Carly?"

She stared off into the crowd of over-excited small humans. "She understands that she hurt her sister and she's trying to make up for it. But when I told her she couldn't live with her father, she didn't take it well. She doesn't want him to be alone and can't rationalize why he could take care of them before and not now."

"I'm sorry, Cupcake. I wish I could help." I stroked her smooth hair and gave her another kiss.

She looked up. "You do help. Having you in my corner helps." A little smile came to her lips and she studied my face. "What sucks is not being able to sleep in your arms. I'm afraid I'm rather addicted to it." Amee nuzzled her shoulder into my armpit and she brought the back of my hand to her lips.

We interlaced our fingers and watched the kids from a distance. The sirens, whistles and bells faded away. There was only us and the kids, their laughter and excitement ricocheting from wherever they were in the restaurant back to us.

The time to leave came too soon. I wasn't ready to let go of the night, to let go of Amee.

In the parking lot, we hid behind my truck for our good night kiss. I pushed her into the cold steel and a deep hunger awoke inside me. My mind told me to be gentlemanly, but my desire was too strong. I buried my face in her warm neck and nipped her ear.

"There's a lot more than my arms that's missing you," I growled.

She let out a whimper and pushed me away with an evil eye. "Don't you dare get me all hot and bothered then leave me."

I caught my bottom lip between my teeth and watched her ass mosey away. "But that's how I like you, Cupcake. And I was just getting started."

She kept walking and flipped me the bird from over her shoulder.

Chapter Twenty-Three

Breadcrumbs

Amee

Pete wiped crumbs from the kitchen counter into the sink. It was a sight I'd seen so many nights before, for so many years. When we'd met in college, I would have sworn on my parents' graves that I would never hate him. And while a big part of me didn't, there was a part that did. I hated that he'd become complacent, that he'd never done anything with his art. And I hated him for turning into a drunk who'd gotten behind the wheel and ruined the lives of our children and another family.

But it wasn't all bad. We'd been young and foolish, but I would never regret having the girls with him. Carly had been one hundred percent unplanned, and when he had told me he wanted to keep the baby, my heart had sung. Maybe that was why she was so special to him, because she almost hadn't existed.

Had we decided to terminate the pregnancy, we would have gone our separate ways sooner rather than later. But the decision to start a family had bonded us for life, and whenever I looked into Shae's eyes, eyes that she shared with the man who stood in my kitchen, my soul beamed that we'd made the right choice.

Which was why I had to bring peace to Pete's and my relationship. We may have done a million things wrong, but we'd done two things right.

I scratched my ankle under my oversized fluffy pink sock then padded into the kitchen. Pete dried his hands on the dishtowel and hung it on its hook.

"Girls asleep?" he asked.

"Yeah. I almost dozed off myself." I slipped onto the barstool. I didn't want to hate him anymore. I wanted to move on…for good.

He leaned against the granite counter, crossed his feet and stared at me with sad eyes. "I want to say this, not to make you angry, but so you understand. The thought of my girls with your boyfriend is killing me."

I opened my mouth to object and but he stopped me.

"I know I need to be better with Shae. I want to be." Pete raked his hand through his hair then scrubbed his face. "Carly is just so easy. She's like looking in a mirror. And Shae, she's…"

"Me."

A quick, airy chuckle married with his nodding head. "Yes. She's you. And I'm still hurt and angry with you." His gaze came back to mine. "I know you and I weren't soulmates and we survived a lot of years on coffee and wine, but you were still my wife, Amee…still my life."

I fiddled with a hangnail. "I know."

"And you can't blame me for wanting to be with them. They were my everything before the accident. I'd felt us falling apart, but I denied the finality, even after the divorce. It was torture not seeing them when I was away, knowing that every day I was behind bars was another moment I was missing their lives."

I brought the hangnail to my teeth and tugged. I could have said so many things. Words that would have revived the anger and thrown the responsibility of his actions in his face — words that had been said to him silently so many times. But I was tired, tired of the tension, tired of the struggle. *The future,* I reminded myself. *The future is where I have to focus.*

"December first. I need you out of the house by December first. No later."

He perched his hands on the waist of his low-hanging jeans. "What about the girls?"

I let out a slow calm breath. "They stay together. And with me."

"But—"

"No buts." I blinked once slowly. "Pete, I know every family judge in the state. We're doing this my way. You need to worry about you for a while. Build your life up. Find new habits."

"So, you're saying I don't get any kind of custody?"

The realization of the burst bubble ran down his face in a single tear.

"I'm saying, not yet. Get your shit together —"

"And get out of your house?" He raised an eyebrow, but there was a small playfulness to his tone, something I hadn't heard in a long time.

I smiled. "Yes. Getting settled into your new place is mandatory."

He exhaled through his mouth and I got down off the barstool.

"Good night," I said and walked toward the stairs.

"Amee?"

I stopped and turned back to him.

"I know I'm not in a position to ask favors…"

No, he wasn't. In fact, considering how calm and mature I'd been in light of his recent deceitful actions with Carly, he was in the opposite of that position. He must have been banking on my goodwill.

"But I'd really like to have Thanksgiving as a family. Since I'll be out the week following, it's my last chance. Plus, Shae told me she wants my apple caramel pie. I was going to show her how to make it."

If he thought I didn't see through his tactics, he was sadly mistaken. But Jude had said she was going away with friends for the long weekend, and anyone who'd ever seen me with a chicken knew there was no hope for a turkey. Maybe Pete didn't deserve a family holiday, but my girls did. Leaving things on a higher note would make it easier for everyone.

"Sure." I wrapped my cardigan tight to my waist and headed up the stairs to my big lonely bed. One step at a time.

* * * *

"A Christmas wedding sounds beautiful." I smiled at Brock Jenssen then over to Jenni Lynn Banks, and even brighter to Chad McFarlen.

The couple and her lawyer sat around the oval glass table in the small conference room at my office.

Brock linked his large hand into Jenni Lynn's smaller one, her long bright pink nails reflected the overhead lighting.

"Yeah, I didn't even know what a 'Destination Wedding' was." He reached for the pen in the middle of the table and signed the document. Without skipping a beat, he slid the papers over to Jenni Lynn and handed her the pen. "Our families are very excited. Although, my mama is a bit disappointed she can't cook for us." Brock winked at Jenni Lynn and gave her his All-American apple pie smile.

Jenni Lynn wrote her loopy signature on the paper and my internal lawyer danced the Bus Stop. I had him. The biggest rookie pitcher in the National Baseball League was my client. I'd protected his assets and secured him to the firm, which might lead to plenty of other work for my colleagues. The partners were going to shit glitter, and I was a step closer to becoming one of them.

I reached for the agreement and tucked it away in an unlabeled manila folder. "When do you get back as Mr. and Mrs. Jenssen?"

"The seventh of January." Jenni Lynn rubbed her thumb on the shiny rock perched on her ring finger.

"Fantastic. Brock, I hate to ask this of you, but if you're around, I'm organizing a fundraiser for a local boxing gym. It would be amazing if you could stop by for an hour and sign autographs. The kids would go insane." I re-crossed my ankles under my chair and sat up straighter.

"I'm sure I can spare an hour of my time. Text Jenni the details. She handles my schedule." He pushed away from the table. "Are we all set here?"

"Absolutely." I stood and took the folder with me on the way up. With it pressed into my chest, I walked over to the closed door and opened it for them.

Brock motioned for his fiancée to lead the way, and when she arrived at the threshold, she stopped.

"Hey, how was that trip to Florida?" Jenni Lynn asked.

I had wondered if she would want to cover all her bases. I had to give her a little credit for bringing it up in front of him. Then again, a girl who dated men for money had to have some sort of confidence.

"Ended up not going." I faked a frown. "Too much work. Did I miss anything?"

A wry, tight smile spread across her pretty face. "Wouldn't know. I've never been."

I held her gaze for a moment before I grinned back. I hoped she could read that I would keep her secret. I wasn't interested in ruining her relationship. The digging into her past had been a means to an end.

I'd needed her soon-to-be husband on my client roster, but it ended there. Even in the event of divorce, their agreement was solid. Unless Brock Jenssen became a wife-beating alcoholic, there was no chance of her walking away with his fortune—if, indeed, he had one.

Careers of professional athletes could be fickle bedmates. Sometimes the money went up their nose or was wasted on cars that lost half their value the minute they were bought and driven home. Sometimes people were injured and played for two years. Sometimes their talent never reached its fullest potential.

I couldn't predict Brock's future, but I could protect it if Jenni Lynn Banks decided she was better off without him.

When we reached the double glass doors of the entrance to the firm, I turned and shook each person's hand.

"Don't forget to send me the date for your fundraiser," she said as her blonde curls whipped over her shoulder.

"I'll do it as soon as I get back to my desk."

I watched them leave and sighed a breath of relief. With a spring in my step, I walked to my assistant's desk and flopped the file on top of his inbox. He raised his left hand and I tapped a high-five as I continued the celebratory path to my office.

When I got behind my desk, I opened the bottom drawer and dug my mobile out of my purse.

"Hey, Mom-fail." My sister's voice chirped from the other end.

"They signed."

"Congrats. And while I'm flattered you thought to call me first with the news, I know you want something else."

"Have I told you how smart you are?" I spun around in my chair and looked out of the window to the crisp fall day. At street level, Brock Jenssen held the door of a massive white pick-up truck open for Jenni Lynn. He swatted her butt and she dropped her head in laughter before she climbed in.

"Blah, blah, blah. Let me guess. You're not coming home tonight."

Damn skippy, I wasn't going to sleep at my house later. Hell, if I was lucky, I wouldn't sleep at all.

"What are you doing this afternoon?" I asked.

"Studying."

"Wrong answer. You are making those chocolate peanut butter cupcakes that Ben and Shae love."

The white trucked pulled away and a red Honda took its spot.

Jude groaned from the other end. "You are so lucky that I love you more than anyone on this planet. And anyway, it will give me something to do with the girls after school. Your ex is out. Apparently, he has a job interview."

"You're amazing," I said and swung my chair back around to face the empty desk.

"I know."

* * * *

I parked my car next to an auburn Buick whose trunk was being held shut by a bungee cord. With a plastic container of cupcakes in hand and my bag over my shoulder, I climbed out. The cool night's breeze shot up my bare legs and sent a shiver down my spine.

I relaxed my shoulders and gave a quick knock on the door of apartment number seven. Three locks unclicked on the opposite side and my gorgeous, freshly showered unicorn stood in front of me.

His gaze drifted to my heels and traveled up the length of me. When he clocked the cupcakes, Ben deepened his grin, bringing out the dimples on his scruffy cheeks. *Jackpot.* Lord, had I known it was all about the sugar for him, I'd have bought a bakery. *Although, to be fair, Jude's cakes are unbeatable.*

"Cupcake brings me cupcakes? This is a first." He closed and relocked the door.

I went right in for the kiss, delighted there was no holding back. When I broke free, I said, "I figured if you burn enough calories, it won't be cheating, and you can eat one right away."

"So very thoughtful." Ben took the container and set it on a sliver of the counter next to the small stainless-steel sink.

Before I could blink, he had my ass against the edge and his mouth was right where it belonged...on mine. I let my bag drop to the floor and reached up to play with the hair at his neckline. It was still damp and cooled my fingers as I twirled it around.

He tugged at the belt of my overcoat. It was a bit trashy and horribly cliché, but I hoped the black lace underneath would make up for the trivial ploy.

After he'd opened the front, he pulled the coat off my shoulders and it fell into the sink behind me. "Jesus, Cupcake. Hard to know where to start." Ben ran his fingers down my chest and goosebumps spread across my stomach.

"What about starting hard?" I arched an eyebrow, which brought back his dimples.

I had no need to ask twice. Ben spun me around and reached into my panties from behind with one hand and slid the other between my bra and my skin. He teased both sensitive targets with perfect pressure. I dropped my head and let out a sound that could only be described as cooing. His touch had turned me into a goddamn pigeon.

A twist and quick circles got my undivided attention. I pushed my stomach into the counter for support and he continued the dual movements. When he added the kiss below my ear and said, "You are so damn sexy," before taking a nibble, he hit the trifecta.

He steadied his hands while the tremors toured my body, and once they'd finished, I leaned into him.

"I love your new place." I spun around and kissed him quickly.

"Get naked and get on the bed. I have a cupcake to earn."

I did as he'd instructed, and he killed all the lights on the way back from the bathroom. With the street lamp beaming in from the window, I couldn't help but stare as he peeled off his T-shirt and sweats.

Ben Mathis was man candy in the flesh. There was no doubt about it. I'd never really considered myself a girl who liked ink, but the band around his biceps was downright edible. And those were the perks.

What I'd never expected was his heart. The gentle giant. Christ, just thinking about him with Shae or Nate made my ovaries ache. He would make an amazing daddy. A fantastic dad. And an ideal father.

Thankfully, he tossed a condom on the bed next to my leg. Otherwise, I might have been convinced to give *au naturel* a try and throw caution to the wind.

"What are you staring at?" Ben bent down over me and faked a bite of my stomach that made me giggle in delight.

"Possible perfection." I wrapped my legs around his solid bare ass and pulled him up to eye level.

"Pff... Me and my shitty little apartment are light years away from perfection." He pressed his shoulder into my forearm as if he was going to move away, but I brought him back nose-to-nose.

"I don't care about where you live. I care about you. You're what I need."

His blue eyes glistened as he searched my face. The seeds of chemistry had sprouted into attachment, circumstances be damned. Our feelings could not be denied.

I brushed my lips over his, staking a gentle claim. Everything slowed down and burning calories morphed into cherishing the moment. Each touch was soft and savored with its intent. My orgasms were hazy and heady instead of fast and thrilling.

Our relationship had clicked into a different reality, one where desire fell aside and was replaced by emotions swirling and connecting around us.

Chapter Twenty-Four

Pecan Pie

Ben

Amee nestled into me like a koala under the covers. I smoothed her hair and kissed the top of her head. These sacred moments could make a man forget he didn't belong with such a beautiful, smart woman, could make me dream of a time when spending the night with her would no longer be the exception but the rule.

Why? Why had I opened myself up to someone so far out of my league? Knowing that our relationship was morphing into deep feelings somehow expanded the barriers between us.

She kissed my bare chest and tightened her leg around mine.

"I'm sure you probably don't want to talk about my ex while we're in bed, but I wanted to let you know that he promised to be out by the end of the month. We're going to give the girls one more family Thanksgiving, then he's gone." She bookended her statement with another kiss.

The canyon I'd been fighting to close in my gut magnified yet again. One more family Thanksgiving. And while I couldn't begrudge her girls their right, there was one word that hung in the air—family. They were and would always be a family.

I'd tried to latch on to Kim and Nate, then done the same with Amee and her kids—to push my peg of need into their hole of existence. But none of them relied on me to be complete. It was me who was searching for open arms, always the second string, never the star player.

Her hair tickled my nose as I whispered, "That's great. I'm happy for you. And the girls totally deserve that. I know it will be hard on them when he leaves again."

I pushed her onto her side so she wouldn't see the disappointment in my face. I kissed her lovely neck one more time. She was too good for me. Too perfect. Even the little sounds she made while falling asleep were elegant.

* * * *

Amee's alarm sounded early, waking me from an unsatisfying sleep. She hopped out of bed in the dark, used the bathroom and was dressed within minutes.

"I'll call you later." She leaned over the bed and zipped up the jeans she'd pulled out of her bag. "Oh! I almost forgot. Shae's Nutcracker show is on the fourteenth. She insists you be there."

The fog of exhaustion cleared with a reminder of the date. *Shit.*

"That's the same night as my final." I rubbed my scruff. The conflict was surely a sign.

"Well, just come as soon as you can. I'll have Carly film it. It will give her something to do." Through the dark, she winked then pecked my cheek. She slipped back into her heels and headed for the door. "Don't eat all those cupcakes in one go. And thank you for the sleepover."

The door clicked shut and I stared at it until my own alarm rang an hour later. I pulled on my sweats and went over to the kitchen. Container of happy cheats in hand, I slid down the barren wall and sat on the hard wood with my knees up.

I opened Jude's edible brilliance and slowly plucked away the green wrapper—a detail of Shae's, no doubt. One bite turned into one cupcake and one cupcake turned into six. I didn't know my next move, only that I didn't belong anywhere.

* * * *

Monday night before Thanksgiving, I had class. We'd already begun our semester review and I tried to care, even though its success didn't matter. I would keep on repairing rich people's cars and barely pay my bills. Pointlessness was my new best friend.

When nine o'clock rolled around and we were freed from the middle-aged boob's overview of credits and debits, I slipped out of the community college as fast as I could. It wasn't that I had anywhere to go, just that I didn't want to be there anymore.

Jemina trotted up to me, her syrupy cloud arriving before her. "Hey, you got a minute?"

Her smile was wide and her tone as sweet as her perfume. *God, to say 'no' would be horrible.* She'd been amazing in helping me understand. But whatever chemistry she'd imagined between us was just that — her imagination. Even if I wasn't involved with someone else, she just didn't do it for me. She tried too hard.

"Sure," I said and motioned to my truck. "You want to hop in? It's cold out here."

We climbed into the cab and I cranked the engine.

Jemina swung her dark hair over her shoulder as she turned to face me from the passenger side. "I was wondering if you had plans for Thursday? My family does a huge pot luck and there's always plenty…"

Oh, no. It was worse than I thought. *Meet her family? No, thank you.*

She continued, "It's just I noticed you've been a bit down lately, so I thought maybe being around a big family might distract you. My great aunt is such a trip…"

I stared into the emptying parking lot and rubbed my cheeks. "Jemina, you're really cool and I appreciate how you helped me more than you know. But I'm not taking any more classes. You can stop making me your charity case."

She blinked slowly and tilted her chin down. *Are those her puppy dog eyes?*

"I…" She tugged at her bottom lip with her teeth. "I don't think of you as charity. I… I like you. I was hoping we could see each other and *not* study." She shrugged. Such an obvious game. A lip bite and sappy eyes.

But she'd been nothing but patient and kind to me. I owed her the gentle Benji Mathis letdown.

"Listen, sweetheart. You are a beautiful and intelligent woman. I just don't feel that spark with you. I'm so sorry. Thank you for thinking of me, but I'm afraid meeting your family would send the wrong signals about my intentions." I frowned, praying the expression would somehow soften the blow.

"Oh." She stared at the floorboard. "Oh, my God. I am so embarrassed. I'm so sorry."

The door creaked open then slammed shut before I could say anything else. *Damn it.* I banged my head a few times against the steering wheel and threw the truck into gear before pulling off.

* * * *

The consolation prize for spending the holiday away from the woman I was pretty sure I'd fallen in love with but couldn't imagine a future where it would ever work out, turned out to be a ridiculously delicious meal — all courtesy of my boxing buddy and his amazing mother.

Kim and Nate had gone to Rob's mother's house two hours south of the city and taken Uncle Teddy with them. My goodwill and previous car fixes for Trev's mom had resulted in the best turkey and stuffing I'd ever eaten. And, mercy me, the woman's pecan pie should have come with a warning label or a stomach pump. I stole a third slice after I'd helped his cousins with the dishes and gone to the den where the men were watching football.

I plopped down in the open spot on the huge sectional next to Trev's older brother. A steady wheeze leaked through his barely open mouth and his neck tilted to one side. *Turkey coma.*

"You working tomorrow?" Trev nodded over to me when the game took a commercial break.

"Black Friday for rich people? Some lucky daddy's girl or trophy wife is bound to get a Porsche and need something added to it." I stretched my arms overhead and claimed more territory for my soon-to-be nap.

Trev stood up and eyed me. "How many pieces of pie did you eat?"

"Do you want the final count when I'm done or just the stats right now?"

He shook his head. "Can you still meet up after work?"

"Yeah. We can even go later if you want. Nate and Devon won't be back yet."

Trev's brother smacked his gums and mumbled contently from his coma.

"No Friday night date?" Trev asked.

"Nah…"

Chapter Twenty-Five

The Turkey

Amee

I pressed the lid down on the plastic container, the leftover turkey just beneath. It had been a quiet and reflective meal — our broken family unit gathered around the large dining room table, picking at Pete's feast atop my grandmother's rose-etched china.

In a few short days, he would be out. Gone. And my stalled state of existence would finally be able to crank itself to life, a life I was more and more sure I wanted to include Ben.

As much as I didn't want to repeat my past by rushing into a relationship, my need for him was only growing — and my feelings.

I opened the door to the packed fridge and wondered where the hell the turkey would fit. The apple caramel pie sat half-eaten on top of a plastic box of grapes. I pulled both out, slid the meat in and piled them back on. I gave a little pat to the long stainless-steel door when it closed, hopeful that whoever opened it next would be lucky enough not to have half of the contents spill on to the floor.

When I spun around, I was surprised to see Pete staring at me from the opposite side of the bar. I brought my hand to my chest and said, "Jesus, you scared me. I thought you were tucking in the girls."

He refocused and wet his lips.

Uh oh.

"You really are a beautiful woman, Amee. I'm sorry I didn't tell you enough." He stepped from around the corner and shortened the space between us. Pete slowly dropped his head to one side and I pressed into the massive appliance behind me. "Thank you for tonight. It was almost perfect."

I'd kicked off my heels when I'd started the clean-up, so I had no choice but to look up into his heavy eyes. My, how they had changed through the years. The crow's feet that had once been barely visible were deep caverns and his eyebrows were speckled with occasional gray hairs that were wilder than the tame bushes of his youth. He was still attractive, even in his thinner frame, but was no longer my type.

"I miss you, baby. I miss us. I don't understand why we can't try again."

Someone needed to break out the hidden cameras, because it had to be a fucking joke. I had given that fucker one inch. One peaceful meal for our girls, and he understood my non-hostile self to mean he could make a move.

I pushed my outstretched palm into his chest. "No. Don't. Do not reach up and tuck my hair behind my ear. Do not think for one second that because we had a civilized evening with our children that it's a sign." I slid out from between him and the fridge and took his previous position of behind the counter with my arms crossed.

Pete dropped his head and spun to face me. "Is it really too much to want my fucking life back? Divorce was never, ever my idea and now you're parading your boyfriend in front of our kids…"

"Stop it right fucking there. Don't you even, for one fucking second, try and play me out to be the bad parent. You were in fucking jail, Peter. You got drunk and took another person's fucking life. Do you have any idea how much guilt those girls have? For fuck's sake, Carly *just* stopped going to a counselor."

"I'm better. I haven't had a drink since the accident. I want to start over again." His hazel eyes did their best to convince me he wasn't lying.

I flung my hands to my face and groaned through my teeth. "Why are we even talking about this? We're divorced. We went through this over a year ago."

"*You* went through this a year ago. Like I said, I never wanted to break up our family."

Zen Garden, where are you when I need you?

"I don't love you. I don't want to spend the rest of my life with a man I don't love."

It wasn't the first time I'd said those words to him. But God willing, it would be the last. Why he thought our evening had birthed some sign of hope was beyond me. Maybe there had been so much bickering in the past that the absence of it equated to the opposite of its presence. Who knew what went on in his confused and fucked up head? But he was off base and every kind of wrong.

"Do you love him?" His eyes searched my body then locked on to my own.

I didn't think it was any of his business, but I hoped admitting my feelings for Ben might put an end to his pointless happy family fantasy.

"Yes. So please, stop. There is nothing you can do to win me back. We are *over*."

Pete's face drooped, and he shook his head. He winced and stared at the floor.

A fragment of me wanted to reach out to an old friend, to apologize for causing his pain. But if he'd proven anything in the last fifteen minutes, it was that he was ready to hang on to any thread, no matter how feeble.

I bent down and scooped up my heels. Pete stayed frozen, no doubt unsure of any next move, be it spoken or physical. I left him in the kitchen, alone and broken. Maybe I was responsible for both in many ways.

* * * *

Spending my weekend without a sight of Ben sucked. But watching Pete pack boxes and driving him to his new house did not. And the girls had a project, since they had a shared room at Pete's. Although they'd never shown any interest in sleeping in the same room before, there was a new excitement for potential bunkbeds and matching comforters — not that they would be using them in the near future.

I poured myself a glass of celebratory red wine on Sunday night and heard the garage door open and shut, the sign my smartass sister was home. I found a matching long-stemmed glass in the cabinet and it clanked when it met the counter.

Jude walked in, lobbed her keys into the community basket and dropped a shoulder to let her bag fall to the tiled floor. She eyed the wine and grinned. "Is Fuckface gone?"

"Well, his ex-cell mate didn't escape and strangle him like you were hoping for, but he has his own place to live." I handed her a glass and we clinked them together.

Jude sipped the wine then tipped her head. "You broke out the good stuff."

"Well, I need to suck up to you again now that my ex-husband is finally out of my house."

The barstool stuttered against the floor as she pulled it out. "Because you want to leave and go get laid?"

She was half right. I did want to get laid, but I didn't want to leave. There was a rich energy to savor from reclaiming my personal space. Ben would never come over for a quickie and going there to see him would have been lovely, as always. But it was a different victory. The healing of a festering wound. It required pause and appreciation.

"Not tonight. Plus, he has a final in two weeks and is using every waking moment to study," I said. "You'll have to endure me in my happy place."

"With his big-boobed study buddy?"

Leave it to Jude to remind me. But even that pendulum had swung my way. "Nope, apparently she hit on Ben for real and he shot her down. I win again."

She rolled her eyes and drank. "Girls okay?"

"I hope so. Oh, Shae says you have to make those peppermint thingies for her recital."

Another eye roll. "I know. She only asked me four thousand times before Thanksgiving."

My phone vibrated and rattled from the granite on the opposite end of the kitchen where it was plugged in to charge. I left my sister and our late-night liquid snack behind and went to answer.

My heart sank before speeding up and I slid the bar. "Hey. Everything okay?" I asked.

My colleague's voice cracked from the other end. "I don't know. Beth started spotting then bleeding. We're at the ER."

"Oh my God. I'm so sorry. I'm sure she's gonna be fine. Are you at Saint Francis?"

"Yeah. Listen. I have the Baker deposition tomorrow. You're going to have to cover for me."

"No problem. What time is it scheduled?" I unplugged the phone and walked back to join Jude.

"Ten a.m. My assistant is emailing you everything now. Sorry, Amee. And thanks."

I dumped my half-finished wine into Jude's empty glass. "Send Beth my best."

My sister waited for me to hang up and, in an act of understanding and solidarity, she stuck out her bottom lip in a frown.

"I hope you like Christmas shopping. I just inherited the messiest divorce in the city."

Chapter Twenty-Six

Candy Canes

Ben

The nerd to my left coughed, breaking the silence of the room. I glanced over to Jemina, who was scribbling away on her test, then back to the eraser-messed-up papers in front of me. There were thirty more minutes before everything had to be handed in and three-and-a-half pages in front of me.

None of my calculations were turning out, and on the previous problem, I'd put all the credits as debits. The fact that I would have been using what I'd learned—or failed to learn—exactly nowhere in the future didn't help me one bit. I reread the question one more time, decided it was gibberish and fake, then moved on to the next.

Jemina cleared her throat and handed in her test with a smile. She gathered her things and quietly left the room. Other students trickled out as well, and when the time was finally up, only me and two other people remained. I hadn't even looked at the final page.

I cursed all my 'follow through' lectures that I'd given Nate over the last year then stood and met the teacher with his tight-lipped smile. He probably thought I would fail. The whole process had been pointless. Not only had I not learned anything about accounting, I'd wasted money to prove to myself I was a dumbass, further confirming my backside's stupidity.

When I got to my truck, I turned on my phone and found several short videos of Shae in a tutu on stage. *Fuck.* I'd missed that, too.

The only stroke of luck was that the auditorium wasn't on the other side of town. When I arrived in front, an Audi pulled away and left a spot for me between all the other luxury cars.

Men in tight-fitting sweaters with collars peeking out at the neckline and women in holiday dresses chatted in small groups in the entryway. They sipped red punch and feasted on homemade cookies and pastries while their equally well-dressed children zoomed around their legs with candy canes in their mouths. I searched the room and my ear caught the giggle of my favorite little girl.

Her daddy held her on his hip and the ribbons in Shae's hair bounced over his shoulder. Her bright eyes sparkled like the Christmas lights I'd passed on the drive over and I'd never seen a bigger smile on her face.

On all their faces.

Amee, who I hadn't laid eyes on in two weeks, had her arms around Carly and they both laughed at whatever Shae had just said. Even stone-faced Jude was beaming.

They were perfect. Christ, they could have been a damn Christmas card or happy family commercial. And they were complete. They didn't need another head at their figurative table. Amee's ex fit the picture of happiness as if it was designed for him — 'upper-class dad' uniform was not part of my wardrobe.

I had nothing to give them. *Nothing.* If I wasn't a man of my word, I would have left — turned around and just let them be. My work coat and jeans were the sugar plum frosting on the cake of me not belonging. But I'd made a promise to that little girl that I would come, and broken promises to kids wasn't who I was. I closed my eyes hard, hoping to find the humility and courage I needed. *For Shae...* I would do it for Shae.

I slid off my stocking hat and shoved it into the pocket of my coat. With my head down, I dropped a shoulder and pardoned my way through expensive perfume and more jewels than I'd ever seen at once, over to the people who didn't need a penniless failure in their lives.

From her perch on her dad's hip, Shae was the first to see me. "BB! You made it!" She wiggled down and threw her laced-up arms around my thigh. When she let go, I bent down to her level and smiled.

"Sorry I'm late, but I watched the videos. You were amazing." I raised my hand and she gave me a high five.

Then it hit me. I had to stand up. I wasn't sure how to greet Amee in front of all these strangers and especially in front of her ex. I didn't want to be disrespectful and I didn't want to make the wrong move. It had been one thing to shake his hand in the privacy of Amee's home. It would be another to kiss his ex-wife in public.

Jude saved me. When I got back upright, she came over and gave me a quick peck on the cheek like we'd been friends our entire life. I man-nodded to Pete, whose face had somehow shriveled up into a prune in thirty seconds. After a little wave to Carly, Amee stepped over to me in her sexy-as-hell boots and oversized silver sweater and reached for my hand. She gave it a squeeze and whispered, "I've missed you."

I understood that kissing her here was off limits and wondered how I'd gotten myself into a situation where I had to hide the fact that I was a boyfriend.

"Well, we should get going. It's a school night," Pete said.

"No, Daddy. Ben just got here. I want to introduce him to my dance teacher." Shae took my free hand and tugged it in the opposite direction.

"Shae, Daddy's right. By the time we drop him off and get home it will be two hours past your bedtime." Amee dropped my hand and went over to Shae. "I'm sorry, baby girl. Another time."

"Smooth move, DQ." Jude rolled her eyes and shook her head. I'm sure it was circumstantial, but it did indeed sound like Amee didn't want me to meet the teacher.

"I'll get our coats." Pete's victory grin was a little too eager. *Ass.*

My girlfriend glared at her sister and Jude said to me, "I'll explain it to her." Then she turned to Amee. "Because that's what I do."

A voice in my head wondered if she should even bother. I bent down again to Shae. "I am sorry I missed your show."

"Did you come as soon as you could?" she asked.

"Yeah, I did."

"Then you did your best." Her simple smile broke my already-cracked heart.

If only she knew how I'd failed my test, how I failed at being a boyfriend to a woman with kids and how I would fail her by backing out of her life. I didn't belong in their picture.

I stood again and said, "Well, it was nice to see you all. Take care." I reached for my hat, smoothed it over my head, gave them my best grin and got the hell out of there. *Sorry, Shae. You deserve better than my best.*

* * * *

"What the fuck was that? Take fucking care?" Amee bolted by me and stopped next to my tiny table for one. She ripped off her coat and threw it onto my bed, then crossed her arms. "Then you don't answer your phone. What the fuck is going on?"

I was tempted to walk out of the door instead of close it, but that would be a chicken shit move. Plus, I was barefoot and only in sweatpants.

"Amee..."

"No. Just fucking *no*. You are a goddamn unicorn. You will *not* do this."

I had to hand it to her for her gumption. The woman did have balls. She was probably a fantastic lawyer. And damn it all, she was gorgeous when she was pissed. But I could not let her charms get under my skin.

The facts were the facts. I didn't know how to swim in her social pool. I had nothing to offer her. There was no long-term plan.

After a long exhale, I walked down the short hallway and leaned against the counter. "I think we may have been a bit optimistic about our future."

She narrowed her eyes, and I swallowed her intimidation like a hard pill.

"What is this about?" Her volume calmed, and she stared at me. Lasers… Her blue eyes were burning a hole in my soul.

I wasn't ready to fess up to my epic school fail. "Why does it have to be about something?"

Her hands flew to her hips. "Don't fucking do that. Answer my question."

"You and I are too different…"

"Oh my God. Is this about money? I told you I don't care about that." She walked over and stood in front of me. Her eyes searched for mine, but I had to look away. "I thought you wanted to take care of me. Be there for me. Jesus, Ben. I'm in love with you."

She wasn't. She couldn't be. She'd had her rebound and could move on and find someone better suited for her. Someone who could wear a dad uniform and buy a ring to put on her finger.

Because I wasn't lying about being overly optimistic about our future. I loved her, too. I wanted to marry her. I wanted to teach Shae and Carly how to kick butt and defend themselves. Have holidays with Nate and the girls. But I couldn't buy her a ring. Shit, I couldn't even pay for her dinner without throwing off my monthly budget. And with the holidays around the corner, there would be no presents from Ben. She was luxury. I was poverty.

Amee reached up and brushed my beard then twirled a lock of my hair with her delicate fingers. "Don't do this. Don't leave me."

"You wouldn't even kiss me hello in front of those people, Amee. Our social status will never change. I can't be with someone who isn't proud to be on my arm."

Her faced dropped and it was hard to know who was suffering more, her or me. But the honesty of my words had obviously dug into her skin.

"I..." she started.

"You discreetly held my hand for ten seconds. When Shae wanted me to meet her teacher, you couldn't leave fast enough. You may think you love me, but you love the escape. We don't have a future. You proved it today."

I pivoted away and her hand fell from my neck. Out of the corner of my eye, I saw her wipe away a tear.

"You should go," I said in a low voice.

"This is fucking bullshit." Amee grabbed her coat and slammed the door behind her.

Chapter Twenty-Seven

Ham Sandwich

Amee

Shae tore open her final present while Pete smiled from the couch. To say he was trying to buy his youngest daughter's love was the understatement of the century.

I'd begrudgingly allowed him to make us another holiday meal. What choice did I have? I couldn't keep them apart at Christmas. I was desperately trying to heed Jude's advice and not be the mother that used her kids as pawns to seek revenge on the asshole ex.

Carly pushed her thumbs into the console she'd asked for and flopped her feet into her dad's lap. Maybe having him at the house was better than having the girls think I was a heartless bitch.

The problem was, I was pretty sure I was a heartless bitch. I'd shunned Ben in public not once, but twice. Jude had said there was no amount of groveling that would fix my blunder. I'd told him money didn't matter, but my actions had spoken way louder.

I tapped on Jude's door and she looked up from her book. "I'm going to lie down. Don't let him move back in while I'm asleep."

"No fucking chance of that on my watch."

I lingered on the threshold a little longer and rolled my shoulder into its sharp corner.

Jude squinted. "Ugh. Don't give me those sad eyes. You fucked up. You'll live."

She was right. I was giving her sad eyes and I had fucked up. And while I would live, I didn't want to move on from Ben. I wanted Ben back. I wanted to be in his arms again.

He'd taken a chance on me and I'd wasted it. He could probably have had any woman and I'd treated him like shit, had reinforced every fear and stereotype he had been fighting. I'd gotten caught up in my own shit and forgotten all about him.

I walked up to my room like a ghost in my own house. My phone sat next to the bed and I still had enough insane hope that he would reach out. Its empty screen confirmed his continued silence.

I scrolled down to the word Unicorn and tapped out my message.

I'm sorry I fucked up. Merry Christmas to you and Nate. Love, Cupcake

Worst of all, I didn't even have anything of his to hold on to. He'd never even seen my bedroom. I should have stolen one of his fucking hoodies when he'd kicked me out the week before. I spooned into my pillow in the fetal position.

There had to be some way to get him back, something I could do to un-fuck the situation. Drawing a blank, I eventually fell asleep.

* * * *

A familiar hand tucked my hair behind my ear and brushed my cheek.

"Hey," he whispered. "It's not like you to take a nap. That Baker case really ran you down, huh?"

I blinked several times and brought my hands to my head. "What time is it?"

"It's nine p.m. Girls ate and are watching a movie. I left a ham sandwich for you in the kitchen. A car is coming to get me."

I looked into my ex-husband's eyes and, for the first time in years, forgot to hate him.

"Thanks for today. I loved being with you guys." Pete's warm tone hinted of more and he licked his lips.

You guys. There it was. The small dig. The faint hint that he wasn't just there for the girls. *Come to think of it, what the hell is he doing in my bedroom?* I was sure I'd voodooed Pete repellent on my doorframe.

"Don't do that." I sat up, moved away from him and stretched. "Don't fold me into your loop. I want to be civil for the girls, but there's nothing more to it."

"Baby," he said.

Baby?

He shook his head. "I get it. You had some wildness left in you. You had your fling but we are a family."

I scoffed. "Fling? I didn't have a fling with him."

"Right." He stood up and gave me a slight smirk. "That's why you didn't want him to meet Shae's dance teacher. That's why you froze when he showed up."

"I..."

Holy crap on a cracker. Pete must have been basting his ego with my fuck up for the last week. I sunk a notch lower into my guilt. If I'd acted like that in front of my ex, no wonder Ben had told me to suck it.

Pete sighed. "It's fine. I get it. And I still want to move forward and heal this family."

Out of his mind. The man was out of his artistic left-brained mind.

"I didn't have a fling. I had a relationship and I fucked it up. And that does not equate to me wanting to reconcile with you. What it does mean is that I'm going to fight like hell to get him back."

Pete stared at me and his jaw shifted. A honk echoed up from the driveway.

His eyes narrowed ever so slightly and he said, "That's exactly what I'm trying to do."

* * * *

Jude was a genius. A smartass, but a genius. After Pete had left that night, she'd knocked on my door and instructed me to pack. She was taking the girls and me to Mexico—four days and four nights in a swanky resort on the beach, all inclusive.

We sipped fruity cocktails, got day-tipsy and watched the girls play in the ocean. It was the art of distraction and some seriously needed rest. The Baker case I'd taken over had sucked the life out of me for three weeks. But after the holidays, my colleague would be back at work and I would be Baker-free.

Ben was never far from my thoughts and I bounced new plans to win him back off my sister on an hourly basis. And she listened. She was a saint, a genius—and still a total smartass. When I explained my long-term idea, she said, "That just might work, DQ."

However, my first step needed to be a huge, massive, in-person apology. And that would require my former stalking skills, because Ben still wasn't returning calls or texts.

By New Year's Eve, I couldn't handle it anymore. Jude rolled her eyes at me on the way out of the door and I hopped into my car, leaving my girls sleeping and my sister in charge once again.

I drove up to his apartment and noticed the lack of lights on and his missing truck. I knocked on the door anyway, but there was no answer. Back in my car, I tapped my fingers on the wheel as the seat heated my ass.

At the boxing gym, I only found Craig's beat-up Ford alone in the lot. Searching three locations was sure to up my crazy-obsessed status, and I promised that if he wasn't at Teddy's, I would go home.

When I turned onto his street, my heart raced. Ben's big black truck was in the driveway. Once I'd pulled up to the curb, I could see the flashing screen of a TV from the living room window.

With a click of the fob, the hazards flashed and my car was locked. I wrapped my sweater — impulse apparently didn't like outerwear — tighter into me and walked up the small pathway to the front door.

Shit. I couldn't ring the doorbell. It was too late if Nate or Teddy weren't awake. While rubbing my shoulders for warmth, I peeked into the window.

My unicorn sat on the couch, flanked by Nate and Devon, all three with video game consoles in their hands. *Knock.* I would knock. *But then what?* I would drop to my knees and plead my pathetic case?

The screen door creaked when I opened it and I rapped firmly.

Nothing. I shivered.

I tried again as I danced back and forth on one foot. Maybe he'd seen my car and was ignoring me. But I was there, and he was just on the other side of the wall. I couldn't give up. If I rang the bell, I risked waking up his uncle, and I didn't want to make him mad before he'd even seen me.

I leaned over to the window again and saw the three of them, all in the same position. I knocked on the window, creating a sharp rattle, and Nate jumped in his seat and stared right at me. Ben turned to him first then narrowed his eyes at me.

I waved, because I was a lovesick fool.

He got up and flung open the front door. After a once-over of my shivering body, he sighed and said, "Come in." The tone was too heavy on the dismissive side and far from welcoming.

The warmth of the house amplified the cold of my skin and my teeth clattered together as I said hello to the boys and walked down the hall to the unlit kitchen.

"Jesus, Amee. I don't know which to call you on first — not wearing a coat or showing up uninvited."

"I'm s...s...sorry." *Crap.* I was colder than I thought. The adrenaline must have been keeping me warm outside.

Ben flipped on a dim light by the sink. "Did you wear those pants on purpose?"

I glanced down to my pajama pants. His favorite. "N...n...no." I shuddered in hopes that some movement may warm me.

"Oh, for Christ's sake. Your lips are blue. Get over here." He stretched out his arms and I'd never moved faster in my life. I was against his warm wall of a body, where I was sure I belonged, before he could change his mind. He rubbed his hands against my icicle fingers. "This doesn't mean what you think — other than you're cold and I'm a sucker."

Ben slowed the friction and dropped my hands. He tucked his chin over the top of my head.

Knowing it wouldn't last, I decided to take advantage of the intimacy for the epic apology I'd been working on for weeks.

"I'm so sorry, Ben. I was a fool. I fucked it all up. I'm so sorry." I held back the tears. It wasn't his pity I needed.

His chest inflated with a slow breath and he let it out with his mouth. He released me and stepped away.

I searched his lovely eyes for any hope. "I'm sorry. And I don't deserve you. I'm not asking you to take me back but I needed to see you and apologize face-to-face." I pressed my lips together as he rubbed his neck. "And despite how I acted, I love you. I fell in love with you. I am truly, truly sorry."

He covered his eyes with his hands then formed a steeple over his nose.

Please let him be considering forgiveness.

Maybe there would be a light at the end of this dark tunnel. He shifted his gaze from my pajama pants to my eyes then over to the dead space across the room. He released his hands and placed them behind him on the counter.

Nate and Devon screamed, "Happy New Year!" from the living room.

I narrowed the space he'd created between us. "Happy New Year, Unicorn." It was everything I had to hold back from repeating that I loved him and going in for the kiss. But Jude had told me I needed to move in small steps.

Ben's posture sank. In a throaty whisper he said, "Happy New Year."

The greeting was a tiny shard of encouragement, but the missing 'Cupcake' was a black hole reminding me of the space between us.

"I'll let myself out." As I walked down the hall, I could sense his eyes on me. I turned around one last time and he blinked up to hold my gaze. It was still there, the energy — the spark he'd identified months prior, the who-knows-why-two-people-fit-together, the 'I never knew what love was until you.' It pulsed strong between us, but he didn't move to me.

A reminder flashed from Jude to go slow. I paused for one more addictive moment then left.

Chapter Twenty-Eight

Chicken and Broccoli

Ben

That made twice in two weeks I'd watched her walk out of my door. Twice I was sure I was making the biggest mistake of my life by letting her go. I ached for her. Christ, holding her in my arms had been everything. I'd told her I'd take care of her and I'd failed. And she'd pretty much ripped my heart out by telling me again that she loved me.

I punched the bag in front of me and wondered what was standing in the way of me giving her a second chance.

Pride. I hit harder.

Anger. Another blow.

Lack of self-worth. I froze.

"I can't believe you woke us up at the ass crack of dawn on New Year's," Devon complained and took a drink from his water bottle. "You realize everyone else in this city is sleeping."

"Yeah, well, while they all turn into noodles, we're getting stronger." Nate flexed his biceps and grinned. He was getting a little bigger and definitely had more power than one would give him credit for. He was becoming a scrappy book nerd. I loved it.

Craig shuffled past and scratched his ass. "You may want to shower, princess. Your ball-busting overly-enthusiastic girlfriend is on her way."

"Excuse me?" I asked. He better not mean Amee Benton. It was one thing to show up at my damn door. It was another to full-blown stalk me. And all that time I'd thought she wasn't crazy. Jesus Christ, and I had the boys.

"Yeah. Well, apparently she has to go back to work tomorrow so she can only drop stuff by today."

Bullshit. I called one hundred percent bullshit. Did she really think her transgression was so simple that she could just show up once in those goddamn pants and we could move on? *Wrong, Ms. Benton.* And this just popping up everywhere I was? *Not happening.* But if I dug really deep and was truly honest, I was afraid. Afraid I'd crack and end up in the same spot of not belonging. Pour salt into the wound of not being good enough.

I glanced over to the boys, who were dutifully groaning through their crunches, and yelled, "Hit the showers. We're leaving."

I ripped off my gloves and stomped to the locker room. Nate and Devon trailed after me, neither one complaining about an early departure and not daring to ask why.

With a final zip to my bag, I swung it over my shoulder and said to the boys, who already had their coats on, "Let's go."

We walked out of the locker room and I realized oh-too-soon that I hadn't moved quick enough. Craig was right. I was a lamppost.

"BB!" Shae ran toward me with open arms and a huge smile. *Didn't Amee tell her we broke up? Does it matter?*

The bag dropped to the ground and I scooped up the glitter bug in my arms. "Hey, Little Mama. You have a good Christmas?" She smelled like frosted sugar cookies. *The perfect child of a cupcake.*

"I missed you. I thought you might come over. Mommy said it's complicated." She looked down then back up. "I know what that means, but I don't know what that means."

The one thing I never, ever, wanted to do was break a kid's heart, mostly because I'd walked that path. And the little one and I had clicked. Lord only understood why, but we had.

I carried Shae over to Craig's office as Nate went to say hello to Carly, who sat in her usual chair near the doors. I gave Shae a peck on the cheek and let her slide down my side to the ground. We smiled at each other and I said, "It was great to see you, Shae. Happy New Year."

Her eyes lit up. "Oh my goodness! I forgot to say that to Nate!" She skipped off in the direction of the other kids.

"Hey." I tipped my chin up to Amee.

She leaned over Craig's shoulder, her hair pulled up. She had on those tight jeans I liked. Damn it, I really had to stop thinking about her in pants. Or out. *Shit. No. Mad.* I needed to be mad.

"Hi, I didn't—"

"You busy later?" I asked in a clipped but somewhat casual voice.

A faint smile appeared on her perfect face. *Not what you think, Ms. Benton.*

"Uh…"

"Without your kids?" Hopefully the frost in my voice would clue her in.

She widened her eyes a little—maybe she understood. "After dinner?"

"Great. I'll be home. I think you know where that is." *Stalker.*

I walked back to get my bag and swiped it up. *Don't show anger in front of the kids, Benji.* "Hey, Carly. You have a nice holiday?"

She grinned. "Yeah, Jude took us to Mexico."

No mention of her dad. I said a silent 'thank you' to her for her omission.

"Nice." Devon bopped his head as if there was a soundtrack we were all missing.

I motioned for the boys to head for the door and Shae climbed into the chair where Nate had been and swung her striped legs.

"BB?" Her sweet voice stopped me from stepping out of the glass door and my chest tightened. Shae slid off the plastic chair and caught the hem of her skirt. Her sparkly nails and ringed fingers smoothed it back into place and she walked over to me.

I bent down. Carly kept her nose in her book and Shae leaned in to me. "I'm doing my best to like my daddy again."

My heart pounded in my throat and I blinked back a tear. The little bombshell had brought me to damn tears. I pulled her in for a hug and whispered, "That's because you are a fortified short stack of awesome, Little Mama."

I turned her around and urged her to sit in her chair. Her mom, who had come from the office and stood next to the first boxing ring, wouldn't get my eye contact. It was one thing to well up for the little one. It was another to show her mom how much I missed them.

* * * *

Back at home and my fridge full of chicken and broccoli from Kim—who'd admitted that sending me home with a week of healthy meals for babysitting payment had been Rob's idea—I waited. I paced around the small apartment over and over.

The knock finally came, and her hopeful look fell when I slammed the door shut.

"I—"

Nope. Not again. I held up my hand. *I will do the talking, thanks very much.*

Amee reached for the buttons on her coat—she'd finally remembered to wear one—and I said, "Don't bother. You're not staying long."

She crinkled her forehead.

"Don't ever fucking do that again. Don't show up unannounced and act like we're buddy-buddy in front of your kids. I didn't return your calls for a reason, *Mrs. Benton.*"

She dropped her jaw but had the good sense not to speak.

"You made it clear that I'm not good enough for you. Don't come rub in my face what could have been with your kids. And stop fucking following me."

"You're angry." Her voice was just above a whisper.

"You cast me aside and forced me to do the same to your kids. And, yeah, I know what that feels like. And it was the last fucking thing I wanted to happen."

"I... I didn't know you were going to be at the gym. I swear."

"And when you saw my truck in the parking lot, you thought that I'd sold it in the last twelve hours?"

Her gaze dropped to the floor.

My voice amplified with her defeat. "And last night... You were driving by my uncle's house in those goddamn pajamas and decided to just knock on the window in the middle of the freezing cold?"

"I knew I was teetering on stalker. Fuck."

"You're not teetering. You've dived off the cliff. You're out of your mind if you think I'm interested in your desperation, especially after you shattered all my fucking dreams." I threw my hands up and walked back to the door. I turned the handle, having said my piece, and I was ready for her to leave, already hating myself for trying to hurt her. But I was somehow convinced it was the only way to prove to her we were through.

"Wait. What exactly did I ruin? What was your dream?"

Maybe it shouldn't have bothered me that she didn't know. But in all fairness, I'd told her. I'd probably tried not to repeat it so that she would think I was interested only in her. But after her first blunder, I had been clear it was the family I was after — a woman who was a great mother and a unit that clicked. Women with their shit together had always been hotter than any pair of panties I'd ever seen.

But she obviously needed a reminder. "A family, Amee. I want a family. This?" I signaled to my tiny apartment and solitude. "*This* is my nightmare."

I turned my wrist on the handle, and the cold air hit my face.

"I made a mistake, Ben. I'm sorry." She dug her hands into the pocket of her camel-colored designer coat and stepped closer until I was looking her in the eyes. "But I don't regret introducing an amazing man to my girls. The only thing I would take back is me not understanding how precious you are." She brought her lips to my cheek, held them for a beat then released. "Any family would be lucky to have you. And I wish I knew how to make it mine."

Chapter Twenty-Nine

Stringy Cheese

Amee

The bedside light leaked out in a sliver from Jude's room. When I pushed the door open, she looked up and frowned.

"Didn't go how you thought?" she asked.

I shook my head quickly and she opened her arms.

"Come here."

Without hesitation, I flung myself on my sister's bed and curled into her.

She smoothed my hair and held me as I silently sobbed in her arms. With every shake of my body, I reminded myself how I'd broken Ben – the magical beast who didn't just want me, he'd wanted my family. *Three for one.* He hadn't been kidding about his deal.

"He wanted us all, Jude – me and the girls – and I fucked it up." I wiped my nose on my sleeve. "Why am I such an ass?"

I'd dangled the golden carrot of his every dream in front of him without realizing how much he'd wanted it. What a fool I'd been—not because he wasn't good enough but because I wasn't.

"There are a lot of reasons you're an ass. But in this case, you did it for the same reason you ignored him at the Cake Walk. You were afraid the bitchy moms there would say something in front of their kids about you dating a younger man. And you were already stressing having Pete back in a social setting. The girls went through a lot of gossip bullshit with him. You don't want a 're-Pete', so to speak. You handled it poorly. Did you tell him why?"

No. Still, Ben Mathis didn't deserve to be a victim of my baggage.

"He was hurt... God, I'm an ass."

Ben was right to be angry with me and he'd had every reason to end it. I'd brushed him off not once, but twice in public. Cast him aside. Time and time again he'd told me he didn't want to be in just a physical relationship and my actions had showed him that he was exactly that.

Jude passed me a tissue and winced when I filled it.

She shrugged. "Maybe I was wrong..."

I plucked another tissue from the box. "Can you save saying you're wrong about something for a moment when I can actually enjoy it?"

"You want me to open some wine?"

"No, that won't help. I want to cry at what a mess I made then figure out a way to explain to Shae that BB is going back to plain Ben." That, however, would require wine. "God, you even told me when I was being a douche."

"Yeah, for the smart one, you are really stupid sometimes." She returned to reading her book and I eventually got up and went to my own bed, where I collapsed fully dressed.

Maybe I'd made a colossal mistake in divorcing Pete. I'd honestly thought my happiness needed to take a priority in my life. But maybe, as a mother, that would never be possible, because, so far, putting myself first had only made things worse — for everyone. I'd brought lightness back into our lives only end up with more darkness. God, Shae was going to crumble.

Having it all was an illusion like a mystical imaginary creature. Ben might remain a unicorn, but for someone else.

My chest ached and a new round of tears stained my pillow. I had ruined all the relationships my daughters were having with men and I'd ruined two men along the way.

* * * *

I still had some loose ends to tie up on the gym's fundraiser, but I didn't want to cross my stalker line, so I met with Craig over my lunch hour to avoid seeing Ben. But walking into that large, cold space, knowing a part of his energy had most likely been left on the sparse equipment that very same morning, only increased my longing for him.

With the checkered box of pizza in hand and a plastic bag of drinks hanging from my wrist, I tapped on Craig's door, causing the clouded glass to rattle. Craig gave me a wrinkly smile at the sight of lunch and he cleared a spot on his army-green metal desk.

When I sat down and blew the steam off my cheese-dripping slice he said, "I just want you to know that I appreciate everything you did. And since you two broke up, I understand that you don't want to go through with the fundraiser."

I stopped just before my teeth sank into the Italian goo. Ben would never eat pizza at lunch. "Did he tell you to fire me?"

Craig chewed on his bite, wiped the orange grease from his lips with the paper napkin and swallowed. "He didn't tell me anything. But he's been here at the crack of dawn for days and my poor old bag has taken a beating. I know enough about men and their *feelings* to know when they're taking their shit out in my gym."

Well, at least Ben was affected by our break-up. I'd given him enough to need to work out. But that didn't change the fact that it was me who had given him one more thing to deal with in his life and I was about to suggest adding more.

"If it's okay with you, I'd like to continue. I have everything in place and have already started promoting it at my kids' school and on social media." I worked my jaw and waited as he finished his slice. The folding chair squeaked as I shifted my weight and drank a sip of my sparkling water.

When he was done, Craig grabbed another piece and ate it in silence. Canceling the event would have been a shame, but I understood his loyalty to Ben. It was the exact same reason I was still ready to keep going.

Maybe Craig and I were in some kind of stand-off. Oh, I could do that. If Craig needed to see I was willing to take it all the way, he had miserably underestimated his opponent. He pulled off a third portion. I smiled.

Number three in his belly, he went for the next. He could eat the whole damn pizza if he wanted. I wasn't leaving until he said yes. I folded my arms and leaned back in the noisy and uncomfortable chair.

With only a dried clump of cheese remaining in the grease-stained box, he finally said, "The thing is, I don't know what to do once it's over. Shiny new dumbbells don't mean new bodies on the mat."

He balled up the final napkin, tossed it onto the cardboard box in the center of his desk and rubbed his belly over his tattered gray sweater.

Perfect. His lead-in was gold.

"I'm glad you thought about that, because so did I." I straightened my posture. "The majority of my contacts are moms." I spread my fingers and lifted a shoulder. "Obviously. And what do moms want?"

"Is that a trick question?" He shot me a side-eye.

"No." I grinned. "Moms want someone else to wear out their kids so they can bring them home and have some peace and quiet. We drive all across this city to ensure it. I have one friend who has four boys. *Four.*" I paused to make sure he understood how horrible that was. "She'll take her mom taxi to hell and back for them, as long as they come home and pass out. It's mom code. Keep them busy, distract them, keep them out of our clean houses…"

Craig scratched his chin. "Okay, but how do I get those moms to drop off their little shits here? And once they're here, what the fuck am I going to do with them?"

His F-bomb spoke to the swearing fiend in my soul.

"Classes. You have to offer classes."

The old man recoiled as if there was a cobra shaking its tail next to the remnants of our lunch. "I'm too old for that shit."

I'd been skirting around his name. Saying it somehow made him more real and the lack of him greater. I found the little fire of courage in my belly.

"Ben isn't." I let the weight of what I'd suggested settle then continued. "Look how he is with Nate and Devon. He's a natural teacher. He taught my daughter to ride a bike in an hour. He's great with kids." I left out the part about him being open to a second income. It would have been a betrayal to say more and I didn't need added reasons for him to be pissed.

"His motivated ass *is* here every day. Did you talk to him about this?"

The cranky bastard had me there. "No. I thought it would be better coming from you."

He raised a wild and ungroomed eyebrow. "And he's not talking to you."

No, he wasn't, not that I was pushing. The days of me sending messages or knocking on his door without being invited had ended the last time I'd seen him, which was *not* okay with my younger daughter. She was sure they could still be friends. She'd even asked me every day for a week if he'd called to talk to her or Lasagna.

"I was thinking that if we could put a schedule on the back of the pictures the athletes are going to sign as autographs, we would be sure that the flyers don't get thrown away. No kid is going to toss out Brock Jenssen's signed photo."

"Brock Jenssen? You're getting him to come to my piece-of-shit gym? Jesus, lady."

Again, his cussing made me grin.

"Not just him. I have three other pros lined up at different times of the day."

Craig stood up and paced around his desk. "And you really think adding these classes will bring up the membership?"

"I know it will." I fished out the folded paper from my bag on the floor, pushed the pizza box to the side and spread out the sheet. "I already did a tiny focus group of moms."

"A *what*?"

I had him. I just had to reel that catfish in. "Here's a list of my suggested classes on nights and weekends."

He peered down at the sheet. "Baby Boxers?"

"You can call it whatever you like. But listen... Moms will eat a thing like that up. You'll probably have more little girls in pigtails than boys."

Craig stepped back and I remembered he was from another age—one where only boys could be boxers.

"You know, equal rights and all that, blah blah blah. The point is, once those renovations are done, you could have a lot of buzz and traffic through that door."

He scratched the salt and pepper stubble on his weather-stained cheek. "When do you need to know by?"

"As soon as you can. If Ben doesn't want to do it, I'll help you find teachers, but he's perfect."

In so many ways.

Chapter Thirty

Oreo Thingies

Ben

"Baby Boxers? Nine a.m. Saturday morning?" Trev raised his eyebrows and flared his nostrils. The stupid smirk would be wiped off his face the next time I had him in the ring.

"She's already got like four kids signed up." I shrugged and told my brain to stop focusing on her. *Jesus and all things Christ, she has to wear the jeans, with the boots, that lead to the ass* and *the low-cut silk shirt?* And her hands in her pockets as she rocked back and forth mulling something over was killing me. I couldn't even figure out why.

Trev chuckled and tossed the flyer onto the folding table. "Don't get me wrong. It's actually a brilliant idea. You're good with kids."

I narrowed my eyes. There was something odd about him giving me a compliment so freely.

"Come on, McDraw," I said and signaled over my shoulder. "Help me set up the other autograph stations."

To say what Amee had pulled off was impressive was wrong. It was beyond my wildest dreams, not that I dreamed about feeding goats popcorn and shaking hands with athletes. My nights, and days, were mostly filled with Amee Benton. Well, in thoughts. Because she'd fried my heart on an open grill and served it back to me in a cheap bun. But, damn it all to hell, I'd thought of her over and over again in the weeks leading up to the event.

And there she was in all her beauty, in charge and with Craig at her complete service, all because she'd cared about something that had absolutely nothing to do with her.

Trev and I finished propping up the final rented table and I said, "Go ask her what she wants us to do next."

He bent over and exaggerated his laughter.

Ass.

"You're afraid of your ex-girlfriend? This is a first." He leaned against the wall leading to the men's locker room. "But, nope. Benji tongue-tied and nervous? This I gotta see."

"You're a dick."

He shrugged.

Ass.

I rubbed my neck and looked back over to her.

Mercy.

I'd thought I would still have been mad at her, but I'd blown off the steam. My anger was just a low simmer, originating more from pride than outrage. Plus, from what Craig had told me, the woman had worked miracles for the event and beyond. She'd found someone to build a website, had a general contractor come in and give him an estimate to revamp the bathrooms and was working on some equipment-sponsoring deals from her sports connections. And I'd thought I'd been helping out when I pushed the broom at night.

With Trev's asshole grin following me, I made my way over to Amee, who was signing a clipboard from the huge video game installation at the far end of the gym.

"Hey…"

The delivery man left us, and she turned to me with a smile. "Hi."

My heart raced, and I failed to blink. *Has she ever been more beautiful?*

Amee kept her simple smile. "Did you need something?"

Yeah. Yeah, I do. I needed an explanation and some fucking make-up sex. *Wait. What?* I gave my head a quick shake.

"Ben?" She squinted. "Are you okay?"

"Sorry. What else can Trev and I do?"

She surveyed the gym. "If you could put the tablecloths on, that would be great. Jude will be here soon with the food and the girls…" She bit her lip and scrunched her shoulders. "Shae has really been chomping at the bit to see you. I didn't know how to handle it. She even stole my phone and threatened never to give it back unless I told her the passcode."

Amee rubbed one of her arms. She was cold. That woman was always cold, except she was hot as hell. *Damn it!*

She continued, "I wanted to give you your space…"

One of the volunteers came up to Amee, dressed in her uniform T-shirt with 'Craig's Boxing Camp' written in block letters over the shoulders. *Jesus.* The woman had thought of everything.

After a brief word, Amee spun to me. "Anyway, I've given you your official Shae alert. I'm sorry, but she'll probably be glued to you all day."

Does she really not understand that it isn't a problem?

"She can call me — or send me picture texts or whatever. I mean, if it's okay with her mom."

Her lovely lips pressed together, and she let out a long, slow breath. "Right. Thanks. Oh, do you and Trev mind being in charge of the video game station after? Otherwise, the older kids will monopolize it."

She was raising money for my crusty old boxing buddy and she wanted me and my best friend to hang out and play video games all day. "Sure."

"Thanks. If any of those little fuckers get out of hand, let me know."

Potty mouth. She came with guns blazing and had absolutely no idea.

As she walked off, Trev approached. His smirk hadn't gotten any more charming.

"Bro," he said, "you're staring at her ass."

"I know." But still kept looking.

"You know what's incredibly stupid?" he asked.

I couldn't imagine what insult he was coming up with, so I just rolled my eyes, still a little drunk on being that close to Amee again.

"That your ego is standing in the way of your happiness. Everybody messes up, Benji. Everybody."

Sure enough, when Shae, Carly and Jude came in, the little sparkly munchkin ran up to me and threw her arms around my quad. I waved to her aunt and gave the thumbs-up that she could stay with us in the back.

In fact, Trev and I were happy to have Shae Benton. She handled the video game station like a boss. Well, like her mom, really. Even Devon didn't dare play more than one game in a row.

I was laughing at her bitching out a mall dad who had cut in line when I saw a familiar face.

In her extra-high heels and her very tight pants, Brock Jenssen's wife swaggered over to me.

"Hey, I know you." She shook a long, bedazzled — a word Shae had taught me — fingernail in my direction.

"Yeah, we met at a game last year." I shot her a tight smile and wondered what Amee had done to get her to sign that agreement thing.

Jenni Lynn's eyes shot back and forth between me and Amee, who was behind the donations table with Craig.

"Your girlfriend throws a pretty mean fundraiser." Her smile was tight. Whatever had happened hadn't left Jenni Lynn a fan of Amee's.

"Not my girlfriend." I wasn't going to embarrass the woman busting her ass to make money for a gym for absolutely no reason.

Jenni Lynn picked up a flyer from the table in front of her. "She ruin your life, too?"

Nope. Not going there. Not with a stranger who had an obvious bone to pick.

"Nah, we just know each other from mutual friends." *Nine-year-olds count, right?*

"Well, she certainly knows how to get what she wants. I'll give her that."

"Uh..." I searched the massive mattresses and pillow area in front of the big screen where people were watching the video games. Shae giggled with Trev while a mom checked him out. No help there.

"She actually dug shit up from my past and threw it in my face." Jenni Lynn turned to me and walked closer, tapping that obnoxious nail on the table as she approached. "Did you know she was like that? A cut-throat bitch?"

Whoa.

I may have still been mad and wounded from Amee, but this chick had crossed a line. I put my hands up, mostly as a defense from her getting any closer. She and Jemina must have shopped at the same horrible soap store.

"Then you know what she does? She calls me last week to have coffee and confirm that Brock will be here today. She gives me the file of my dirt and says she's glad she didn't have to use it. What the hell? She thinks she can be all buddy-buddy after she stole my paycheck. Uh? No."

"Who are you?" Shae, my own personal short savior, asked as she peered up at Jenni Lynn.

"My husband is Brock Jenssen. He's over there signing autographs." She smiled down at Shae.

"Oh." Little Mama checked out the long nails and shrugged. "Pretty glitter." She pulled at my hand. "Come on, BB. You're shirking your duties."

I waved a happy goodbye to the athlete's wife.

"Where did you learn the word 'shirking'?" I asked with a chuckle.

We walked back, hand in hand, to the huge screen where Nate was racing cars on an animated beach with a kid I recognized from his school. Little Man was kicking the other kid's ass, proper.

Shae sighed. "I heard Jude say it to my mom. She said, 'Fucking Pete better not shirk on his duties now that he found a job.'"

I pulled her to a stop and squatted down. "I don't think you're supposed to be saying that F word."

"I'm not supposed to be saying BB, either. I'm shirking my word duties."

How the hell does Amee find a way to punish that child? I leveled my eyes and tried to act the adult, but her little smile was too much. "Shae Benton?"

"Yeah?"

"I absolutely adore you."

She flung her arms around my neck and squeezed me tight. I scooped her up with one arm. All was right in my world for the first time in a month.

"Can we get cupcakes? Jude and I made your favorite. Oh, and Logan's mom brought these Oreo thingies. You *have* to try them."

"Damn skippy we can."

Chapter Thirty-One

Magical Beasts

Amee

Shae lay snoozing on the one of mattresses in front of the blank video screen. Her BB sat against the wall next to her, his hands on his bent knees. The unicorn watched the dictator breathe. A slap of what could have been hit me hard.

What would that man do if I didn't give up? If he knew I was ready to fight for it all? A long exhale steamed through my tight throat and I stepped forward. When he looked up, he didn't smile.

More time… He needs more time.

Craig shuffled past me to the stairs leading to his apartment above the gym. "I'm beat. You're a damn miracle worker, but I'm beat. You'll lock up?" The question was for Ben, who nodded his agreement, still on the floor by Shae.

I motioned with my thumb over my shoulder. "I need to put some stuff in my car and I'll be back for her."

"You want me to carry her out?" He ran his hand across his beard, which was longer than usual.

Yes. Yes, I did. I wanted him to carry her out, buckle her up and drive home with us. He hated me and had spent the entire day being nothing but polite. As predicted, Shae had never left his side, and it pained me to know I would have to separate the dynamic duo yet again.

But instead, I said, "It's okay. I'll just be a sec." I grabbed the huge bags of tablecloths and coffee pots and wobbled away before I said something I would regret and upset him by telling him how perfect he was.

The brisk air whipped up my blouse and I shivered. *Where the hell is my coat, anyway?* When I got to my car and clicked the fob, nothing happened. I set the bags down on the concrete parking lot and clicked again. I walked around the back to find the hatch open. *Shit.* I'd left it like that the whole day. *Idiot.* Jude was right. For someone with a law degree and a six-figure income, I was a dipshit.

Even worse, I only had one way to turn. Back into the gym I'd just helped refinance and ask for a favor from the one person who owed me nothing.

I stored the bags in the opened hatch, and as I slammed it shut, I caught a glimpse of my coat on the passenger's side in the front. *Genius.* I'd left it outside in the cold. How had I organized an entire fundraiser? Jude had taken Carly home hours before, but did Shae even have a coat? Wasn't that like the first rule of motherhood? Bundle them up?

I shook my head all the way to the other end of the gym, where I found Ben and Shae just how I'd left them, except his head hung into his hands.

"Um..." I said in a quiet voice, feeling like an intruder to their privacy. "You're never going to believe this, but my battery is dead. I left the fucking hatch open all day."

Our eyes met, and I had to blink several times to understand what I was seeing. He wiped his nose on his sleeve and sniffed once.

"I'm sorry. What?"

A magical, beautiful, sensitive beast, right there on the floor watching my daughter. I hated to bring him out of his moment. It would only be further proof of my selfishness. But it was late, and I was dead on my feet.

"My battery is dead because I'm a fucking idiot."

"Oh." He took a long breath then pushed to his feet. The unicorn walked over to me and held out his hand. "Give me the key. I'll jump it." His gaze traveled the length of my body. "For someone who's always freezing, you should consider a jacket." I didn't imagine that he stopped for a fraction longer at my chest. "Or a second layer."

I placed the fob in his palm and watched him walk away. When he was securely on the other side of the door, I glanced down at my boobs. Yep. I was very obviously cold.

I called Jude to tell her the delay, and Ben was back within ten minutes. There was no objection to him carrying Shae, though it was an odd compensation for his help. He settled her into my already warmed up car and shut the back door.

When I turned to thank him, he was closer than I expected. Ben hung his arm on the door frame and was gazing into my eyes. What I wouldn't have given for permission to stroke his beard, loop my fingers through his hair…put my head into that nook in his chest where I'd previously fit so perfectly.

He said, "You'll probably need to drive around for a bit so it doesn't die again by morning."

"Seriously? Fuck. I'm —"

He had his mouth on mine before I could finish, and he grabbed my ass. Ben pulled me closer and dug in. *Everything.* I whimpered and fought back tears. His kiss was *everything.*

I wrapped my leg around his thigh and tried to eliminate any space, dust or light particle between us.

"I fucking missed you so much," I confessed into his ear when he finally broke the kiss.

But instead of him deepening the embrace, he pulled away.

Ben lifted his chin, motioning me to the other side of the car. "Get in. I'll drive. You'll talk."

I searched his face for a sign of a joke.

"Come on, before I change my mind."

I ran past him and around the car, and was buckled up before he was back from locking up the gym.

As he moved the seat to accommodate his height, he nodded to the jacket in my lap and he said, "Nice coat. Ever think about using it?"

Shae's sweet grumbles of snoozing from the back seat were our safety net of calm. The blinker clicked as he turned onto the main road, and when it stopped, it left a silence only my words could fill.

I began, "What I'm about to say doesn't make up for how I treated you but it may help explain it." The street lights passed in a lulling rhythm and I begged the ounce of intelligence I had to not fuck up. "You didn't know me when Pete had his accident. So, you didn't know what it was like for the girls. We went from being the idea of a model family — even though behind closed doors we were the furthest thing from it — to the subject of a lot, and I mean a *lot*, of gossip. Carly had it the worst because she'd just started school. It was an easy reason not to like her. And if it weren't for Jude, a great therapist and a power mom I had in my corner, we would have changed schools."

He kept his eyes on the road and the leather beneath him crackled as he readjusted.

"I hadn't thought about how it would be the day of Shae's recital."

He glanced quickly to me.

"It was the first time we'd been in public since Pete's release and I was sure I'd heard snickering from some previously horrible moms. Then you showed up and — "

"Made it worse?"

"No... Yes... Maybe." I needed to get it together, loop us around to a better place. "I *am* sorry, Ben." I edged closer to the center and him. "I panicked. I understand now that what I did was the worst thing I could have. I am sorry. I will forever be sorry."

He pulled into a strip mall and put the car in Park. "You done?" The seatbelt unclicked, and he shifted to face me.

I had one more thing I had to say, even if it brought back a story I wanted to put behind me. "I was never embarrassed by you, despite my actions."

Maybe I was insane, but he didn't look angry.

Ben took a long blink before saying, "You know when we first started seeing each other and you would ask me to tell you something about myself?"

I nodded, afraid more words would shatter the shaking foundation we may have been repairing.

"I didn't want to. I didn't want to tell you anything because I was embarrassed — about Kim, about me and my classes, about my income. Well, *lack* of income."

Shit. I'd only made things worse with my confession.

"This last month or so without you, I thought about that a lot."

I reached for his hand and uncurled it. We interlaced our fingers. I dared not squeeze. My heart was already racing with the contact and leaping with its acceptance.

"You are, Amee Benton, everything I've ever wanted. I couldn't have concocted a more perfect woman of my dreams. I know there's still a lot of work I need to do with Carly, and maybe it never will be as solid as I'd like, but that can't change what I have with Sparkle Pants in the back seat" — he brushed his beard against the back of my hand — "or you."

He smiled, those goddam dimples deep in his scruffy cheeks and giving me the first sign of hope I'd had in far too long.

I swallowed hard. "What are you saying?"

"I'm saying there's one thing I should have told you and never did." He licked his lips then whispered, "I love you, too."

* * * *

Six months later...

I stood next to Michelle Simmons at the renovated entrance of Craig's gym as her son Logan, Nate and a few other boys finished their class with Ben.

"Is it wrong that I love how he tortures them?" she asked. "Remember how sensitive we used to be about teachers treating our kids with respect?"

With a to-go metal coffee mug in her hand, she rolled her eyes.

Another mom who I'd never seen before walked up and nudged my shoulder.

"You think he gives private lessons?" She pointed over to Ben with a dirty smile on her face.

"I know he does. That's my boyfriend." I leveled the woman with my eyes.

She smiled back and said, "Well, color me eighteen shades of jealous. Go you."

Her kid hopped out of the ring and Michelle smirked as they left.

"Does anyone not comment on his looks?" my old friend asked.

"Every single mom. I swear."

And I didn't mind. In fact, claiming my boyfriend was a badge of honor. Hotness aside, the kids loved him and his classes were really starting to fill up. He was even making some good side money.

Not that he cared about money. In fact, fancy gifts made him uncomfortable and I tried to avoid them at all costs.

But, for his birthday weekend, I couldn't help but reserve the same cabin we'd gone to the fall before and my present was a small box I was sure he would love.

Pete had miraculously kept a job and the girls were staying with him, although Jude was on call should he decide to fuck up our lives just for the hell of it. I'd even seen him flirt with a single mom at school, so maybe there was real hope that he was moving on.

Because I certainly had.

Ben and I weren't exactly living together, but he had finally seen inside my bedroom and had a drawer where he kept a few things. The weekend in front of us was to talk about the next steps and I wanted him to be crystal clear what that meant for me.

We drove up to the cabin in comfortable silence and mindless banter about the events of the week behind us. Easy. My time alone with Ben had become the Zen garden to my chaos. After checking in and unpacking, we went outside with a blanket.

Red sparks flew off the camp fire as he prodded it with a stick. I handed him a beer — cheat days had changed to Saturdays — and scooted next to him with my glass of wine.

"Thanks, Cupcake." His nickname would never grow old. And I loved that I wasn't 'baby' or 'honey', I was always his Cupcake.

I dug the small box out of my sweater and presented it. "Happy birthday."

He eyed the green square in my hand, then me. "I thought we agreed that the cabin was my present."

"It's really nothing. Just open it."

He reached for the gift with a curious eye. Bringing the box up to his ear, he shook it, but only the ribbons let off a light shuffle.

"Open it and see. I promise, it's nothing." I sipped my wine to hide the childlike glee inside me. It really was better to give rather than to receive. Well...some things.

With care, he slipped off the ribbons and they fell to the forest floor. He lifted the clear tape on both ends. The paper crinkled, and he let it drop between his legs. He examined the shiny box.

"Condoms? Ah, thanks, Cupcake. We can always use these." He shot me a wink and pecked my cheek.

"Look inside." I bit my bottom lip and my toes wiggled in my boots. I'd been dying to give him the present since I'd had the idea.

His blue eyes twinkled in the warm sun. "Okay…"

The box, having already been put to very, very good use, opened easily. Ben squinted and looked inside.

"It's empty."

"I know." I grinned.

"You were right." He laughed. "You gave me nothing."

A breeze rattled the leaves and the smoke drifted away from us. I dug a stable spot in the dirt for my wineglass.

"Well, not yet. But I want to give you a baby."

He looked back at me and his chest rose and fell quickly. "What?"

"I want to give you a baby. Whenever you're ready, but kinda soon because I don't want to have to worry about collecting social security when my kid's in college."

"You don't have to…"

That was the point. I didn't have to. He was amazing with my girls and still a huge part of Nate and Devon's lives. And while his commitment to those children would never waver, he deserved to know the bond of truly being his. Plus, I was horny just thinking about him holding a baby. I'd have to beat the PTA moms back with a stick.

"I want to…with you." I smiled and edged a little closer to him. "If you want to with me."

Ben moved to his hands and knees and crept closer, causing me to fall to my back. He hovered his mouth and gorgeous face over mine. "Only if you'll marry me."

My heart stopped. We'd hinted at a union but had never discussed it. "Are you asking?"

"Damn skippy, I am. Marry me, Cupcake."

"I would be honored."

In the months of dating — public dating — Ben had been nothing but perfect. Yeah, there had been snickers about our age difference at first, but the bitchy moms had moved on to their friend's swollen lips or the latest divorce. We had kept a pretty low profile anyway, being sure to check in with the girls and their adjustments before worrying about what others would project onto us.

Ben bent down and kissed me then said, "I suddenly understand shotgun weddings. We start now."

He kissed me again, deeper. The love between us solidified yet again. And with it the confirmation that I *had* deserved a better life. It might not have been easy to get, but it was worth every effort.

Unicorn and I, his Cupcake, would live happily ever after.

Want to see more from this author?
Here's a taster for you to enjoy!

Luca's Lessons
Deana Birch and Amelia Foster

Excerpt

Luca

A silver foil wrapper tumbled down the stone walkway along the Limmat River, and Luca stepped to the side, his arms crossed. A giggling young couple with too many piercings for his personal preference hurried by, unaware of the menacing, forgotten paper. In his dark suit, crisp white shirt and matching silk navy tie, he waited.

The improperly disposed-of litter flopped one more time, trapped itself at the edge of the stone wall and, away from the light breeze, rested. Satisfied by his small conquest — surely it was his will that had brought its journey to an end — Luca smirked. He walked over, picked it up and secured its fate in a wire bin. A pestering thought of germs poked at his side, but he brushed his hands together at a job well done and continued on his path to the private bank.

While the inconvenience had been a distraction, it had been welcomed. Early and eager were two qualities he admired, but not in himself. He reached for the door of the gray, historic building at exactly seven minutes past his scheduled appointment. *Perfetto.*

After a brief check through security, including a confirmation of his identity, he climbed the two flights of stairs to the private bank of Steinmetz and Favre. The heavy wooden doors of the suite opened to sleek metal-and-cream marble that created a stark contrast to the building's dated exterior. But the interior did not surprise Luca. He'd already seen the clean, powerful reception in the magazine article about the youngest woman entrepreneur in the history of private banking.

And it was no mistake he'd sought out Claire Favre. Young, driven and on-the-rise was exactly the kind of mind he wanted handling his soon-to-be-acquired secret business. The piece about her and her partner in the weekly publication inserted into the Sunday paper had done more than pique his interest. Fortunately, Luca's reputation and family history had provided enough of a motivation that he'd obtained an appointment without too much delay.

He gave his name to the young, just-above-cheap-suited man behind the massive desk and took a seat in the black leather club chair. Magazines in four different languages were fanned on the iron table next to him. He aligned the one on top to sync with the others and the rhythmed echo of high heels ricocheting off the hallowed walls made him look up.

Madonna mia.

The picture had done her no justice. Claire Favre's sharp hip bones pointed behind the fabric of her tight black skirt and they swayed in a hypnotizing motion as she drew nearer. The formfitting blazer matched the skirt, and a pink silk blouse formed a deep V below. Different from the photo, where her blonde locks had been loose and casual as she'd smiled, her hair was now pulled back into a low, tight bun and her lips remained firmly locked together.

Luca stood, happy his height put him at an advantage, and buttoned his jacket at the waist. The momentary shock of her in-person beauty sank into his gut. It had no business in his throat or chest.

"Herr Bernardi." She extended her small, manicured hand but barely smiled.

"English, please." Luca ignored the slight jump in his heart rate as they touched.

"As you wish." Her light shrug remained formal.

Surely a coincidence.

He narrowed his eyes.

Ms. Favre's smile grew tighter and she spun around. "My office is just down the hall."

Luca followed the banker and stared at the back of her exposed neck. He would not check out her ass, not in a professional setting where the woman deserved respect. He would not.

He did. He most certainly did. And damn it all to hell and back if his palm didn't twitch with desire.

When the penance of being a gentleman and walking behind a woman to whom he owed respect — not ogling — had finished, he squared his shoulders at the threshold of her office and renewed his purpose — business.

Ms. Favre ushered him to a cubed leather chair opposite her desk and he reached for the button of his jacket while she floated to the other side of the impressive oak plank.

A quick glance of her surroundings revealed nothing — no framed photos of her and the late husband the article had referred to or children it had not hinted at. Truly nothing. This woman was clean, uncomplicated and professional—everything Luca desired in a banker…and perhaps other things.

"Please," she said and motioned to the seat behind him. With a quick brush on the back of her skirt—*is hand jealousy a thing?*—she gracefully sat. "Tell me what brings you here, Mr. Bernardi."

Where to begin? The long and challenging path of fully respecting and refining one's own needs? The obvious motivation of a man-made success? Best to start with the not-so-shocking. One never knows.

In the warmest, most casual tone he could muster he said, "I am in negotiations to buy a business. A private club, actually. And I was hoping to keep said investment separate from my others."

Her blue-gray gaze pierced him and she drew her light, thin eyebrows together. "You have a business you'd like to hide, and you want to use my bank to do so?"

"No." Convincing her was going to take some massaging, especially since the bulk of his wealth would not be coming along for the ride. "I have a business I'd like to keep to myself, but I'd like you to handle investing and growing the worth of the account."

Claire crossed her fingers on the desk and circled a thumb slowly into the opposite palm.

"Is it an illegal business?" she asked.

"No, but it is private, much like your bank." Luca flattened his lips and fought a smile. The woman calmed herself with touch. He admired and recognized the gesture. In a cold room full of stark decorations, her softness slammed into him.

He blinked. Business. And the need to hide his new project.

"And what is this soon-to-be-acquired oppor-tunity?" She creased her pink lips.

There was the catch. The hitch. The hard-sell.

He stared into her eyes. "A private club."

She stilled her hands and cocked an eyebrow. "A misogynistic group of racist old men smoking cigars and plotting world domination?"

Interesting choice of words.

"No." This time he allowed the smile to shine. Her spunk and terseness must have helped her along the way.

But what way? According to the magazine article, she was barely thirty years old, and her private schooling, with winters in Gstaad and springs outside of Geneva, had assured her enough wealthy contacts for life. Her path and its perks had been easy — a silver spoon and a glass slipper.

"Are women welcome in your club, Mr. Bernardi?"

Her chest rose then fell slowly.

"Very much so." He dipped his chin.

She'd mentioned it twice now. Maybe empowering women was her motive.

Luca continued, "I welcome all to my club, Ms. Favre. The members and I pride ourselves on acceptance."

This brought a slight tilt to her head and what Luca hoped was a glimmer in her hazy eyes.

"All? That doesn't sound too private."

Her objection was welcomed with fervor, the familiar heat Luca longed for in a challenge. That, and her 'As you wish' comment from reception, braided into a perfect rope of feisty and submissive — not that the powerful woman before him would ever admit to wanting to surrender herself to the will of another.

But, contrary to what were probably her beliefs, she had all the signs. Her manners were impeccable. Her attention to detail...perfection. And that softness... The gentle side of her that Luca would bet his portfolio she didn't think people saw — but he did. He knew exactly the kind of woman who sat in front of him.

"I assure you that the membership fee secures the privacy," he said with a quick nod.

"And what is the membership fee? If I may ask?"

You may. Such lovely manners.

"Fifty thousand euros initially, plus another fifty thousand a year. On top of that, there are certain benefits that members may or may not choose to acquire. But, essentially, ten million would be my earnings in the first year."

She smiled curtly. The minimum balance to open most private banks in Switzerland was usually around a million francs. With a promise of more, maybe the risk of taking on what appeared to be a seedy client would dissolve.

"What exactly transpires at your club, Mr. Bernardi?" Her business etiquette remained flawless.

Well, that would depend entirely on which room one would peep into. But there was no reason to beat around the bush.

"Exploration of one's boundaries, Ms. Favre." Luca met her stare with heavy eyes.

"Sex. You plan to run a high society sex club." Her tone was flat, almost bored.

How could she hold his gaze? He was certain she was more a bottom than a top.

"I'm interested in continuing the initial goal of the founder, who provides a safe environment for all genders to escape without worries or hassles. It has been a tradition for years that every member sign a confidentiality agreement. It covers everything done and witnessed behind the closed, or sometimes open" — he tilted his head — "doors of the club."

Claire Favre appeared to remain unfazed. *Is she?*

She looked past Luca and he studied the pale, sweet skin exposed from her neck to her chest. From the lack of freckles and spots, it hadn't seen much sun over the summer. He knew its shade well, the perfect cream that would flush pink with proper stimulation.

Luca lifted his gaze. He would not be caught dreaming about bunching up her skirt and examining the most sensitive areas of her body. *Business,* he reminded himself.

"Might I ask why you thought *I* would be the right banker for your secret investment?"

Luca was still very much denying the answer himself. The woman had intrigued more than his financial affairs when he'd seen her in the photo.

"Empowerment, Ms. Favre. We're in the same business. You want to empower—"

She raised a hand and scoffed. He'd finally rattled her.

"I fail to see how tying up women and spanking them with riding crops is empowering." Her expression must have been attempting to scold him.

Hilarious.

Ah, the misconceptions. The fantasized, glorified, utter wrongness in the perception of the lifestyle… Luca had hoped a woman of Claire's status would have been better read than what popular opinion had painted as the BDSM culture. But alas, stereotypes were indeed festering wounds.

Luca curled his index finger around his mouth and tucked the opposite hand under his elbow.

She sat behind her desk, eyes slightly narrowed and waiting, oh so patiently with her hint of challenge, for his response. The blend was intoxicating.

Before the stirrings of his under-thoughts could bubble to the surface, he said, "I'd like to prove you wrong. The best way to do that I think would be to show you."

Her eyelids fluttered and the rosy flush he'd been trying to deny he craved crept up her neck. Claire swallowed hard.

Sorry, Ms. Favre. Flexing my mental muscle is an unbreakable yet delicious habit.

"Excuse me?" she managed.

Luca cleared his throat. "There are, perhaps, images you have about what goes on in a private setting such as my future club — images that, while they may scratch at the surface of truth, do only that...scratch."

Her skin returned to its cream natural state and Luca grieved the departure of the pink.

He continued, "Why don't you visit? Take a tour. I'm sure you'll find that it's just as much a legitimate business as the pesticides that kill millions of bees every year. Hopefully, more. I assure you that no one gets hurt unless they want to." Another man might have winked, but Luca only shifted his jaw instead.

She stiffened her posture. "You want me to come to a club and watch people get spanked and have sex?"

He grinned. "You seem rather fixated on the spanking part."

She rolled her eyes.

That would never do.

"I'm not fixated on anything. I'm just wondering... If your business is so much on the up and up, why would you want to hide it in my bank, because it doesn't seem like any of your other sources of income are shifting into my vaults with it? And secondly, why then, would I take a risk on you, a stranger to me, for a venture that you would like to brush under the rug?"

Luca crossed his foot over the opposite knee and adjusted in his chair.

"To answer your questions..." He twisted the platinum watch below his starched cuff. "For starters, perhaps I am interested in having some privacy on this matter and wish to not mix it with the accounts that have been in my family for decades. I am well aware of the labels that accompany my lifestyle. I still have a sweet, aging grandmother, and I have no intention of killing her with rumors of my sex life."

Claire's hands folded once again, but this time she rolled her shoulders back and shivered.

"And secondly, I read about you. I know you are a perfect balance of risk-taker and security. Much like anyone, I'd like to see my money grow. As I have no friends who are clients of yours, I feel the risk is mutual."

She sat back and tapped her delicate thumbs together three times.

Stalemate.

Her gaze ran the length of Luca and when it met his, she gave a slight purse of her mouth. "When?"

He wet his lips.

"Friday or Saturday night. You'll need to sign a non-disclosure agreement and you won't be able to visit the higher floors. But you will get a sense that the members are as normal as you and me." He paused at the brief fantasy of her in his private suite. "And you will see the respect and consent of a tight community."

Her eyes raked over him again. *A good sign?* He couldn't tell.

"I'll think about it."

She rose, as did he, and he followed her to the door.

"I'll see myself out." Luca nodded. There was no way he could follow that ass down the hall after he'd discovered how her skin could blush with just a few words.

"As you wish," she said.

Despite the brakes halting in his mind, Luca exited her office.

How had she known? How could she have possibly known the symphony of music those words were to his ears?

Home of Erotic Romance

Sign up for our newsletter and find out about all our
romance book releases, eBook sales and promotions,
sneak peeks and FREE romance books!

About the Author

Deana Birch was named after her father's first love, who just so happened not to be her mother. Born and raised in the Midwest, she made stops in Los Angeles and New York before settling in Europe, where she lives with her own blue-eyed Happily Ever After. Her days are spent teaching yoga, playing tennis, ruining her children's French homework, cleaning up dog vomit, writing her next book or reading someone else's.

Deana loves to hear from readers. You can find her contact information, website details and author profile page at https://www.totallybound.com